MW01052821

# Assateague Dark

Other Emerson Moore Adventures by Bob Adamov

| | |
|---|---|
| • *Rainbow's End* | Released October 2002 |
| • *Pierce the Veil* | Released May 2004 |
| • *When Rainbows Walk* | Released June 2005 |
| • *Promised Land* | Released July 2006 |
| • *The Other Side of Hell* | Released June 2008 |
| • *Tan Lines* | Released June 2010 |
| • *Sandustee* | Released March 2013 |
| • *Zenobia* | Released May 2014 |
| • *Missing* | Released April 2015 |
| • *Golden Torpedo* | Released July 2017 |
| • *Chincoteague Calm* | Released April 2018 |
| • *Flight* | Released May 2019 |

Next Emerson Moore Adventure:

• *Sunset Blues*

# Assateague Dark

**_Bob Adamov_**

Packard Island Publishing
Wooster, Ohio
2020
www.packardislandpublishing.com

Copyright 2020 by Bob Adamov
All rights reserved
No part of this book may be used or reproduced in any manner whatsoever without written permission from the author except in the case of brief quotations embodied in critical articles or reviews.

www.BobAdamov.com

This book is a work of fiction. Names, characters, places and incidents are either products of the author's imagination or are used fictitiously. Any resemblance to actual events, locales or persons, living or dead, is entirely coincidental.

First edition • May 2020

ISBN: 978-0-9786184-9-0
(ISBN 10:) 0-9786184-9-1

Library of Congress Number: 2020900872

Printed and bound in the United States of America

Cover art by: Denis Lange
Lange Design
890 Williamsburg Court
Ashland, OH 44805
*www.langedesign.org*

Printed by:
Bookmasters, Inc.
PO Box 388
Ashland, OH 44805
*www.Bookmasters.com*

Layout design by: Ryan Sigler
holePUNCH Studios
6775 N. Etna Rd.
Columbia City, IN 46725
*www.holepunchstudios.com*

Published by:
Packard Island Publishing
3025 Evergreen Drive
Wooster, OH 44691
*www.packardislandpublishing.com*

Dedication

This book is dedicated to my dear wife, Cathy, for her continued support of my writing adventure and her enduring love. Thank you Honey!

Assateague Dark is also dedicated to my hero, Clive Cussler, who passed away on February 24, 2020. Besides being the Grand Master of the American action/adventure novel, he was a shipwreck hunter, classic car collector and a extraordinary influence on my writing style. He was a gentleman and all-around rascal. You are missed!

*They that wait upon the Lord shall renew their strength;*
*they shall mount up with wings as eagles;*
*they shall run, and not be weary;*
*and they shall walk, and not faint.*

**– Isaiah 40:31**

Acknowledgements

For technical assistance, I'd like to express my appreciation to Chuck "Big Daddy" Meier in Cudjoe Key, one of the most interesting characters I've met during my book research. I also thank Roe Terry, Chuck Gove, Bill Lawhorn, Billy Joe Tarr and Carleton Leonard for their technical expertise and sharing their experiences.

I'd like to thank my team of editors: Cathy Adamov, John Wisse, Peggy Parker, and Julia Wiesenberg of ImProof Editing.

For more information, check these sites:

*www.BobAdamov.com*
*www.VisitPut-in-Bay.com*
*www.MillerFerry.com*
*www.chincoteaguechamber.com*

*Lake Erie Islands*

# DELMARVA PENINSULA

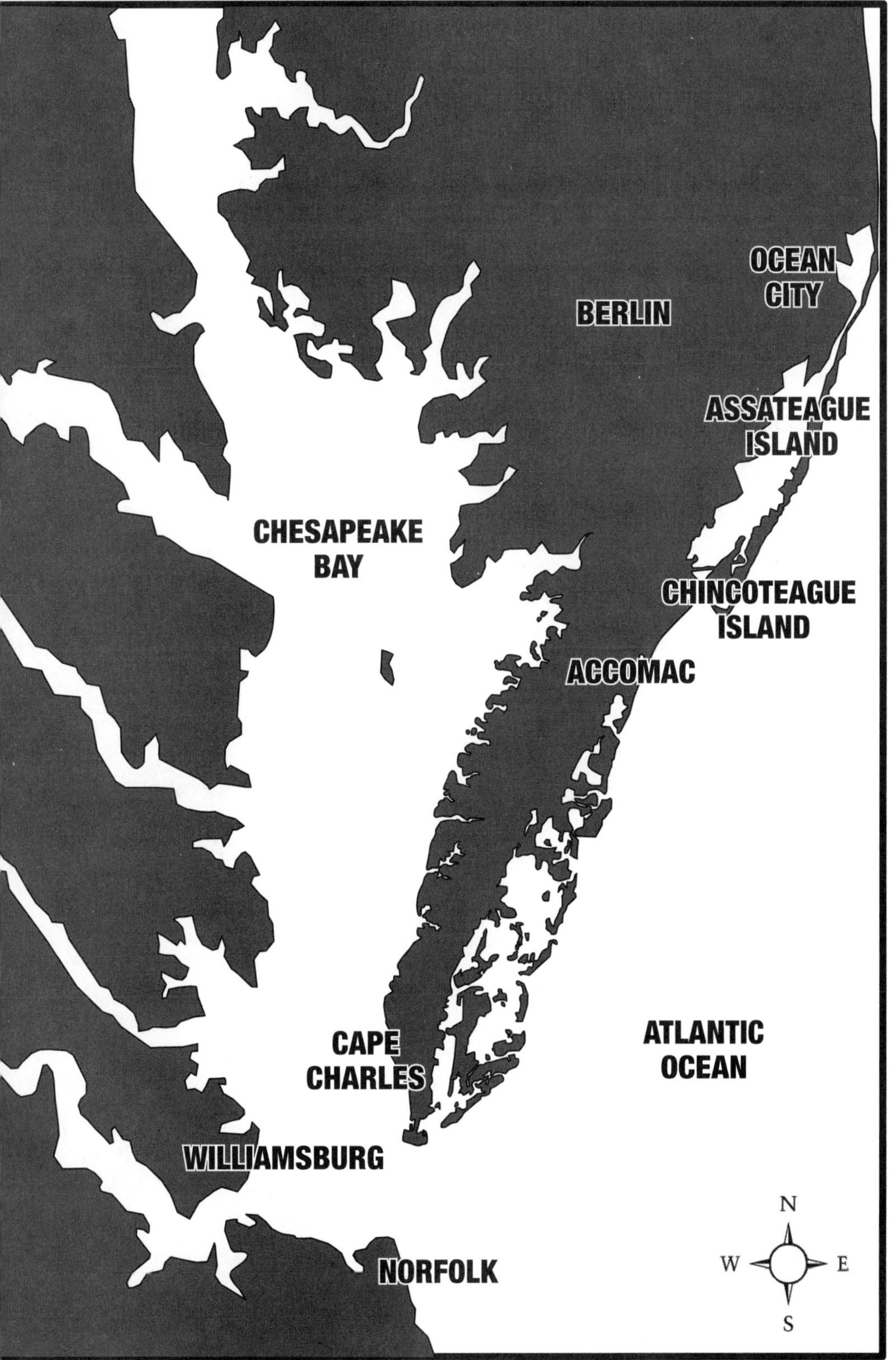

# Assateague Dark

# CHAPTER 1

## U.S. Naval Hospital
## Guantanamo Bay, Cuba

"Welcome back to the living, Emerson," Chuck Meier said as *Washington Post* investigative reporter Emerson Moore moaned and slowly opened his eyes.

Moore took in the hulking military veteran looming over him and the white polystyrene tiles overhead. "Where am I, Chuck?" Moore asked from his hospital bed where he was lying on a crisp, but thinning sheet.

"If you turn that beaten body of yours a bit, you can see Guantanamo Bay out your window. You're still in Cuba my friend...at Gitmo's hospital."

"I believe you," Moore sighed as he began to slowly turn his body. "How did I get here?"

"Just look outside for a minute," Meier urged as he observed how the six-foot-two, dark-haired man had changed.

Moore, who was in his early forties, had narrowly escaped death in Cuba's jungle. His once tanned body was now a pale white. It had been beaten and bruised—and it showed.

Meier pulled back a thin curtain which hung limply from a rusted chrome rod attached to the ceiling. He was trying to encourage Moore back to health following his recent near-death escape.

Moore groaned as he shifted his body and looked out at the

tranquil, azure-colored bay. "Nice. Peaceful. I know where I am," Moore commented with a hint of relief.

He gently moved back to his prone position. "I'm so weak."

"You should be, boy. You almost met your maker. The sand almost ran out of your hourglass," the red-haired, bearded six-foot-four-inch giant of a human killing machine commented.

"How long have I been here?" Moore inquired.

"Two days now, and you're going to be here a few more," Meier replied.

"I remember getting into the river, but how did I get here?" Moore asked as he tried to comprehend the recent events.

"I'd guess that you floated down from the Sierra Maestra mountains. They found you in the Guantanamo River, washed up against the base's perimeter fence."

"I think I remember that. It's all so foggy," Moore weakly acknowledged.

"The medical staff here didn't expect you to live," Meier continued. "You had a gunshot wound in your left shoulder and a stab wound in your right side. Fortunately for you, it barely missed your vital organs. Those open wounds caused your problems."

"What do you mean?" Moore asked.

"You decided to swim in a bacteria-filled river. The wounds went septic on you. The docs said that you had a foul-smelling, green liquid oozing out of them. You smelled worse than the stinkiest thing you could find in a rendering plant! They really thought you were going to buy the farm, my friend," Meier offered.

"I'm so tired," Moore sighed painfully.

"This is the first time you've been awake in the last two days and you've lost a lot of weight there, skinny boy. I'm going to let you rest, and I'll be back tomorrow. We can talk more then."

Meier looked at Moore. "If you're not feeling good, I can bring a priest with me. He can give you your last rites," Meier teased.

"I don't need one. I'll be fine," Moore said weakly. He just wanted to sleep, so he closed his eyes.

Meier reached down and felt Moore's hands. "Your hands are ice cold, Emerson. You sure you're going to make it?"

Moore didn't respond. He had already fallen back asleep.

Meier smiled, glad that his reporter friend had survived. He walked out of the room and left the hospital.

The next day, Meier returned to Moore's bedside and was pleased to see that Moore was sitting up in bed.

"You awake, Emerson?" Meier asked.

Moore's eyelids opened, and he looked at his rowdy visitor. He remembered that Meier once explained how three improvised explosive devices (IEDs) went off under his vehicle one day during his deployment in Tikrit, Iraq. Meier had barely survived the third explosion which took off his leg from the knee down.

"Yeah. I'm feeling better, Chuck," Moore nodded. "I've been dozing off and on."

"You look better. The other day you looked like something that I drew with my left hand," Meier chuckled.

"That bad?"

"Worse."

"What are you doing here, anyway? I thought you told me that you were a marked man in Cuba," Moore asked.

"I am, but I'm on U.S. soil here on the base. I actually did a tour of duty here years ago. When I heard about the explosions up in the mountains at El Patrón's place, I figured you had a hand in it and just maybe needed some help. So, I hitched a flight from Key West. What happened up there?"

Moore gave Meier a recap of the events from when he landed in Cuba and then infiltrated El Patrón's compound above Santa Lucha. The Cubans knew Cuban drug lord Henri Baudin as El Patrón.

Moore talked about blowing up the cocaine processing lab and money counting operation. After that, Moore told him how Baudin was stung to death by a huge swarm of bees.

Meier couldn't resist laughing. "That's a real buzzkill," he chortled. "How fitting!"

"Better him than me," Moore agreed as he continued relaying his painful escape down the mountainside through the dense forest and jungle. He explained how he tried to hide under rock outcroppings so that the Cuban helicopters couldn't find him.

Meier interrupted Moore's explanation. "You hid from us, too."

"What?"

"We were in the air at night when the Cubans wouldn't fly. We couldn't find you either, even though we had heat-sensing monitors. At least we were all looking for you until the rainstorms grounded us."

"I had no idea."

"Of course you didn't."

"That was risky for you," Moore said.

"What's a little risk from time to time?" Meier grinned.

"Have you heard about a woman named Peaches Babbit?" Moore asked.

"No. Why?"

"She did a con job on me. Pretty lady. She pulled me right in and spied on me. She worked for El Patrón."

"Never heard of her, but I can see what I can learn about her," Meier offered.

"Chuck, I'd appreciate it. I'd like to know what happened to her."

"I take it you didn't kill her," Meier said with raised eyebrows.

"No. She took off down the road in one of El Patrón's cars. I don't know if she made it back to Santiago or where she was headed."

"She could have driven to Havana or El Patrón's marina in Santiago and hightailed it out of Cuba on one of his go-fast boats," Meier mused. "Sounds like she's more slippery than a pocketful of pudding. I'll poke around a bit."

"I've got one piece of good news," Moore smiled. He thought back to his reporting assignment that had taken him to the Florida Keys, back before he ended up in Cuba. That assignment had included a search for a missing plane and a lost treasure train from 1928.

"I'm sitting still for it," Meier said with a twinkle in his eye.

"Remember the sunken treasure train by Seven Mile Bridge? The one you showed me?"

"Yeah. What about it?"

"I found the missing Ford trimotor and the Pinkerton," Moore declared.

"You did?" Meier asked, stunned.

Moore explained how he found the plane and what happened to the treasure.

"So, there was never any treasure on that train?"

"Nope. It was a misdirection from the get-go. It was on the trimotor, and El Patrón's family took it all when they found the crash site on their estate."

"Nice way to bankroll their business," Meier said thoughtfully.

"Yeah. Did you hear anything about our little buddy, Bones Aiken?"

"The guy who worked at the strip club in Key West?" Meier asked.

"That's him."

"No. He disappeared about the time you headed for Cuba. You remember that car he drove?"

"Who could forget it?" Moore asked as he recalled the quirky Gremlin that Aiken drove.

"I saw that it was found half-buried in a swamp near Florida City, but there was no sign of your buddy."

"I hope the mafia in Miami didn't catch up with him. I wouldn't be surprised if they put a contract out on him," Moore surmised.

"I don't know. Bones seemed like a survivor to me. He'd be savvy enough to ditch his car, steal another and get out of Dodge," Meier suggested.

"You might be right there. Bones was a funny guy, but smart in his own way."

Meier reached over to the nightstand and picked up a phone message. "You better call your boss at *The Post*, Emerson, and brief him on what happened here in Cuba with El Patrón."

Moore's eyes widened. "How did he know I was here?"

"I called him a day ago," Meier replied. "I figured he was anxious to know about you since you'd been off the grid for a while. He's very concerned about your health."

Moore groaned at the thought of calling John Sedler. "I'm sure he's going to give me a piece of his mind about being careful."

"That wouldn't surprise me one iota," Meier grinned and stood up from his chair. "I'll leave you alone so you can call. I don't need to hear the grief that you're going to get," he smirked.

"Thanks," Moore said without a hint of appreciation.

"You rest up, and I'll be back tomorrow. I'm going to make a few calls and see what I can learn about your Peaches friend and if anyone has a contract on you—like termination for cause."

"I need to get out of here," Moore muttered.

"Don't rush it, Emerson. You're safe here on a U.S. naval base while you recuperate a bit longer. Can't get much safer," Meier said confidently.

"I brought your laptop and cell phone with me. They're both charged up, but don't overdo it," Meier warned as he set them on the nightstand.

"I guess you're right. I'll call Sedler," Moore said as he reached for the phone.

"Happy trails until tomorrow, amigo," Meier chortled as he departed. He expected that Moore was going to have a painful conversation with his boss.

Moore's call to Sedler was answered on the third ring.

"There's my wayward reporter," the African American's deep voice boomed with seriousness mixed with relief. "MIA on another assignment. How are you feeling, Emerson?"

"Better, but still weak," Moore responded.

"I heard about your rescue at Guantanamo from your buddy Chuck Meier. Emerson, you're very lucky to be alive, from what he told me about the condition you were in when they found you. You were at death's door!"

"I know," Moore agreed.

"I've warned you over and over to be careful. You do some foolhardy things at times. You take too many risks," Sedler admonished Moore.

"They're calculated risks," Moore explained weakly. "I do get the story," he added.

Sedler was going to counter the comment, but decided against it. "Meier didn't have the details from the time you took that luxury cruise on my nickel with Captain Congo to get you into Cuba. I've been watching the newswires, but there hasn't been much coming out of Cuba about that El Patrón. Bring me up to speed."

Moore quickly recounted what had transpired after he boarded Congo's charter boat for Cuba, what happened in El Patrón's compound above Santa Lucha, and his perilous escape through the jungle.

"Another close one, Emerson," Sedler observed. "Maybe a little too close," he added.

"You know me, John. I've got nine lives like a cat," Moore countered.

"I'd say more like twenty lives the way you've been going through them," Sedler suggested. "When you feel up to it, I need a story."

"I knew you'd be asking. I have my laptop here and will start pecking away as my strength returns."

"What about the loose ends, like that Peaches woman?" Sedler asked.

"Chuck is running her down to see what he can find out. I'll figure out what the next steps in the story will be. It could end up as a series."

"Keep me in the loop."

"Will do."

"How long are you staying in Cuba?" Sedler asked.

"Not sure. I'll have to check with the docs here to see when they can release me. I'm still weak. I guess Chuck will guide me as far as how I actually get out of here. I certainly can't go back to Santiago and take a commercial flight out. I'm sure I'm on somebody's hit list."

"Be careful," Sedler cautioned his incorrigible reporter.

"I will."

"One more thing. Your buddy from Put-in-Bay recently called me to see if I heard from you."

"Mad Dog?"

"Yeah. Your entertainer friend who invited me up on the stage at that Round House Bar and embarrassed the hell out of me when I visited your island a few years back. I'll never get over getting on the stage with him and blowing a conch shell."

"What did he want?"

"He was with your aunt, and they both were worried about you since neither had heard from you in a long time. You better give them a call, and I'd suggest calling your aunt first," Sedler proposed.

"Will do," Moore agreed as they ended their call. Moore opened the water bottle on his nightstand and took a sip before calling his Aunt Anne.

She lived on South Bass Island in the western basin of Lake Erie. Her two-story, East Point home overlooked Put-in-Bay's harbor and its boating traffic. The scenic resort village of Put-in-Bay has long been a vacation mecca, and with its many festive visitors, is fondly known as "The Key West of the Midwest."

Moore had moved into her home a few years earlier, after the loss of his wife and son and the death of her husband, Frank.

"Land sakes. Look who is calling me!" Aunt Anne exclaimed as she answered her cell phone. The excited tone in her voice conveyed her exasperation from not hearing from her nephew for some time. "Are you okay? Are you still in the Keys?" The questions poured out like a torrent.

Moore didn't want her to worry, and he thought of a quick response. "I'm looking out of my window at calm blue seas," Moore said as he glanced out of his hospital window at Guantanamo Bay.

"Are you okay?"

"Of course I am!" he immediately replied.

"You sure about that?" a familiar, gruff voice boomed.

Moore instantly recognized Mike "Mad Dog" Adams' voice. They had been friends for years and had shared several dangerous adventures where Moore drew upon Mad Dog's experience as a former Navy SEAL.

"What are you doing at my aunt's house?" Moore asked the island entertainer, a local legend who had performed for over forty years at the island's Round House Bar.

"Just flirting with this pretty lady sitting across from me," Adams teased.

"I don't know who he's talking about," his aunt retorted. "He's sitting here on the porch with me, and we were worrying about you over a cup of coffee."

"Maybe she was worrying more about you than me because my coffee has two shots of whiskey in it," Adams countered in jest.

"I'm glad you're both doing well," Moore said.

"When are you coming home, Emerson?" Aunt Anne asked.

Moore shifted in his bed and moaned slightly from the pain it caused. He did his best to muffle his groan. "I'm not sure. Maybe in a week," he responded cryptically as he tried to buy time.

"Don't take too long there, Emerson. I might try to sweep this pretty little lady off her feet," Adams joked.

"And I might let him if you don't get yourself back here, pronto," Aunt Anne pushed back in a teasing tone.

"I know. I know. I have a few things to wrap up before I head back to the island," Moore explained.

They bantered back and forth for a few more minutes before starting to end the call.

"I better go," Moore said. "And Aunt Anne, you be careful hanging out with that Mad Dog guy! He may take you out dancing," Moore teased.

"Oh honey, my Saturday night fever has been replaced with Saturday night hot flashes—and that's only if I'm lucky," she teased back.

"I could take her over to the Round House. I just had them install a stripper pole on the stage for me," Adams joked.

"Oh Honey, please take me over there right now," Aunt Anne ribbed Adams in a seductive tone.

"Okay you two. I can tell that I've been gone too long," Moore countered quickly.

Chuckling, Adams added, "Emerson, don't you worry none. I'll make sure that she's taken care of while you're gone."

"That's what worries me most," Moore shot back as they ended the call.

Exhausted, Moore placed his cell phone on the nightstand and relaxed. Within minutes, his ravaged body was asleep. His sleep was punctuated by tormented dreams and horrific images as his mind replayed his dangerous escape through the jungle and down the river.

Two hours later, he suddenly awoke. His body was covered in sweat even though the air-conditioned room was cool. His head ached. Forgetting about his healing wounds, Moore sat up abruptly, wincing in pain as he did. Gingerly, he laid back down and thought about the reality of his brush with death.

He turned his head to the side and looked out of the window on moonlit Guantanamo Bay. His mind focused on his near-death experience. So many times, he had narrowly escaped it. Doubt began to fill his mind and he wondered if it was time to give up his job as an investigative reporter. Maybe it was getting too dangerous. Maybe this was a warning that he should make a change. Maybe he should return to Put-in-Bay and work on the Miller Ferry.

Maybe. Maybe. Maybe. His head was filled with maybes, uncertainty and confusion. He lay awake for the next two hours as his usually sharp powers of sound reasoning short-circuited. His psyche was plagued with self-doubt.

Finally, he fell into a restless sleep. When he awoke in the morning, he still had a nagging feeling that he was finished with investigative reporting. It was becoming too dangerous the way he conducted his investigations. He couldn't perform anymore to his own level of expectation.

After his breakfast, the nurse assisted him and his IV pole to a nearby chair and wheeled the over-bed table in front of him. She set his laptop on the table and plugged it in for him.

"Thank you," Moore said appreciatively as he settled carefully in the chair.

"If you need anything, Mr. Moore, just pull on the call cord," she smiled before leaving the room.

Moore powered up the laptop and watched its screen as it opened. He stared at the screen. His mind was blank. He couldn't think. Moore shook his head from side to side as if to clear the cobwebs from his brain. He had nothing. No drive. No ambition. He had no desire to write anything about his encounter with El Patrón's drug operations. Nothing. Nada.

Reaching for the power button, he pushed and held it. He simply didn't care. The screen went blank just like Moore's face. No one was home and there were no lights on. The Pulitzer Prize-winning journalist was absent from the whole world. He was missing. Moore muttered to himself, "People say Emerson often goes off into his own little world, but that's okay—they know me there."

An hour later, that's how Moore's visitor saw him—staring into nothingness.

"Looks like you're a few beers short of a six-pack," Meier's voice roared as he entered Moore's room. "What are you doing there, boy?"

Moore snapped out of his trance as Meier's question brought him back to his surroundings. "Just thinking," he responded.

"By the look on your face, I better go out and bring back some jumper cables to attach to your head. Your brain needs a jump start. Looks like your thrusters aren't on full burn there," Meier countered.

"I was just thinking," Moore commented. "Deliberating, actually. Pondering."

"If that's what you want to call it. It looked to me like the wheel wasn't turning because the hamster was dead. You okay, Emerson?" Meier asked with genuine concern.

"Of course I'm okay."

"Sure you are. Your face is filled with doom. I've seen that look on some of my battle buddies. You may have a dose of PTSD going there—you know, Post Traumatic Stress Syndrome."

"You're pretty perceptive," Moore said.

"Reality hit you?"

"Yeah. Last night I woke up. Had all kinds of nightmares."

"About your escape?"

"Yes."

"It had to hit you, but you've got to understand that you're a survivor. You made it, Emerson. Now, once we get you all healed up, it's time to take another adventure," Meier encouraged.

"I don't know. I tried to write this morning. There was nothing there. I'm just not motivated. I think everything has left me," Moore lamented.

"It will come back to you," Meier reassured Moore. "You'll see."

"Did you find out anything more about Peaches or Bones Aiken?" Moore asked as he changed the topic. He didn't want to talk about his future.

"Like I said before, Bones has disappeared," Meier explained. "Probably got himself another false identity—if he knows what's good for him."

"What about Peaches?"

"Nada. I used what limited resources I have here in Cuba, and no one seems to know what happened to her. They did find her car in Santiago, but she flew the coop."

"She said she was from Atlanta," Moore reminded him.

"I've got my contacts checking up there to see if they find her. I'd bet you anything she gave you a false trail," Meier added. "I can't tell where or how I got this information, but there is no record of anyone named Peaches Babbit entering or leaving Cuba."

"That's strange."

"She's like a ghost," Meier suggested.

"What about the boys in Miami? Anything about a contract out on me?"

"Not from what my contacts could dig up. They're still checking, but I'd guess you're in the clear."

"Good, but I'd like to know for sure. I don't like this work anymore. I think it's time for a change," Moore sighed. "I mean it, seriously Chuck, a real change."

"Give it some time, Emerson. You're just burned out from this recent adventure. Time will help with your recovery."

"When do you think I can get out of here? More importantly, how, Chuck?"

"We'll have to check with the nurse when she comes in," Meier noted. "Where do you think you want to go? You need some place to relax for a bit."

Moore thought for a moment and smiled. "Chincoteague Island."

"You want to go and hang out with our buddy, Roe Terry?"

"Yes. I think it would be a good place for me to relax. I can't go home to Put-in-Bay like this. My aunt would be beside herself. Besides, Chincoteague is a lot calmer than Put-in-Bay. It's like Put-in-Bay on valium." Moore surprised himself by smiling.

"I think that would be a good idea. I can probably get you on a transport flight over to Boca Chica in the Keys. I'll then drive you up to Chincoteague to make sure you get there in one piece. Sound good to you?"

"Sounds like a plan," Moore answered. "If you can hand me my cell phone, I'll give Roe a call and see if I can stay at his place."

"Sure," Meier said as he handed the phone to Moore. "He and Monnie are real good people."

Moore and Roe talked for fifteen minutes as Moore gave him a brief update on his near-death adventure. Roe readily agreed to host him at his home as Moore completed his recovery.

After he ended the conversation, Moore turned to Meier. "We are all set."

"Good. I'll check with the powers to be and see when they can release you. I'll also see about getting our flight out," Meier said as he stood and walked out of the room.

# CHAPTER 2

## *Captain George's Seafood Buffet Williamsburg, Virginia*

A week had passed since Moore spoke with the Terrys about recuperating at their Chincoteague Island home. Meier and Moore had successfully departed Cuba for Boca Chica in the Keys, then to Meier's home in Cudjoe Key, Florida. Following a day of preparation for their road trip, the dynamic duo boarded Meier's unique special edition Ford Raptor truck and proceeded north for the Eastern Shore and Chincoteague Island.

The four-wheel-drive black truck reflected Meier's commanding personality. Each fender was painted with the open jaws of a shark. This was a visual warning that he wasn't a guy to mess with.

The first leg of their drive from Cudjoe Key took about twelve hours to reach Charleston, South Carolina, where they spent the night off of Interstate 95 at a motel. The next day, they enjoyed a leisurely breakfast before continuing their drive. They had driven seven hours when Meier caught Moore off-guard with a little detour to Williamsburg, Virginia.

"I've got a surprise for you, Emerson," Meier grinned as he headed down Richmond Road.

"What's that?"

"You like seafood, right?"

"Yes."

"I'm taking you to the biggest seafood buffet in the entire state of Virginia. It seats 900 people at a time, and they have great food. It's called Captain George's Seafood Buffet. Besides great seafood, there's something else special about the place," Meier said with an air of mystery.

"Oh?"

"It's run by my Navy buddy, Tom Long. We served together."

"I've met some of your friends. He must be a real character," Moore said all-knowingly.

Meier smiled. "You'll like him. He's a singer, too. At Christmas time, he becomes the area's singing Santa Claus. Entertains all kinds of kids."

"Not exactly what I'd expect from one of your friends. I bet he has to tone down his personality a lot if he's like you," Moore guessed.

"Nah. He's not as rough around the edges as me," Meier retorted.

"I look forward to meeting him," Moore said as the truck slowed in front of a building with a ship's bow in the middle. It fit right in with the Williamsburg colonial architecture.

Meier turned right and drove along the side of the building where people were lined out the door to the back of the building.

"Busy place," Moore observed.

"That's because the food is so good," Meier said as he found a parking spot behind the building.

After parking the truck, they headed to the line where they waited their turn.

"Two?" a young man with a thick mop of blond hair asked at the hostess stand. His name badge read "Noah."

"Yes, but I'm looking for an old Navy friend of mine. His name is Tom Long," Meier answered.

"That's my dad," Noah replied.

"Don't you look just like your dad at your age!" Meier smiled.

"I'll go get him," Noah responded and walked around the corner while Meier turned to talk with Moore as they waited.

A couple of minutes passed, and a male voice asked, "How many are in your party?"

Meier turned and saw that Noah had returned. "Your dad isn't here?" Meier asked perplexed.

"Oh. You want to see my dad?"

"Yes, just like I did two minutes ago when you asked," Meier replied, a bit confused by the young man's apparent memory loss.

The young man looked equally bewildered. "I'll go find him."

As the boy left the two at the hostess stand, Meier turned to Moore and commented, "In the pinball world of life, I'd say that boy's flippers are farther apart than most."

"That was strange. It was like he didn't recall your request at all," Moore agreed.

"Can I help you gentlemen?" a voice asked from behind Meier.

Before Meier turned, he noticed that a broad grin had appeared on Moore's face. When he completed his turn, he saw why.

Standing between the twins was their father, Tom Long.

"Big Daddy, how in the world are you doing, my old friend?" Long asked as the tall, broad-shouldered Long clasped Meier in a bear hug.

"Better now. I was worried about your son having short-term memory loss, but I see that you've got twins," Meier said with a chuckle. He quickly explained what had transpired and the five men snickered together.

"Now that we've got that cleared up, let me show you two to a table," Long suggested. "And is your friend a veteran?"

"Of life? Yes. Of the armed forces? No. This is Emerson Moore. He's a buddy of mine who works for *The Washington Post*," Meier explained as the two men shook hands, then walked to a table.

"Nice place you have here," Moore said appreciatively as he looked around the nautical décor.

"The food is even better," Long assured them as they arrived at the table. "Your server will be here to take your drink orders, but go ahead and grab a plate to start the buffet. I've got a couple of things to do, but I'll be back to talk with you."

"Go ahead," Meier said. "We're big boys."

Long disappeared to tend to his duties, and the other two helped themselves to the sumptuous buffet. Twenty minutes later, Long returned to their table and eased his well-built frame into a chair.

"How did you enjoy your meal?" he asked.

"It was delicious," Moore responded. "I focused on the shrimp, scallops and fish. And the barbeque ribs were tasty!"

"Good. Glad you enjoyed it," Long beamed as he turned to face Meier. "How was yours, Big Daddy?"

Meier patted his belly. "I destroyed the oysters and Alaska snow crab legs."

Long smiled. "It was that good?"

A mischievous smile appeared on Meier's face. "Tom, great food is like great sex. The more you have, the more you want!"

Long and Moore joined in chuckling at Meier's quip.

"Emerson, when Tom and I were in the Navy together, we used to call him Tommy Gun," Meier said.

"Oh, I can see this one coming," Long smiled as his eyes widened.

"He used to go off like a tommy gun. He'd spit out one-liners faster than me. Looks to me like he slowed down a might," Meier remarked.

"That's what getting older does to you. Hopefully I'm getting a bit wiser, too," Long countered.

Meier wasn't going to stop. "Tom used to speak ten words a second with gusts to fifty."

"You're not going to stop until I give you one, huh?" Long asked with a look of pure innocence on his face.

Meier just sat back and waited with a large grin on his face.

Long erupted. "When I first met Big Daddy, he was fresh in from West Texas. That boy was so country that he thought a seven-course meal was possum and a six-pack. I'm surprised you didn't ask if we had possum on the menu."

Laughing, Meier replied, "I did ask one of your folks who was refilling the buffet. You should have seen the look she gave me."

"Of course you would."

"What do you think, Emerson? Should we swap spit with him and hit the road?" Meier asked.

"I don't know about swapping spit, but I'm ready to hit the

road," Moore replied.

The intrepid reporter had been unusually quiet during the meal. The long road trip was taking more out of him than he previously expected and he was rapidly becoming fatigued.

The three men rose from their chairs. Meier settled up their meal tab and server tip before bidding Tom Long a hearty farewell and returning with Moore to the truck. Before long, the pair encountered bumper-to-bumper traffic along Interstate 64 heading east for the Norfolk tunnel.

"How long of a drive do we have?" Moore asked.

"It's about three more hours to Chincoteague after we get through this mess," Meier responded as he eased the big truck forward. "Once we get to the turn-off for Route 13, we're going to need to gas up this beast."

"It's later than I expected," Moore said as he glanced at his watch.

Forty-five minutes later, they exited onto Route 13. It was nearing midnight when Meier wheeled the truck into a gas station a mile down from the exit.

"Not sure that I like what I see," Meier said as he squinted his eyes.

A low-riding car with two thugs in it pulled up next to a police car parked at the side of the gas station. They were eying the police officer. An officer was finishing a cup of coffee that he had purchased inside.

"Open that glove box, Emerson," Meier said in a grave tone.

Moore did as he was told and popped it open.

"Take that Smith and Wesson and hold onto to it. You're going to be my backup."

"Trouble?" Moore asked, curious as he looked toward the

two vehicles.

"Could be. You never know," Meier said cautiously as he parked the truck. "I've got something back here in the crew cab that might come in handy." He released his seatbelt and leaned into the back where he picked up a dangerous looking weapon.

"What's that, Chuck?"

"This here is a M249 light machine gun. It's known as a Squad Automatic Weapon or SAW for short. I call it my equalizer," he grinned.

"You're going to use it?"

"To serve and protect a fellow officer, I'll use anything if I have to," he said. Meier intently watched one of the thugs get out of the car and walk in front of the police car where he turned and started yelling at the police officer. The thug pulled out a .45 caliber semi-automatic handgun from his waistband and began shooting.

The officer instantly ducked onto the seat of his car and struggled to withdraw his service weapon while the thug continued shooting.

Meier jammed his foot on the gas pedal, and the truck leaped forward as it raced to the police car. The approaching truck caught the thug's attention, and he began to swing his gun arm toward it.

Meier brought the truck to a screeching halt and shoved open his door. He emerged from the truck like a screaming banshee as he opened up with the SAW. The thug ducked in front of the police car and edged his way to the right front end where he peeked around, firing off two rounds at Meier.

Avoiding any stalemate, Meier advanced toward the vehicle, laying covering fire as he moved forward.

The thug popped up and began to take aim at Meier when

several rounds from the SAW caught him in the chest, killing him. Meier ran up to be sure.

Suddenly, he heard Moore yell, "Drop it." The shout was followed by Moore's Smith and Wesson firing twice.

Meier turned and saw that Moore had left the truck to cover him. The second thug, the driver, had also left his car and had sneaked behind the police car to get a shot at Meier. Moore's two shots had eliminated the threat.

Meier walked over to the second thug and made sure he, too, was dead before looking at Moore.

"Thank you, Emerson. I owe you one," Meier spoke gratefully.

"I told you I have your back," Moore grinned as he leaned against the police car.

Meier peered inside. "You okay, officer?"

"As far as I can tell," the officer replied as he sat up and exited the vehicle. "Thank you for saving my life," he said as he eyed the SAW. "Nice weapon," he added as he wrinkled his brow.

"Comes in handy. Don't worry. I'm licensed. I'm one of you guys."

"Here?"

"Florida. Cudjoe Key and wherever I'm needed. I train law enforcement officers," Meier explained. "You know these guys?"

"No. Probably some drug runners that are pissed off about our more aggressive approach with them," the officer replied.

"How's that?" Meier asked.

"This road here," the officer began as he pointed to the highway, "is known as the Cocaine Express."

"It is?" Moore asked.

"Yes. It's a faster drive through here since you don't have to go through the D.C. traffic on I-95. And usually, there are fewer traffic stops."

"Usually?" Meier asked as he picked up the word.

"Yeah. We've started pulling over more vehicles out here and ended up doing quite a few drug busts. Really pissed off the drug runners," the officer explained.

"I'll say," Moore agreed.

The sounds of sirens signaled the approach of a number of law enforcement vehicles responding to the reports of a shooting.

"That was an awesome weapon you fired," Moore said as he looked at the SAW that Meier was cradling in his arms.

"Emerson, you never go to battle with a slingshot. Overwhelming firepower is what you want. This little baby can fire at a rate of 800 rounds per minute at a range of 800 meters. But I only have a 30-round M16 magazine in this one. If I let loose with 800 rounds, we'd all be slipping and sliding on the cartridge shells," he snickered.

"Nice," Moore said appreciatively, before looking back at the body of the man Meier had cut down. "I bet he was surprised."

"You can count on that. He should have dropped his weapon when he saw me approaching." Meier paused before continuing. "Emerson, I have a billion nerves in my body, and that guy irritated all of them. He could have lived if he had dropped his weapon."

The men spent an hour explaining their role to the arriving law enforcement officers and then returned to Meier's truck. Meier set the SAW on the floor of the cab and covered it with a blanket as Moore returned the Smith and Wesson to the glove compartment.

"It's really late," Moore said as he glanced at his watch.

"Yeah. You might want to send our buddy Roe a text and let him know we're rolling in late," Meier suggested.

"I can do that," Moore said as he reached for the phone and sent off a quick text message.

When Moore's cell phone beeped, he looked down and saw that Roe Terry had responded. "He said we should take our time," Moore read to Meier.

"That we will," Meier said as he pulled the truck out on the highway and headed north. Shortly they would be paying an $18 toll and driving along the 17.6-mile-long Chesapeake Bay Bridge and tunnel across the mouth of the Chesapeake Bay. The route linked Norfolk, Hampton, Chesapeake and Virginia Beach with the Delmarva Peninsula and Virginia's Eastern Shore.

# CHAPTER 3

## The Causeway
## Chincoteague Island, Virginia

A couple of hours later, Meier turned right onto Route 175 and headed for nearby Chincoteague Island.

"They've got a lot going on here," Meier observed a few minutes later as they rode past the well-lit NASA Visitor Center and the huge NASA/NOAA complex with its satellite dishes, hangars and runways on Wallops Island.

"I was surprised on my first visit here, too," Moore said as he recalled his adventure not so long ago. It involved NASA rockets mysteriously exploding. That was his first trip to the area.

They followed the causeway through the marsh and across the Black Narrows and Chincoteague Channel onto Chincoteague Island, a nine-square-mile barrier island off the Virginia coast with about 3,000 year-round inhabitants. The subtropical island's highest point is only three feet above sea level.

As they approached the traffic light at the foot of the bridge to the island, Moore glanced to his right where the shadows hid the remains of the Clam Shells Pub. It had been destroyed by an explosion during his prior visit and he recalled how he had narrowly escaped death there, too. They turned left and headed north on Main Street.

When they neared Terry's house, Moore spotted several signs at the corner of Main Street and Winder Lane. The signs announced waterfowl carvings by Roe "Duc-Man" Terry at 5191 North Main.

"Pull in here. This is it," Moore instructed Meier.

Meier turned left into the driveway of the one-story, yellow vinyl-sided ranch home with a large front porch. He parked behind the house in the well-lit parking area in front of a low building which housed Terry's retail outlet and workshop.

In front of the wooden deck was an array of weathered clam shells, carved wooden ducks, floats and buoys. It had a nautical theme. A yellow flag with a rattlesnake and the saying "Don't Tread on Me" flew from the corner of the deck. Another sign read, "Prayer is the best way to meet the Lord. Trespassing is faster."

Looking at the signs, Meier spoke admirably, "I think I know why you like being here."

"It sure captures the flavor of who Roe is, doesn't it?"

"Oh yeah," Meier agreed.

The door to the side of the house opened, and a man appeared. He looked to be in his forties, had long graying hair with a matching goatee and wore a headband. He was wearing a sleeveless t-shirt and cutoff jean shorts. He looked like a cross between a hippie and someone out of the TV show "Duck Dynasty."

Roe bounded down the steps to greet his visitors. "You sure took your time in getting here," he stated.

"We ran into a little trouble as we left Norfolk," Moore said.

"That wouldn't surprise me, seeing as you two hombres are together. What kind of trouble did you two get yourselves into?" Roe asked.

Meier and Moore explained what had transpired earlier at the gas station shootout on Highway 13.

"Yeah. I've known about the trouble they've been having on

that Cocaine Expressway. Doesn't surprise me."

"You don't get much blow over here, do you?" Moore asked.

"Nope. Nothing like they have over there," Roe responded.

"What do you having going on here, Roe?" Meier asked as he eyed a sign attached to the workshop. It read "Open when I'm here. Closed when I ain't."

"You like that?"

"Sure."

"Come on. I'll show you my workshop and showroom. Emerson saw it last time," Roe said.

"And I'd like to see it again," Moore said enthusiastically as he followed the two men up the short flight of steps and entered the retail outlet.

"Nice," Meier said as he stepped inside and gazed at the wood-paneled walls. They were covered by shelves displaying expertly carved waterfowl, in addition to a diverse collection of oyster cans, deer antlers, shotguns and traps. A large, oval rug covered the painted green floor as a ceiling fan turned lazily overhead. A display table in the middle of the room held a variety of carving books and an island mystery adventure author's books for sale.

"Come on over here and see the workshop," Roe said proudly as he opened a door and walked through.

Meier's eye swept the shelves on the two walls in the small hallway. They were packed with duck carvings. "Oh my," he said as he walked into the main working area which was filled with the aroma of freshly chipped wood. He glanced at the floor and saw wood chips surrounding a tree stump with a carving hatchet buried in it. A worn office chair was behind the stump.

"That's where you carve?" Meier asked.

"Yep. That's where I spend a lot of time," Roe answered.

The walls were filled with oyster cans and waterfowl carvings. Several shotguns hung from the walls as did three calendars of bikini-clad females.

"I've got to compliment you on your wall art," Meier said as he took in the scantily-clad women posed on the calendars.

"Roe, tell him which one is your wife," Moore teased.

"Your wife is one of them?" Meier's eyes widened as he looked closer.

Roe and Moore laughed.

"No, Emerson's joshing you."

"But she could be," Moore countered.

"The only centerfold that my Monnie will be is mine," Roe kidded.

"I get it," Meier said as he shifted his attention to the work table with two shelves over it. The top shelf displayed unpainted ducks while the second shelf held freshly painted ducks. The work tabletop was covered with a variety of carving tools, paint cans and containers filled with paint brushes.

"There's plenty of beer in the fridge. Help yourself," Roe said as he nodded to an old refrigerator that had seen better days.

"I'm good," Meier said. "We actually should be hitting the hay. Right, Emerson?"

Moore stifled a yawn. "Yes. I'm tired."

"Let's quit jabbering out here then and get to the house. You need help with your gear?" Roe asked.

"We've got it," Meier said as he and Moore headed out the shop door and grabbed their gear from the truck. They caught up to Roe and followed him through a side door into the house.

"You're going to love what you see here," Moore said to

Meier as they entered. "I think I told you that I stayed here for a week some time ago."

"You did," Meier said as he followed the two men into the house. He stopped and stared as a smile filled his face. "I like this. I like this a lot."

The family room featured a cathedral ceiling with wood paneling. The walls also were wood-paneled, and a brick fireplace with a large mantel was positioned on the north wall. Gracing each side of the mantel was a mounted white-tailed deer head featuring a large rack of antlers.

Wooden shelves lined the walls and displayed hand-carved ducks, including bluebills, hooded mergansers, canvasbacks, goldeneyes, blue-winged teal and pintails. Various taxidermy waterfowl also graced the walls of the family room, along with several framed original paintings of duck hunting scenes common to the Eastern Shore and Chesapeake Bay.

A 65-inch, QLED 8K TV was flanked by two steel cabinets that contained Terry's collection of shotguns, rifles and handguns. On the other side of the room were a more modest green plaid sofa and two recliners.

Meier spotted the large head of an alligator with sharp teeth. "You shoot him?"

"Yep. I was in Louisiana with my swamp buddies. That one was eleven-foot long. You should come with me on one of my gator hunting trips," Roe proudly stated.

"I'd like to do that," Meier responded. "I've hunted all kinds of animals, but nothing like gators. You going to join us, Emerson?"

"Not me, Chuck," Moore commented quickly. "I've been in those swamps, and I've seen how big those gators can get. Besides, Roe told me about one he shot, pulled aboard and it came back alive."

Meier laughed. "How did you know it was alive, Roe?"

"Well, you see, I felt something gnawing at the back of my boot. I turned around, and there was this ornery gator chomping on me."

"You jump in the water or take him out with your knife?" Meier asked.

"Neither. I just put a round through its skull," Roe explained as if it was an everyday occurrence.

"And through the boat?" Meier asked.

"Nah. The skull was thick enough. It took him out."

"Where's Monnie?" Moore asked as he looked around the room.

"She got tired of waiting for you boys and went to bed. She'll see you at breakfast."

"Speaking of bed, I'm ready," Moore said.

"You're in the same room as last time. You know your way," Roe replied. "Chuck, you can follow me and I'll show you your room."

The next morning, the rich aroma of bacon cooking mixed with freshly-brewed coffee filled the kitchen. Roe and Moore were seated at the table as Roe's wife, Monnie, scurried around the kitchen to make breakfast.

"I smell something good!" Meier roared as he walked down the hall into the kitchen.

"Did the smell of breakfast wake you?" Moore grinned as he looked up from his coffee cup.

"It sure helped," he suggested as he sat in the chair next to Moore and across from Roe. He sniffed the air again and wrinkled his nose.

"You okay?" Roe asked.

"Speaking of smell, something smells bad, like horse manure," Meier declared as he looked at Moore.

"I just got in from a long walk," Moore explained. "It was hot out."

"You need a shower, Emerson."

"Right after breakfast," Moore answered.

"And who is this beautiful woman cooking breakfast for us?" Meier asked as he turned his attention to the svelte brunette in her late forties who flashed him a warm smile.

"Meet my wife, Monnie," Roe offered.

"Hello, Chuck," Monnie greeted Meier before turning back to the skillet. "Sorry I missed meeting you last night. You boys got here too late."

"No problem," Meier said before looking at Roe. "Is this the sweet thing you met at the stripper joint?"

Roe guffawed as he decided to play along with Meier. "Yep. There were two of them to choose between. Since the other one was as big as Shamu, I chose this one."

"Now Roe Terry, don't you be going on with made-up stories about me!" she scolded her husband light-heartedly.

"Who, me?" Becoming serious, Roe said, "Chuck, now you know that's not true." He took a sip of coffee. "And I'd advise you, son, to be careful. Otherwise, she just might slap you on the side of the head with that hot skillet," he teased.

"My husband knows me well," Monnie cheerfully joined in as she took the skillet off the stove and took a step toward Meier.

"I was just busting your chops," Meier explained hurriedly.

"Honey, this boy just wants to make a great first impression on you," Roe smiled.

"I'm the one who might make a great impression on Chuck.

Right on the side of his head," Monnie teased back.

They continued their good-natured exchange over breakfast. When they finished, Meier spoke.

"I hate to treat you all like a drive-by shooting, but I've got to head up to Annapolis for some business."

"Like Blackwater stuff?" Moore asked.

"You never know," Meier said as he winked slyly.

"You gotta do what you gotta do," Roe commented.

"I should be back in a few days. I'd like to take a tour of your island and get in some fishing, Roe."

"No better place to do it. I'll be here when you get back."

Moore added to the conversation. "And thanks, Chuck, for being my guardian angel and chauffer. I can't thank you enough."

"I've been called a lot of things in my life, but never a guardian angel. That's a new one for me, Emerson, but I'm glad I could help save that scrawny neck of yours."

Within thirty minutes, Meier had showered, packed and hit the road for his meeting in Annapolis.

As Moore and Roe stood in the driveway and watched Meier drive away, Roe commented, "He's quite a guy, isn't he?"

"I'll say. One of the most unique people I've ever met. Such a rascal, but he has a soft heart underneath that gruff exterior."

"That's for sure. So, what do you have planned for today?"

"I thought I'd drive around the island a bit and refresh my memory," Moore offered. "Want to join me?"

"I can't. I've got a load of cottonwood being delivered this morning and I need to work on it. But you're in luck."

"How's that?" Moore asked.

"That Jeep Patriot over there belongs to my son. He left it here while he's gone overseas and I have the keys. You can use it while you're visiting with us."

"Thanks, I appreciate it," Moore said.

"But you better get in there and take that shower. I agree with Chuck. You smell a bit ripe," Roe chuckled as the two men headed back to the house.

Thirty minutes later, a freshly-showered Moore hopped into the front seat of the Jeep. Turning right out of Roe's drive, he drove south along Main Street. He wanted to reacquaint himself with the island and reflect on his last visit to the area.

He passed through the charming downtown filled with antique shops, art galleries, souvenir shops and restaurants. He smiled when he saw Don's Seafood restaurant with Chattie's Lounge on the second floor. He loved their clam chowder and made a mental note to stop by for lunch.

On the right, he saw a number of chain hotels and independent boutique hotels dotting the waterfront as well as several fishing piers. As he drove by the Waterside Inn, he spotted Donna Mason getting out of her car and tooted his horn as he pulled into the parking lot.

"Emerson," the attractive blonde started. "Are you back on my island?"

"Yes. Just got in last night?"

"And you're not staying here?" she asked with a pouty little frown.

"Not this trip, Donna. I'm staying with Roe."

Moore felt bad because he had met Donna on his last trip and had toured her inn. He liked it and told her then he would stay there the next time he visited the island.

"Bad boy," she teased.

"Next trip," he said.

"Promises, promises," she kidded. "You want to come in

for a coffee?"

"I'd love to, but I'm heading down to Captain Bob's Marina."

"You have a good time, dear," she said as she waved.

Moore pulled out of the parking lot and continued his drive south. He had a little boyish smile on his face and briefly replayed in his mind the encounter with the friendly Mason. He admired her winning personality.

As he drove past the carnival grounds, he saw the signs announcing the upcoming pony swim and auction. Saltwater cowboys herded the wild ponies from nearby Assateague Island into the channel between the two islands. The ponies then would swim to Chincoteague Island where they were herded through the street to the carnival grounds for the pony auction.

It was a huge annual summertime fundraiser for the Chincoteague Volunteer Fire Company and it attracted thousands of tourists. The event also allowed the pony herd to be properly managed as part of a natural resources management plan for Assateague Island as it could only support so many ponies.

Moore was pleased that he would be on the island for this year's pony swim and auction. He had missed it on his last visit.

As he drove, Moore thought how satisfied he was that he had chosen Chincoteague as the site to extend his recuperation. It was so peaceful and alluring. It was like Put-in-Bay on valium. The island seemed so calm compared to Put-in-Bay. Moore was experiencing a sense of contentment. What he didn't know was that it wouldn't last for long.

Within another five minutes, he turned right into Captain Bob's Marina, the largest marina on the island. His tires crunched on the limestone parking lot as he parked in front of the marina's office.

Moore exited the car and looked across the bay at Wallops Island and its NASA rocket launch pad where a number of Antares rockets had exploded during launch. Moore's first Chincoteague vacation became pervasively interrupted and was filled with another puzzle of suspense, intrigue and investigative journalism as he uncovered the source of the explosions.

His subsequent stories of the rocket explosions, which were published in *The Washington Post*, made Moore even more determined to one day return to Chincoteague Island for another opportunity of real rest and relaxation. It was difficult in the present moment though, not to allow his mind to be filled with memories of his encounters with Hala Yazbek, Russian General Orlov, Wu Tang and Maya Simon as well as the pompous head of NASA Security, Hal Horner. He wondered briefly if Horner still worked at Wallops Island, but quickly decided that he really wasn't interested in learning anything more about the jerk.

Moore's eyes followed the flight of a passing seagull until he saw the 20-foot-long shipping container sitting on the other side of the marina's restrooms. It had once been the home of Bo White, who had painted the container white and then named it "The White House." White had provided Moore some valuable insight during his investigation into the rocket explosions.

He recalled how much he had enjoyed his time with Bo White. It was a special time and one that would not be relived since White had been murdered. He sincerely missed him.

"You going to stand there all day, or come in and say hello?" a voice snapped from behind and broke Moore's thoughts.

He turned and saw an attractive blonde in her early fifties standing at the open marina doorway. It was Donna Roeske, the marina owner.

Smiling, Moore walked over to Roeske and gave her a big

hug. “Donna, it’s so good to see you, my friend.”

“It’s been a while, Emerson,” she said warmly as she placed her arms around his waist and squeezed him. He responded with a groan.

“What is this groaning noise? You becoming a big baby, man-child?” she asked as they separated and walked inside the building.

Following her to the sales counter, Moore explained. “Not me, but I’m a bit tender from a recent wound.”

“There you go, getting hurt when I’m not around to rescue you,” she shot back.

Moore cheerfully smiled as he recalled her saving his bacon. “Still have that rifle?”

“Right there,” she said as she pointed to the weapon. “And I’m still a crack shot.”

“I bet you are.”

“Are you here on a pleasure trip this time? No business? No investigating?”

“That’s the plan,” Moore said, without mentioning what had happened in Norfolk on the way up.

“You picked the right place, provided you don’t go sticking your nose into stuff like you did the last time you were here.”

“Donna, sometimes I can’t help myself,” he explained.

“You need to just hunker down and enjoy life, Emerson.”

“That’s my plan this time,” he smiled.

“You going fishing on this visit?”

“Wouldn’t miss it.”

“I can charter you with Captain Oz Morgan like last time.”

“Maybe. I’ll see what Roe wants to do.”

“You staying with Roe?”

“Yes.”

"He's such a good guy."

"I know." Moore looked around the jam-packed retail space before adding, "I better go. I just wanted to stop by and see you."

"Where you off to?"

"I'm heading out to Assateague Island."

"You running again?"

"Not yet. It's a bit painful. Just walking, but I'll be running within a week," Moore answered.

"Now don't go and reinjure yourself. Slow down a bit and enjoy life," she instructed.

"Will do," Moore smiled as he headed out the door and returned to the Jeep.

Shortly afterward, he turned left out of the parking lot and drove back through town to Maddox Boulevard where he made a right turn and followed it eastward. He took in familiar sites from his last trip, including the local bike rentals and ice cream stands like Mr. Whippy and The Island Creamery. He drove by H&H Pharmacy, and Steamers and Maria's restaurants, before spotting The Village Restaurant, one of his favorites for their flounder dinners. He also passed AJ's on the Creek and Woody's Beach BBQ, an outdoor restaurant with a captivating collection of beach and hippie memorabilia that included an old flower power VW minibus.

After driving through the roundabout where the Chamber of Commerce office was located, he continued driving east along the boulevard past the popular Refuge Inn onto the causeway to Assateague Island. He paid the gate fee at the entrance booth and followed Beach Road through the thick woods and past the red and white striped, 142-foot-tall Assateague Lighthouse.

A short distance later, Moore pulled to the side of the road where he spent a few minutes watching a herd of wild ponies grazing. It made him feel good to realize there still exist many good things in nature to enjoy as well as life. Wild ponies are really cool to see, Moore thought to himself.

A few minutes later, Moore pulled back onto the road and drove to the beach where he turned right into a parking lot and parked the Jeep at the farthest point south. He locked the vehicle and walked atop one of the sand dunes and stopped.

Moore took in the wide expanse of pristine beach that lay before him. He loved this beach because there were no cottages, condos or hotels overlooking it. He especially enjoyed early morning jogs on the beach before any of the day-trippers arrived. Looking north, he saw a number of beachgoers enjoying their day in the sun, sand and sea.

Moore turned his attention to the south as he walked through the heavy, dry sand to the wet, hard-packed sand at the water's edge. This was where he liked to jog. He started to run, but quickly halted as he felt a few sharp twinges of pain in his side.

Too soon to try that, thought Moore.

Instead, he took a leisurely walk south along the water's edge toward Toms Cove Hook. Twenty minutes later, he slowly pulled off his t-shirt and sat down on the beach. Not only was this a perfect area for jogging, but the peaceful solitude of the southern end offered Moore an ideal time to think.

What about his future? What would he do if the desire to write had left him? A number of thoughts about his career raced through his mind as he watched the seagulls flying overhead.

Forty minutes later, Moore didn't have any answers to the flood of questions his mind had raised. He stood and returned to the parked Jeep. He was carrying his t-shirt in his hand while beads of perspiration covered his face and chiseled chest.

He reached inside his insulated cooler and grabbed a bottle of water that he had purchased at Captain Bob's Marina and took a long drink before pouring its remainder over his head, shoulders, chest and back as he enjoyed the water's cooling effect.

He climbed into the Jeep and drove back to Chincoteague. After crossing onto the island, he wheeled the vehicle into a parking spot at Pony Tails—a place well-known for their saltwater taffy, fudge and unique souvenirs.

Walking into the store, he heard a voice shout at him, "Well, look who has returned to our island."

Moore looked to the center of the store and saw the store's manager, Pamela Ireland. He returned the attractive redhead's greeting. "Hello, Pamela."

"You back causing more trouble in our peaceful paradise, Emerson?" she asked.

Shaking his head as he smiled, Moore responded, "Nope. Just a little R & R." He had met Pamela on one of his visits to the Pony Tails Candy Company the last time he was on the island.

"Are you back for some of that root beer taffy that you liked so much?"

Moore nodded as she walked over to the taffy counter.

"How much would you like?" she asked as she picked up a scoop.

"Three pounds."

"Whoa! You going to eat that all by yourself?" she teased.

"I'm sharing it with Roe and Monnie," he replied.

"You staying with them again?" she asked as she filled a sack with the individually-wrapped pieces.

"Yes. They're such good people."

"I know what you mean. This island is filled with good people," she said with pride.

"Most of them," Moore agreed. "And please, I'll take two pounds of that chocolate fudge," he added.

"I'll be watching tomorrow to see if I spot you jogging by. With all of this sweet stuff, you're going to have to start your running again," she said as she remembered him taking long jogs out to Assateague Beach and back.

"Maybe next week for jogging," he said. "I'm going to be busy just relaxing."

"You picked the right place to relax. No place around like a Chincoteague calm."

"I agree," he said as she handed him his items and he headed for the cash register where a tall blonde cashier waited. Moore remembered meeting Donna Speidel on his last visit.

"Hi Donna."

"Stocking up on that root beer taffy, I see," she teased with her winning smile.

"Always," he answered as he watched her weigh his purchases and paid her.

"I bet we see you in a couple of days for a refill," she said wryly as he picked up his packages and headed for the door.

"Maybe," he smiled back. He really did like their root beer taffy.

After returning to the vehicle, he drove back to Roe's house. Parking the Jeep, he grabbed his purchases and started to walk to the side entrance of the house.

He stopped when he heard what sounded like someone chopping wood behind Roe's workshop. He decided to surprise Roe with the fudge and taffy and headed around the corner.

Suddenly, Moore froze. Roe had his back to Moore and was chopping a piece of cottonwood. But it was the man behind him that caused immediate concern.

It was the remaining Kronsky twin, and he was walking up to Roe. In his hand, Louie was carrying a hatchet. Moore had killed Louie's twin brother Luke when he broke into Roe's house during Moore's previous stay.

Reacting quickly, Moore dropped the sacks and launched himself through the air at Kronsky, knocking him to the ground. The two rolled over while Moore groaned in pain from his almost-healed abdomen wound. The two fought for control of the hatchet before they heard Roe's voice thunder.

"Stop it. What are you two boys doing?"

"Saving your life, Roe. He was sneaking up on you with a hatchet," Moore said as he separated himself from Kronsky while holding the captured hatchet and giving Kronsky a wary eye.

"You mean the hatchet that I asked him to get for me?" Roe inquired.

"Louie works for you?" a bewildered Moore asked as he stood, wincing from his still-tender wound.

"Yes. Louie is rehabbing with me. Aren't you, son?" Roe asked as he smiled at his protégé, who also stood up.

"Helping Roe any way I can," Kronsky nodded.

"Louie is working hard at changing his life. No more drug running, right?" Roe asked.

"No, sir. I put all that stuff behind me," he answered before turning to Moore. "It got both of my brothers killed."

Moore recalled that his other brother Joe, the meanest of the three, had his body fished out of Chincoteague Channel. The young man in front of him had gone through his share of tragedy.

Contritely Moore offered, "I'm sorry about killing Luke."

Before Kronsky could comment, Roe interjected, "Nothing to be sorry about, Emerson. Luke broke into my house. That's breaking and entering. You were just protecting my property. Besides, he was gunning for you, and you had to defend yourself. Luke was plain wrong. And one other thing that you probably didn't know, Luke was high on cocaine that night. At least, that's what the autopsy showed."

Kronsky shook his head in agreement as he looked at Moore. "You don't owe me an apology. What my brother did was wrong, and he got what was coming to him. All three of us were doing some bad things back then."

"You were," Roe concurred. "And Louie here was the only one who woke up to doing the right thing. He's doing his best now to follow the straight and narrow, aren't you, son?"

"Yes, I am," Kronsky nodded.

"And part of that straight and narrow is that path over yonder. I need you to bring some more of that cottonwood from that pile and stack it here."

"Right away," he said as he scurried off.

Moore turned to Roe. "You have no idea what flashed through my mind when I saw him approaching your back with that hatchet," Moore explained.

"I'm sure you had my best interests at heart. Thanks anyway."

"What are you guys doing?" Moore asked.

"I've got some cottonwood to use for my decoys. We're debarking it and splitting it down to a workable size for me. Louie's helping me."

"It's nice that you've taken Louie under your wing," Moore

said. "He's doing things right, now?"

"Pretty much. He's a real talented carpenter if he'd focus on it. It's amazing some of the things he can build."

"Nice skill to have," Moore commented.

"That kid had a rough life growing up. His brother Joe was the worst of the lot. He took the twins down the wrong path with the drug running and breaking and entering business. But you still have to keep an eye on Louie."

"Oh?" Moore asked.

"Yeah. He tries really hard, but he drifts back into some of his old habits at times. And when you ask that boy a question, many times he gives you a relaxed version of the truth. He's come a long way, but he still has a long way to go to clean up his act."

"He's still involved with drug running?"

"I'm suspicious. Primarily because of some of the crowd he'll hang out with down in Accomac and Cape Charles. Then he can disappear for a few days up to Ocean City. Probably using drugs."

"Oh boy," Moore muttered. "It does come down to who you associate with, doesn't it?"

"And it didn't help with his old man verbally abusing him. He'd tell the boy things like he was as useless as the letter 'g' in the word lasagna."

Moore shook his head sadly. "That had to be tough. And hanging with the wrong crowd is a lot of the problem."

"I give him credit for trying to break out of it. He's a good kid, and he's got good carpentry skills. I think one of the reasons he keeps coming back here is that he finds a sense of stability here."

"I can see that. You and Monnie are two of the most stable

people I know."

"You're going to put us in a horse stable?" Roe teased.

Moore grinned. "You know what I mean, Roe."

The sound of a vehicle's door slamming caught their attention. Roe turned toward Kronsky. "I'm going around front. You keep working at that pile, okay?"

"I got it, Roe," Kronsky yelled back.

"Come around front and let's see who pulled up. Might be someone who wants to buy some duck decoys," Roe said as he headed around the building, followed closely by Moore.

When they walked in front, they saw a deeply tanned, lean man with short-cropped, white hair. He was wearing a sheriff's deputy uniform, and his Ford Explorer had the markings of the Accomack County Sheriff's Department.

"Billy Joe, how's it going?" Roe greeted his friend.

"Good. Stopped by on my break to pick up that decoy you were holding for me."

"It's inside. Come on in," Roe said as he turned and walked up the steps to his workshop. "This is my buddy, Emerson Moore," he added as he introduced Moore.

"Nice to meet you," Moore said as the two men shook hands.

"Likewise," Deputy Tarr said as he followed them into the workshop. "Nice and cool in here, Roe."

"I like it that way," he replied as he picked up the decoy and showed it to Tarr.

"Another masterpiece," Tarr said as he reached for the decoy and examined the mallard. "Beautiful," he added.

As Tarr was paying Roe, Roe commented, "Billy Joe, you'd be interested in my buddy here. You both are a bit involved in the same line of business."

"Oh?" Tarr asked.

"The investigating line. He just returned from a drug investigation in Cuba where he got pretty banged up. Almost died."

"DEA?" Tarr asked as he looked at Moore.

"No. I'm an investigative reporter," Moore replied. "*Washington Post.*"

"What happened to you in Cuba?"

Moore gave Tarr a quick *Reader's Digest* version of his misadventure in Key West and Cuba.

"Bad stuff and you're lucky to be alive," Tarr concurred with Roe.

"I'm hanging out here with Roe and Monnie while I recuperate from my wounds. I can't think of a better place to be," Moore explained.

"Makes sense to me," Tarr agreed.

"And you're involved in drug investigations?" Moore asked.

"Yes. I'm on the task force for Accomack and Northampton counties and we work with the folks from Salisbury and Ocean City."

"No DEA?" Moore asked.

"I was trying to give you a short answer, but we do work with the DEA, the Virginia State Police, the ATF and the local law enforcement agencies in Eastville, Exmore, Cape Charles, Chincoteague, Onancock and Parksley."

"Sounds like a lot of coordination," Moore said as he digested the answer.

"There's one more group we work with."

"Who's that?"

"One source of good information is the Virginia Department of Corrections."

"How's that?" Moore asked.

"The inmates use our phones to connect with their families and their partners on the outside. They exchange a lot of intel that is good for us to have—and we get it because all of their phones are tapped," he grinned.

"What a source for intel!" Moore agreed.

"You know about Route 13 being called the Cocaine Expressway?" Tarr asked.

"Yes. I heard that."

"Last week, we had a tip about a box truck running a 20-kilo load of cocaine from a warehouse in Virginia Beach to a location in Ocean City. We tailed them to their destination and busted them as they exchanged the drugs for cash."

"Did you get whoever the ringleader is?" Moore asked, his curiosity piqued.

"No. That would be Max Steiner. Steiner's too slick. Has layers of gang members for the dirty work. What we've been able to glean is that Steiner has a place in Cape Charles. Steiner flies in and out on a seaplane. Very low profile and very elusive. The DEA is working hard to get something on Steiner."

Moore was warming up to the idea of doing a story on Steiner's drug running, especially with the area being so close to Washington. "I'd be interested in going along with you on a raid sometime."

"Maybe. I'd have to clear it."

"I've got some security clearances, if that helps," Moore offered. "I've got a couple of friends in law enforcement who can vouch for me." Moore grabbed a piece of paper and wrote down the cell phone numbers for Sam Duncan and Chuck Meier.

Tarr took the paper that Moore handed him and looked at the names. "I don't know them, but let me see what I can do. It could be at the last minute, if you're cleared," Tarr suggested.

"That's fine with me," Moore said.

"And all of this coming from the guy who's supposed to be here recuperating," Roe teased.

"You know how it is, Roe. You can't keep a good man down," Moore retorted. He was surprised with himself. Maybe his passion for writing was returning, he thought.

Tarr looked at Roe. "You still have that Kronsky boy working for you?"

"Yes. He's doing a good job."

"I gather he's staying out of trouble," Tarr said casually, but with a sharp eye toward Roe.

"As far as I can tell."

"Good. Well, I better hit the road," Tarr said as he picked up the decoy and headed for the door where he paused. He looked at Moore. "I'll get back to you about going with us on a raid."

"Thanks, Billy Joe," Moore said.

"See you, Roe," Tarr said, walking through the doorway and out to his car.

"Next time, son," Roe called.

While favoring his healing wound, Moore spent the rest of the day helping Roe and Kronsky move and cut cottonwood behind the workshop. After they finished, Kronsky headed home and Roe and Moore went into the house to clean up for dinner.

# CHAPTER 4

## The Village Restaurant
## Chincoteague Island

An hour later, Roe pulled his Toyota SUV off of Maddox Boulevard into the white limestone parking lot of The Village Restaurant and Lounge. The long, white, one-story restaurant was set on stilts on the edge of the marsh along Eel Creek.

Moore, Monnie and Roe exited the vehicle and walked up the ramp to the raised restaurant. As they entered, Roe greeted Lisa Hudkins and Candi Connor, the two owners.

"Hello, ladies. Looks like a full house tonight. Think you can squeeze the three of us in?" Roe asked.

"Always for Roe," Hudkins smiled before looking down at the seating chart on the hostess stand.

"Hi Monnie. How have you been, Roe?" Conner asked.

"Good. You remember my buddy, Emerson Moore? He visited here last year," Roe asked.

"I do. And you loved the flounder if I remember correctly," Connor flashed Moore a big smile.

"Good memory. And that's what I'll be having for dinner tonight," Moore replied.

"Follow me," Hudkins said as she grabbed three menus and led them down the hallway. She turned left and walked over to a window table that overlooked the marsh.

"How's this?"

"Perfect," Roe answered as the three sat.

"Great. Your server will be right with you."

"Aren't you going to look at your menu, Emerson?" Monnie asked, noticing that Moore turned his menu over.

"Nope. I'm a creature of habit. I'm having their flounder. It's the best flounder I've had," he smiled.

"Everything is good here," Monnie commented as she glanced through the menu.

"I love their flounder," Moore repeated.

The server appeared and took their drink and food order.

Before anyone could make another comment, a tall, lean man with close-cropped hair approached their table. "Hello, Roe," he said.

"Carleton, how are you doing?" Roe replied as he turned in his chair to greet his visitor.

"Good. Hello, Monnie."

"Hi Carleton," she responded.

"You want to join us?" Roe asked.

"Just finished my dinner and heading out."

Turning to Moore, Roe introduced the man. "Meet Carleton Leonard, Emerson."

As Moore stood to shake hands, Roe continued, "He lives up north of me and owns Daisey's Island Cruises."

Roe gave Leonard a quick overview of Moore's background.

"So, you're the guy who was causing all that mess with the exploding NASA rockets on Wallops Island a while back," Leonard offered.

"Not so much causing as exposing who was behind it," Moore promptly replied.

Leonard chuckled.

"Son, you've got to take a tour on one of Carleton's pontoon boats," Roe urged.

"They're really nice boats, Emerson," Monnie added.

"I can fix you up with one of the Chincoteague nature cruises or take you out for bird and dolphin watching," Leonard suggested.

"I'd like that," Moore nodded.

"We also coordinate beach weddings on Assateague if you'd like one," Leonard added as he arched his eyebrows.

"Oh, no," Moore said with his hands extended. "Not for me!"

"I know a few single ladies on the island," Monnie smiled mischievously.

"No. No," Moore repeated. "I'm just fine," he nodded vigorously.

"Well, you need to take one of their pontoon-boat cruises," Monnie added. "Carleton's got the biggest pontoon boat hereabouts."

Leonard nodded. "That'd be the *Martha Lou*. She's fifty feet long and has a bathroom and running water. She's even got a roof over the whole boat to provide shade. Nothing like her around here."

"Carleton, next week is Pony Swim Week. You have room for Emerson?" Roe asked eagerly.

"I believe we do. Want to see the wild ponies swim across from Assateague to Chincoteague?"

"I would. It sounds like fun," Moore confirmed.

Leonard reached into his pocket and withdrew a business card. "Call the office tomorrow to make sure we can fit you in. It's on South Main Street."

"Do you put out from behind the office?"

"No. Do you know where Curtis Merritt Harbor is?"

"Yes. On the south side of the island." Moore turned to Roe. "Isn't that where you keep your boat?"

"The same place," Roe answered.

"That's where you board. They haven't announced the pony swim time yet, but we can let you know. It'll be on Wednesday."

"I'll call in the morning then."

"I better get going," Leonard said as he offered his good-byes and departed.

"Nice guy," Moore said as the waterman walked away.

"One of the nicest on Chincoteague," Roe concurred.

"Next to my Roe, that is," Monnie chuckled as their meal arrived.

"Look at the serving size!" Moore exclaimed. His inquisitive eyes surveyed the large helpings of crab, shrimp, oysters and clams as well as the lobster tail and flounder on the plate which Roe and Monnie were sharing.

"And look at my serving of flounder. It's hanging over the plate," Moore added with glee as his eyes relished his meal.

"They have great food here. You'll enjoy it. Bon appétit!" Roe said as he attacked his crabmeat broiled in cream sauce.

As they were eating, Roe asked Moore, "Do you know what butt dust is?"

Moore's eyes widened. "Can't say as I do," he answered after he swallowed a tasty piece of flounder.

"I heard a funny story about it. It happened last week during the sermon at the island's Baptist church. The minister raised his arms toward heaven and said something like, 'Dear Lord, without you, we are but dust.' My friend's four-year-old daughter asked in a loud voice, 'Mommy, what is butt dust?' Had the whole congregation snickering when she did."

"That's hilarious," Moore laughed softly. "Did the mother

explain?"

"Not on the spot. She told her daughter she'd explain it later."

"The things kids say!" Moore smiled as he brought a fork full of flounder to his mouth.

"And they are so cute," Monnie added.

They continued to chat over their meal. When they finished, they returned to the Terry home.

The next day, Moore followed up with Leonard and learned that he could get a ride on the pontoon boat for the swim event. He walked out of the back of the house and spotted Roe who was helping Kronsky.

"I'm all set for the pontoon boat ride," Moore said as he approached the two.

"Good. What do you have planned for today?" Roe asked as he looked up.

"Nothing."

"Then son, I've got a plan for you."

"You do?" Moore asked in mock surprise.

"Yes. You can help Louie," he said. "I need to go inside and paint some decoys."

"Sure."

"Louie, you show him what he needs to do." Roe turned and went into the workshop.

"It's really easy," Kronsky explained as he showed Moore what needed to be done to debark the cottonwood.

As they worked, Moore asked Kronsky about his days growing up on Chincoteague. Kronsky warmed right up to the conversation and talked about the good things on the island.

Eventually, Moore began to shift the conversation to the rough home life that Kronsky endured while growing up. Kronsky reluctantly shared about the physical and verbal abuse he received from his father and how he followed his older brother into petty crime. That progressed to drug use and eventually drug selling to pay for the drug use.

The more the men talked, the more Kronsky appreciated the compassionate approach that Moore offered. Moore tried to give Kronsky examples of the positive things in life and, most importantly, provide hope for a better life. Kronsky willingly took it all in.

For the next four days, Moore fell into a routine. He'd rise early and drive out to Assateague Beach where he took a brisk walk as his condition improved and then returned to the Terry house to clean up. He worked with Louie and grew to admire his woodworking skills. They also developed a good friendship which pleased Moore. He felt sorry for the young man and his struggles.

On Monday, Moore's cell phone rang. He answered it on the second ring. "Hello."

"Emerson, it's Billy Joe. Ready to go on a raid with us?"

"Ready. Oh yeah!" Moore answered quickly. He was ready for a change of pace.

"Good. It's on for tonight." Tarr gave Moore the details for the meeting point.

"Great. I'll meet you there," Moore said as they ended the call.

"Evening plans, Emerson?" Kronsky asked.

"Yes. I'm going to meet up with an island friend," Moore said. While he was becoming more comfortable with Kronsky, Moore wasn't going to reveal that he was going on a drug raid. One could never be too cautious.

Late that afternoon, Moore jumped in the Jeep and made a thirty-minute drive to his meeting point on the mainland.

# CHAPTER 5

## Accomack County Sheriff's Office
## Accomac, Virginia

Moore turned onto Wise Court where the Sheriff's Office was located. As he pulled into the parking lot, he spotted Tarr standing with six deputies. He parked the Jeep and walked over to Tarr.

"Hello, Billy Joe."

Tarr grinned at the new arrival. "Glad you could make it. Boys, this is Emerson Moore, investigative reporter with *The Washington Post*. He's doing a ride-along with us."

"Are you writing a story about our raid?" one of the deputies asked.

"No. I'm not on assignment. I'm actually in the area on R & R," Moore responded before Tarr introduced him to the other deputies.

"You should put this on," Tarr advised Moore and handed him a bullet-proof vest.

"I don't like wearing these," Moore protested as he took the vest and looked at it. "It rubs against my wound that's not completely healed."

"If you're planning on going with us, you have to wear it, Emerson—department policy. It's all part of the protocol," Tarr explained sternly.

"I guess I don't have a choice," Moore said reluctantly as he slipped on the vest.

"You don't."

Seeing the others were armed, Moore asked, "And where's my weapon?"

Tarr grinned. "Not for you, my friend. You are just along for the ride—to observe, not participate."

"But I'm weapons trained," Moore countered.

"Doesn't matter," he said. "Let's saddle up, men," Tarr directed as he led the team to two Ford Explorers.

"Emerson, you can ride up front with me," he said as two officers got into the back seat of Tarr's vehicle.

"Good," Moore said as he walked around the Ford and settled in the front seat. "Where are we headed?"

"Just north of Exmore, about twenty minutes from here. We're meeting up with the Northampton Sheriff's Department for a small raid. There should be twelve of us in all."

"Is it a house raid?"

Tarr chuckled. "Sort of. It's a trailer, ya know—a mobile home. We had a solid tip that a couple of guys are selling coke out of the trailer. Both of them are there now. We've had eyes on them all day."

"I'm looking forward to this. I'm glad my contacts helped me out so that I could come along," Moore said.

"Did they ever! My phone lit up like a Christmas tree when I inquired about you, Emerson. You know a lot of people in high places."

"It's all a part of my job. And they know I do my best to do the right thing. I don't betray confidences and try to shoot straight."

"That always helps," one of the deputies in the back cracked with a chuckle.

Tarr's cell phone rang. He looked down to see who the caller was and smiled. "It's your buddy, Chuck Meier," he said to Moore as he answered, placing the phone on speaker. "He was one of the guys I talked to on your behalf. This is Tarr."

"Billy Joe, are you guys on the way?" Meier's voice boomed as it always did.

"Yep."

"Is my buddy Clark Kent there with you?"

"Yep. He's sitting right here next to me, and you're on the speaker."

"You still working in D.C. at the *Daily Planet*, Clark Kent?" Meier asked although he knew better.

"No. I'm on R & R," Moore laughed.

"Sure, you are. That's why you're going on this drug raid. I have just one question for you, Clark."

"What's that?"

"You have to tell me. Is Lois Lane as hot as I think she is?" Meier teased.

"She's just as you picture her in your dreams," Moore replied.

"How do you know about my dreams?" Meier came right back at Moore.

"I can only imagine," Moore countered.

"I could write some erotic thrillers if I wrote down my dreams," he sniggered before becoming serious. "You be careful, Emerson, and don't go trying to play Superman when these guys go in."

"Not to worry," Moore responded. "I'm just an observer."

"Make sure that's all you do."

"How's your business trip going?" Moore asked.

"Good. Helping the DEA out here in Baltimore now. I'm

not too far away from you."

Tarr interrupted their conversation. "We're getting close. You better end your call."

Moore and Meier complied and immediately finished the call.

Tarr turned off the road and followed a couple of side streets. "There they are," he said as he spotted two Northampton County Sheriff's Department vehicles parked on the side of the road next to an Accomack County Sheriff's Department SUV.

"The lead for this raid is that thin guy with the beard. His name is Nick Relle. He's works with me in Accomac. The guy next to him wearing the crazy bright socks is Zak Sherman. He's the number two guy," Tarr explained. "He loves to wear wild-colored socks," he added.

The men emptied out of the vehicles and Tarr introduced Moore. Relle reviewed the plans for going in. The officers climbed back into their vehicles and quietly drove the two minutes to the trailer.

The five vehicles pulled up to the trailer and surrounded it. After the officers exited, they took protective cover. Relle and Sherman walked rapidly to the trailer entrance door while the others provided cover.

"Police," Relle shouted as he knocked hard on the door.

"Isn't he concerned that the occupants are going to start firing on him?" Moore asked Tarr as they crouched behind the hood of their vehicle.

"You always have to assume that can happen, but these two are repeat offenders for selling drugs. The good thing is they aren't the violent type," Tarr explained. "But you never know when they can turn on you."

"Come on out DeShawn and Jalen," Relle yelled.

From where he stood, Moore could see that someone had raised a window shade slightly. He saw two eyes peering out the window.

"Come on, boys. You know the drill. This isn't something new to you. Walk out backwards with your hands clasped behind your heads," Relle ordered.

Slowly the door opened about four inches, and a voice called out nervously. "We're coming out. We're unarmed. Don't shoot."

"Come on, then. No one's going to get shot today," Relle answered back.

The door swung wide open, and the two black men walked out as instructed. As they stepped onto the ground, several officers ran over and secured their wrists behind their backs with plastic ties.

"Anybody else in the trailer?" Relle asked as he kept a wary eye on the doorway.

"No," DeShawn answered.

Relle nodded to Sherman who led two officers inside to confirm that the trailer was empty. Within two minutes, Sherman returned. "All clear."

The captured suspects were escorted to the two Northampton Sheriff Department vehicles. They were placed in the back of each vehicle.

Two white vans arrived, and four men exited them. One van was a K-9 unit that included a trained detection dog. They and the dog stepped out of the two vehicles and approached the trailer.

"Now that the work is done, you show up," Relle teased the arriving officers.

Moore looked from them to Tarr. "Detectives?"

"DEA. They're going to help us find where the drugs are stashed. The two drug sellers aren't volunteering any information. These two typically don't, but we end up finding the stuff," Tarr explained. "Come on. This should be interesting."

I'll say, Moore thought to himself as they approached the junk-strewn trailer lot. There were several worn tires stacked three high, an old boat on a trailer with a flat tire and a fenced-in area behind the trailer which housed a dilapidated vegetable garden. Half of the tomatoes were drying up, and weeds threatened to take out part of the garden. There was one area that looked like it had been recently tilled.

"That's a likely spot," Tarr said.

"They're growing drugs here?" Moore asked in surprise.

"Not quite, but these boys may have buried drugs there," he said as the agent with the drug-sniffing dog entered the area. The dog searched around the other parts of the garden with no results, but it was a different story when it got to the freshly-tilled area. It's where the dog cued an alert to its handler by pawing and digging at the ground.

"He's found something," Tarr explained as the handler led the dog away and pulled out a white towel. He then began playing a game of tug of war with the dog and the towel, much to the dog's enjoyment.

"What's that towel about?" Moore asked as an agent walked over and began digging.

"Drug sniffing dogs are trained by taking a clean towel and rubbing marijuana on it and then playing tug of war. These dogs eventually tie the marijuana smell to playing and are rewarded by their handler with a game after finding the drugs."

"And they alert the handler by pawing and digging?" Moore

asked.

"In this case, yes. That's called an aggressive alert, but you don't want a bomb-sniffing dog to give you an aggressive alert. Its pawing could detonate the bomb. They're trained to give a passive alert. When they discover an explosive, they sit next to it," Tarr explained.

"I see," Moore said.

"We sometimes call drug-sniffing dogs 'probable cause on four legs.'"

"Why?" Moore asked.

"If we don't have the vehicle owner's permission to search his car during a traffic stop, we'll have the dog walk around. If it gives an alert, then we have probable cause and can search the vehicle," Tarr added.

"Interesting," Moore said quietly as he took in everything.

When the search of the trailer and property were concluded, they had found cocaine hidden in plastic bags taped to the bottom of the toilet tank, on the underside of the bedroom dresser drawers and in the battery compartment of video game controllers. They also discovered a hole cut into the bottom of the bed mattress which was used as a place to stash more cocaine.

Outside, the men found cocaine hidden in two boat fenders and shoved up through the base of a large lawn ornament. The garden yielded a metal container filled with bags of marijuana.

Moore was stunned by the hiding places. "This is the first time I've been on a raid like this. These guys are pretty clever with hiding drugs," he said to Tarr, Relle and Sherman.

"This is nothing," Sherman responded. "We've found drugs in stuffed animals, thermos jugs, pop cans, cold air return vents, fake electrical boxes, and behind light switches and outlet plates."

"That's right," Relle agreed. "We've seen drugs hidden behind picture frames and above ceiling tiles."

Tarr jumped in. "I've seen them hidden all over cars. Drugs can be stashed under the hood, floor mats and seats or in the glove compartment or ashtray. You can find them in the trunk, too. They'll put in a false trunk floor and stuff the area between the real floor and the false floor with bags of coke. One time, a guy had filled the spare tire with bags of drugs."

"Creative!" Moore said in response to their comments. "This has been a real learning experience for me."

"It's worth their while to be creative," Sherman said. "They're making a lot of money."

"And so is Steiner. I wish we had more concrete evidence so we could nail that kingpin," Tarr said.

"One of these days," Relle said confidently.

After another hour at the trailer, Tarr rounded up his team and headed back to Accomac while the others remained at the trailer. When they reached Accomac, Moore thanked Tarr and returned to the Terry house on Chincoteague.

# CHAPTER 6

## The Next Morning
## The Terry House

"Sounds like you had a good experience last night," Roe said as he sipped a cup of coffee and looked across the kitchen table at Moore, who had just finished relaying his prior day's adventure.

"It was," Moore agreed.

"You get anything to write about?" he asked as Monnie placed a plate full of pancakes on the table and sat.

"Did I ever! Billy Joe is going to keep his eyes open for other raids where I might tag along."

"Any shooting?"

"No. These guys were pretty tame."

"You wear a bullet-proof vest?"

"Yes, but it wasn't necessary. I don't like them. It was a bit tender around my wound."

"You never know, son."

"Dig in, boys," Monnie said as she reached for the pancake syrup.

They did as she instructed and placed pancakes on their plates.

"They look good," Moore offered.

"Son, my wife is the best darn cook on this island. No one can cook like her," Roe boasted with a large smile.

Monnie giggled. "Emerson, he just said that because I'm making his favorite meal for lunch."

"What's that?" Moore asked.

"My husband just loves corned beef and cabbage."

"There you go," Roe grinned. "I just can't get enough of the stuff. Folks on the island surprise me and bring over pots of it."

"I like corned beef, but I'm not a big fan of cabbage," Moore offered.

"Hey, did you notice how much traffic was on the island yesterday when you drove off for your adventure?" Roe asked.

"I did. The closer I got to the light at Maddox, traffic became bumper-to-bumper. I saw a long line of traffic stretched out on the causeway to Wallops, too."

"That's for the pony swim. It's going to be on Wednesday. You're all set with Carleton to go out on his pontoon boat, right?"

"Yes, I am," Moore answered. "How many people come to the island for the event?"

"Tens of thousands show up from all over the country."

"Wow!"

"Yesterday was the Beach Walk," Roe continued. "The saltwater cowboys herded the ponies to the southern corral on Assateague. Today, the veterinarians will be checking the ponies to be sure that they are healthy enough for the swim. Some of the ponies will be selected to be auctioned off.

"Tomorrow morning, sometime between 8:30 and 10:30 during slack tide when there is no current, the saltwater cowboys will herd the ponies into the water. The ponies then swim across the swim lane to Chincoteague. My boat will be one of the four herding boats guiding the ponies across the channel."

"How close to the action will Carleton's pontoon boat be?"

"You'll be in a line of boats from shore to shore on both sides of the crossing area to watch. There will be a lot of people watching from the shore, on the docks and in Memorial Park."

"This is really a big deal."

"It is," Roe agreed.

"People come from all over to watch it and see which foal is the first to make it to Chincoteague. That foal is crowned King or Queen Neptune and will be raffled off at the carnival grounds," Monnie added.

"They'll rest up the ponies for about forty-five minutes after the swim, then they have the pony parade down the streets. The saltwater cowboys herd them to the pens on the carnival grounds. Thursday morning, the Chincoteague Volunteer Fire Company auctions off the foals," Roe explained.

"Why do you sell the ponies?" Moore asked.

"Assateague Island can only sustain so many ponies. Auctioning off some of the ponies helps control the pony population and pays for the cost of the vets to take care of them. And part of the proceeds goes to the Fire Company."

"I didn't think about the cost of the vets," Moore said.

"A lot of people don't. Would you like to join me Friday morning? My boat is one of the herding boats when they swim the ponies back to Assateague," Roe asked.

"I would," Moore answered. "Sounds like fun."

"You can ride out with me Friday morning," he said as he pushed back his chair from the table. "You ready to get to work? We're burning daylight, son."

"Oh yeah," Moore said as he stood and followed Roe outside. As they walked behind the workshop, Moore asked, "Where's Kronsky?"

"He called me this morning and said he's got a big carpentry job down in Cape Charles. He expects to be gone a few days."

A skeptical look crossed Moore's face. Putting it behind him, Moore focused on helping Roe for the rest of the day.

# CHAPTER 7

## Wednesday Morning
## The Pony Swim

Twenty-five boats rocked gently on each side of the Pony Swim lane. There were other boats that arrived late and had to be content with watching from where they could anchor. A slight breeze from the ocean helped cool the onlookers on board and those ashore as they waited for the swim to begin.

Inside the swim lane, a small Coast Guard boat patrolled to make sure no boats other than the four herding boats entered the swim lane.

From the deck of the *Martha Lou*, Moore could see Roe in a floppy hat maneuvering his 21-foot Carolina skiff with a Honda 100 HP outboard in the swim lane. Each of the herding boats had a red flag hoisted to identify them as one of the official herding boats. In addition to his herding responsibilities, Roe had to chaperone two TV news crews who were on the island to record the event. He had his hands full, Moore thought to himself.

The *Martha Lou* was at full capacity. Her passengers were well-protected from the bright, early morning sun that beat down on its covered roof. It was captained by Bill Birch, a local waterman and fisherman. He had frosty gray hair and a mustache to match. Being a Sunday School teacher, he regaled his passengers with quotes from the Bible as he offered coffee, water and soda to his charges.

They had arrived at their spot two hours ago, and Moore was thankful they had a head on board. Not only did he have to use it, but several others also took advantage of this luxury.

Thirty minutes passed, and Moore saw one of the Coast Guardsmen speaking on his radio. Next, the officer shouted a command to two of his crewmen in the bow. The two set off orange smoke flares to signal the start of the swim.

The herding boats positioned themselves two on each side of the entry point into the water as the saltwater cowboys started cracking their whips in the air and yelling at the ponies to drive them into the water. The cowboys rode their horses into the water until it was too deep for them to continue.

The herding boats then took over. Roe and his fellow boat herders also started yelling and driving the ponies toward the Chincoteague shore. When a couple of ponies tried to turn around and go back to Assateague, a herding boat would quickly move in and cut them off, forcing them to turn toward Chincoteague.

Within ten minutes, the ponies emerged on the Chincoteague shore where they were greeted by the waiting crowd and saltwater cowboys. The ponies then were herded to a resting area before being paraded to the carnival grounds.

"That's the end of the swim, folks. I'll take you back to the harbor so you can drive over and watch the parade," Birch directed as he hoisted the anchor and started the engine. He deftly swung the boat around, then motored the short distance to Curtis Merritt Harbor where his passengers disembarked.

Moore headed for his Jeep and drove toward the carnival grounds. Parking spots near the parade route were at a premium and difficult to find. He lucked out as a car pulled out of a parking spot and he was there to grab it. Taking a cold water from the small ice chest in the vehicle, Moore walked around the front of his vehicle and waited.

Ten minutes later, he heard the sound of whips cracking and cowboys hollering. He looked south on Main Street and saw two trucks approaching him. They were filled with TV camera crews filming a line of saltwater cowboys who led the parade. The ponies were boxed in on all sides by the mounted cowboys who drove them to the carnival grounds.

Moore's face broke into a wide smile when he recognized one of the approaching riders. It was Denise Bowden, the town's vice-mayor and chief spokesperson for the Fire Company. She had given him a tour of the island on his first visit and they had dined together.

Moore waved to attract her attention, and she spotted him.

"Emerson," she called out in her deep voice from atop her horse, "I didn't know you were back on the island."

"I'm spending some time with Roe," he shouted back.

"Don't get into trouble like last time," she warned as she cracked her whip.

Moore shook his head from side to side. "No way. I'm just relaxing."

"Famous last words," she said skeptically as her horse trotted by.

After the ponies went by, Moore saw an Indian chief, mounted on a brown horse. He was the last rider and signaled the end of the parade. Ten minutes later, Moore had driven up Main Street and parked. He headed for Chattie's Lounge, which was above Don's Seafood Restaurant.

The red-haired manager, Anne Clark, greeted Moore. "Nice to see you again. Did you see the parade?"

"I did," Moore replied as he followed her to a window table overlooking Chincoteague Channel. When she offered him a menu, Moore waved his hands. "I don't need one, Anne. I already know what I'm having," he affirmed.

"I remember from last time. You like our clam chowder, right?"

"Good memory," Moore smiled.

"It seems like you were in here almost every day for our clam chowder when you were here the last time. I'll send the server right over," she acknowledged as she walked away.

When the server arrived, Moore said, "I'm going to have a bowl of your delicious clam chowder and the flounder sandwich. I love your chowder."

"That's good to hear," the server said.

"You are a must-stop because you folks make chowder without onions. I can hardly find chowder without onions anywhere," he said.

"This man bothering you?" a voice inquired as Moore turned to see Tommy Clark, the smiling, bespectacled owner walk over and pull out a chair. He was wearing his usual ball cap and a t-shirt with Don's Seafood printed on the right chest.

"He's no bother at all, Tommy," she said as she scurried away to enter his order.

"Did you come down for the Pony Swim?" Clark asked as he settled in the chair.

"No, but the timing worked out. This was the first time I've been here for the Swim."

"You enjoy it?"

"Oh, yeah. I was on one of Carleton's pontoon boats. I had a great time."

"Did you see the parade?" Clark inquired.

"Yes, and then I headed straight over here. You know how much I love that clam chowder."

"I do."

"Friday, Roe is taking me on his herding boat so I can experience the swim back."

"That should be fun. Any time with Roe is a fun time," Clark smiled. "What brings you to Chincoteague this time? We don't have any rockets exploding."

"Actually nothing. I'm just here to relax a bit. I'm staying with Roe and Monnie and helping Roe out."

"You're not staying at the Bare Necessities?" Clark chuckled as he recalled the trick Roe pulled on Moore when he first visited the island and Roe took him to the clothing optional B&B for senior citizens.

"No. Not this time," Moore laughed. "Honestly, I'm here to relax."

"Listen, if you get a chance, come on out to Tom's Cove Aquafarms, and I'll show you how we raise clams and culture salt oysters."

"You do that?"

"Yep. The cool, ocean-fed waters around the island yield some of the finest shellfish on the East Coast. We grow them and harvest them, then ship them to some of the most prestigious restaurants in the United States and Europe."

"I'd like to see that if I get a chance," Moore said as he took the business card that Clark handed him.

"You call me when you want to come out, and I'll give you a personal tour," Clark said as the server arrived with Moore's chowder and Clark stood. "I'm going to let you enjoy that chowder you told me you were looking forward to enjoying so much."

"Thank you. I'm sure I will," Moore said as he reached for a spoon and Clark walked away.

# CHAPTER 8

## Late That Evening
## Norfolk, Virginia

Four rough-looking men stood together on a dock along a water channel near an obscure, empty warehouse. Above them was a crane which had a small steel cage attached to its cable. A wide-eyed man stood bent over at the waist inside the cage where he had been shoved with his hands tied behind his back. He was panic-stricken.

"I don't know who's behind it," he moaned.

"If you're a wise head, Vegas, you'll fess up and tell us," Zimo said in a dangerous tone.

The brawny, bearded man with a shaved head looked like he belonged in a lawless biker gang. He was well-inked with a diversity of tattoos on his arms, chest and neck. Carl Zimmerman (aka Zimo) was a member of drug lord Max Steiner's inner circle.

Someone, possibly a Norfolk gang, had been hijacking Steiner's box trucks filled with cocaine as they ran up the Delmarva Peninsula. Zimo's job was to find out who was behind the heists. He now had a likely suspect in front of him.

"I don't know anything," Vegas said nervously.

"I know how you like to gamble, Vegas. But don't gamble your life by not telling me what I want to know," Zimo warned.

"Like I told you, man. I don't know anything," Vegas pleaded.

Zimo nodded to the crane operator nearby who lifted the cage off the ground and swung it above the water. It then was slowly lowered into the water until it reached the man's knees.

"Have anything to tell me?" Zimo demanded.

"I don't know anything!" Vegas repeated as he looked down with frantic fear at the water.

"Lower him."

The crane operator lowered the cage so that the water was up to the man's neck.

"No!" Vegas screamed. "I don't know anything."

Calmly, Zimo looked at the crane operator and instructed him. "All the way."

The crane operator lowered it until water completely covered the cage.

After thirty seconds, Zimo signaled to the operator to raise the cage.

As the cage broke the water's surface and Vegas' head appeared, Vegas began desperately gasping for air.

"Have anything to say now?" Zimo asked. He was a fiend when it came to torturing people from whom he needed information.

"I don't know!" Vegas cried out in fear.

"Do you think that's an answer that would be acceptable to Max? You sure you don't know anything?"

"I don't."

"Drop him!" Zimo ordered the crane operator, who released the cable to allow the cage to again fall into the water.

Thirty seconds later, Zimo had the operator raise the cage, and a gasping Vegas reappeared.

"How's your memory now?" Zimo asked.

"There's one thing that I did overhear," Vegas blurted as he tried to fill his lungs with air.

"Swing him over here and release him," Zimo instructed his men.

A look of relief appeared on Vegas' face, but he didn't know how short-lived it would be. The men helped Vegas out of the cage and surprised him by placing a noose around his neck. The men then affixed the end of the rope to the crane cable and placed a stool in front of Vegas.

"Step on the stool," Zimo ordered.

"But I'm going to talk. You don't need to do this," Vegas pleaded as two men roughly lifted him on top of the stool.

"Let's see what you tell us and then I'll decide," Zimo said as he motioned for the crane operator to take up the slack.

Vegas choked and had to stand on his tiptoes in order to breathe.

"Go ahead. We're listening."

"I was in a restaurant, and I heard two guys talking about knocking off one of your trucks."

"Who were they?"

"I don't know."

Zimo walked over and kicked the stool out from under Vegas' feet, allowing his body to swing in the air. Vegas instantly felt the noose tighten around his neck and begin to strangle him.

Zimo signaled the crane operator again, and he eased Vegas to the ground where he gasped to regain his breath as two henchmen loosened the noose.

"Remember now?"

"It's coming back to me." Vegas gagged for air.

"Put him in the chair and bind him," Zimo instructed his

two henchmen. They grabbed a white resin chair and sat Vegas in it, then wrapped duct tape around him to secure his thighs and upper body to the chair. They also placed the noose around one of the chair legs and tightened it.

"See. I'm not such a bad guy," Zimo said with feigned concern.

Vegas knew better. He was filled with terror, just as Zimo had planned.

"It was Stumpy Smith."

"Who was the other guy?"

"There was no other guy."

"You just said you heard two guys talking," Zimo probed.

"I'm not thinking straight right now," a panicked Vegas replied.

Zimo skeptically eyed Vegas. "Then how was Stumpy involved?"

"He told me about the truck heists. I was going to help sell the coke once he had it. He was bragging about it to me."

"Anything else you can add?" Zimo asked.

"That's all I know."

"We know where to find Stumpy. So, I guess we're all done with you."

"You're going to let me go, right?" Vegas asked with a look of desperation.

"Yes. I'm going to let you go. Right over the side," Zimo sneered. "Toss him."

The two henchmen picked up the white plastic chair as Vegas struggled hopelessly to free himself. They carried him the few feet to the edge of the dock and tossed him into the channel.

"Fish him out after ten minutes and get rid of the body," Zimo ordered as he walked inside the nearby warehouse to his office. He wasn't surprised to hear Stumpy was involved. He needed to call Clawson and discuss the action they would take against Stumpy. Zimo made the call on his cell phone.

"Did he talk?" Clawson asked when he answered and saw that it was Zimo calling.

"Yeah. It was Stumpy Smith," Zimo replied.

"You know what to do."

"Got it," Zimo said as they ended the call. Zimo gathered two of his henchmen and left to take out Smith.

# CHAPTER 9

## The Next Day
## Pony Auction

It was going to be a hot summer day, Moore thought. He was glad to have arrived early at the carnival grounds for the pony auction and to get a seat in the bleachers that was close to the action.

Two Chincoteague firemen were restraining a five-month-old pony with pinto markings. It was the sixth equine to go up for auction, and the bids were already up to $2,000 for it.

Moore enjoyed listening to the auctioneer's rapid-fire voice. The words shot out of his mouth as fast as one of the rockets from Wallops Island. There were several spotters watching for bidders to raise their hands and signal the auctioneer. Unlike other auctions where bidders had to register, bidders here just had to raise their hand in order to respond to a bid request. Once they won the bidding, they paid cash or credit card for their pony. Checks weren't accepted.

After an hour, Moore stood and walked toward one of the coffee stations on the carnival grounds. He bought a cup and was adding cream when a voice behind him offered, "Hello, Emerson."

Moore turned around and smiled when he saw Evelyn Shotwell and her husband, Holt. Evelyn was the president of the local Chamber of Commerce and Holt worked at the nearby NASA base. Emerson had met them on his last visit to Chincoteague.

"Hi, guys. Looks like your Pony Week is going well."

"It always does. We have a great team of volunteers on this island," Evelyn said proudly.

"And the biggest volunteer is the one right here," Holt teased his wife good-naturedly.

"Did you buy a pony, Emerson?" Evelyn asked in her sweet southern drawl.

"No, I just stopped by to see what it was like," Moore replied.

"It's a lot of fun."

"Sure looks that way."

"You coming to the carnival tonight?" Holt asked.

"I think I will. I love good carnival food," Moore answered.

"That they have here," Holt commented.

"We better let you go. We have to get back to the auction," Evelyn said as the two turned and walked away.

"I'll see you tonight then," Moore said as he raised his cup to his lips and sipped his coffee. Taking two more sips, Moore started walking to the parking lot to retrieve his vehicle. It was across South Main Street on the other side of the entrance to the carnival grounds.

As he crossed the street, Moore failed to notice that the driver of a passing car stared at him. The driver recognized Moore and pulled over to the side of the road to wait for the reporter to exit the parking lot. The man tailed Moore and followed him a short distance north on Main Street to Sundial Books, the island bookstore. He discreetly parked and again observed Moore's activity.

Moore walked into the quaint two-story building where a bearded man wearing metal frame glasses looked up from where he sat behind the counter.

"Can I help you?"

Spying the man's name on the name badge he was wearing, Moore replied, "Thank you, Jon. I'm just looking."

"Are you here for Pony Week?" Jon asked inquisitively.

"Yes," Moore answered.

"Did you see the Swim yesterday?"

"I did. I was on Carleton's boat. You folks have a good thing going here."

Jon nodded.

"I just left the auction, and I'm heading back to my place."

"Where you staying?"

"Roe Terry's house. Roe's a friend of mine."

"He's good people," Jon offered.

"That he is."

"We've got a great selection of books about the ponies in that case over there," Jon pointed. "And next to them are a number of books about the island's history."

"Anything about those NASA rockets exploding?" Moore asked.

"Now, I know why you look familiar. You were here last year. You broke the story on the sabotage that was going on over on Wallops. I think I remember your name. Something like Morrison. Is it Morrison Moore?" Jon asked.

Moore smiled. "Emerson Moore. You were close."

"I have a way with names. Take your time and let me know if I can help you."

"Thank you," Moore said as he walked around the store that was cheerful and well-lit.

Ten minutes later, Moore walked over to the counter.

"Find one you like?" Jon asked.

"Yes. This particular book looks interesting," Moore suggested.

As Jon rang up the purchase, he noticed that Moore also had been eyeing a section of books concerning the history of Chincoteague and Assateague islands. Moore paid for his lone book purchase, but offered no further conversation.

"You picked a good one. It's been an island best-seller. Stop in again. We like seeing new faces," Jon smiled. "Thank you."

"Sure. I like your store, especially the selection of books you have," Moore offered as he walked out the door to his vehicle. He jumped inside and headed back to Roe's house.

Jon was at the back of the bookstore when the rear entrance door opened. It was the man who had been tailing Moore, and he recognized Jon.

"You remember me?" the man asked in a low voice.

Jon looked closely. "Hold on a second."

His eyes then widened as he recognized the man. "You son of a bitch. What the hell are you doing here? Especially with what happened in Nicaragua."

"You remember?"

"You still sore about that?" Jon asked.

"You still owe me money."

"I thought you'd forget about that," Jon said hopefully.

"You don't forget about money like that!" the man said.

They both laughed and embraced.

"I did the best that I could. You know my hands were tied. The government boys weren't going to give me the money you were owed. Can't trust them," Jon groused. "You still doing mercenary work?"

"Yes and no. Did you ever marry Jane?"

"How do you think I got out of Nicaragua? It was her nonprofit that got me out." Jon turned and called toward the side of the store. "Jane, come here. You remember Sam Duncan?"

Jane walked over from where she had been stacking books on a shelf. She smiled as she took in the blond-haired, rugged, former Navy SEAL.

"I certainly do," she said as she gave Duncan a big hug. "I had a hard time deciding between you two," she said as she placed her arm around Duncan's muscular waist.

"She picked the right one," Jon said quickly.

"I don't know about that," Duncan teased as he put his arm around her waist and pulled tight her against his side. "I think she made a mistake."

Breaking free of Duncan, Jane spun around and looked at him. "What brings you to town? Pony Swim?"

"I wish. No. I had some business."

"I thought you got out of the business," Jon said with a perplexed look.

"Jon, I just can't stay away from the dark side. You know that," Duncan retorted. "By the way, was that Emerson Moore who was in here?"

"Yes. You know him?" Jon asked.

"Yes. He's not long for this world," Duncan said with a conspiratorial look.

"You're after him?" Jon asked with surprise.

Duncan laughed. "No, we're good friends. We've been on some adventures together, and we're both lucky to have come out alive. Emerson's one very lucky guy when it comes to survival. He could draw a pat hand from a stacked deck."

"He's staying at Roe Terry's house."

"I know Roe. I invited Emerson to join us on a fishing trip here last year, then I had to bail on him."

"So that's how he ended up finding our special island," Jane mused.

"You going to stop by and visit him?" Jon asked.

"No. I'm not supposed to be here. I just wondered if that was him and when I saw him come in here, I remembered something about you owning the store. So, I decided to stop in and see you both."

"We're glad you did," Jon said, grinning broadly.

"Give me a second." Duncan walked over to one of the shelves featuring best-selling books. He then picked out one and brought it back to the register where he paid for it.

"I better go. And remember you never saw me," Duncan offered as he lifted his forefinger to his lips. "Not a word."

"No way," Jon assured him as he gave Duncan a hug and Jane walked over to embrace him.

Duncan walked out the back door and back to his car.

As they watched him walk by their windows, Jon turned to Jane. "That was strange."

"You mean Duncan stopping by and not seeing his friend?" Jane asked.

"No. He and Emerson bought the same book," Jon explained.

"What?"

"*Chincoteague Calm*," Jon smiled.

"I'm sure they'll enjoy it," she smiled. "Remember? We met the author."

"I do. He's a real character!" Jon laughed.

Outside, Duncan returned to his car and drove to the meeting he had on the island. He hoped he wouldn't run into Moore. He knew Moore would be all over him with questions, and he needed to stay undercover.

# CHAPTER 10

## Friday Morning
## Pony Swim Back

"Was that chicken good last night, or what?" Roe asked as he guided his boat in the swim lane.

"It was, but I really liked the carnival fries," Moore added. "I didn't know that you could get chicken like that at a carnival."

"You can on Chincoteague!" Roe bragged. He was so proud of what he and his firefighter friends had accomplished.

"They have the best chicken," Joanne Moore added. The tall, dark-haired Mrs. Moore worked for the Chincoteague Chamber of Commerce and was on the boat to take photos of the pony swimming back.

"I have a question for you, Joanne," Roe said as he positioned his skiff.

"What's that, Roe?"

"Are you related to my buddy, Emerson?" Roe skeptically inquired.

"You'd need to ask my husband, but I don't think so," she responded.

"I'm not aware of any relatives down here," the reporter added. He allowed his eyes to focus on the saltwater cowboys who were moving into position to herd the ponies into the channel.

The four herding boats waited in Assateague Channel to guide the ponies back to Assateague. The Coast Guard patrol craft was again there to make sure no boats wandered into the swim lane. Like Wednesday, a bevy of watercraft lined the edges of the swim lane to watch the wild ponies on their return swim.

Moore was enjoying the privilege of being on Roe's boat. He had a front seat for the action.

Suddenly, the red flares were lit, and red smoke filled the air around the Coast Guard boat. It was quickly followed by the sound of whips cracking and men hooting as the saltwater cowboys drove the herd of ponies off Chincoteague into the water.

The four boats moved into position, and the occupants started hooting at the ponies to urge them to swim for Assateague. Moore joined right in as he was caught up in the moment.

After they herded the ponies to the opposite shore, Roe's radio crackled. "Roe, we're missing a foal. She got separated from her mother, and she's still on the other side. Can you go back across and get her?"

"Roger. I got it," Roe spoke into the radio. "We're going to make a pick up," he said to Moore as he expertly swung his boat around and returned to Chincoteague. "Mama's baby was left behind."

As they approached the shore, they saw the foal. It was restrained by one of the saltwater cowboys who had dismounted. When Roe was close enough, he eased the craft to a gentle stop. The saltwater cowboy picked up the foal and carried it as he waded in knee-deep water to the boat.

Moore and Roe helped lift the foal into the boat, and Moore held it while Roe assisted the cowboy in climbing aboard. Moore and the cowboy then held the foal steady for the short ride across the channel.

As they crossed the channel's midpoint, the foal suddenly bucked and surprised Moore and the cowboy, who lost his balance. The cowboy then fell backward and hit his head on the gunnel as he tumbled unconscious into the water.

"You take the pony. I'll get him," Moore yelled as Roe put the craft into idle and raced over to secure the foal. Moore shucked his shoes quickly and dove into the water.

While Moore swam over to rescue the cowboy, one of the other herding boats pulled up next to Roe's boat. Two occupants then stepped aboard Roe's craft to help restrain the foal. This allowed Roe to return to the center console and navigate the boat toward Moore who had the unconscious cowboy in tow.

Another of the herding boats moved next to Moore and two men reached over to pull the cowboy out of the water. Once they had him on board, they headed to the Chincoteague shore where two Chincoteague Fire Company paramedics were racing with a gurney from their parked ambulance.

When the boat reached the Chincoteague side of the channel, the men carried the cowboy through the mucky swamp to the paramedics. They, in turn, took the cowboy to the ambulance for treatment. Within a few minutes, the ambulance's siren announced it was transporting the cowboy for further medical attention.

Meanwhile, Moore had climbed aboard Roe's boat where he promptly sat on the deck and took a well-deserved moment of rest.

"That was a little excitement that I bet you didn't expect," Roe said as Moore rose and worked his way back to the console to stand dripping wet next to Roe.

"Not what I had planned," Moore said. "At least I had a chance to cool off a bit."

Roe laughed. "Not only that, the TV crews got you on film. You'll be on the TV news tonight." He pointed to the TV crews on the nearby dock who had been covering the rescue.

Moore groaned.

"Those TV folks will want to interview you," Roe said with a smile.

"Not me. I don't need any TV exposure," Moore protested. "I'm just here to recuperate and enjoy a low profile."

"Too late for that. The cameras have been rolling," Roe grinned.

"You're going to have to get me out of here."

"I can do that. I'll radio Denise. She's coordinating the TV people since she's the fire company spokesperson. I'll ask her not to identify you."

"Thank you. I appreciate that."

While Roe radioed Bowden, Joanne made a suggestion. "Emerson, I'll call Evelyn at the Chamber. She's standing on the dock over there by some of the media people. They may ask her about you."

"Thanks," Moore said as Joanne made her call.

When they reached the Assateague side of the channel, the two men who had boarded Roe's boat to help with the foal jumped into the knee-deep water. They carried the struggling foal to shore where they released it and watched it quickly re-join its mother.

"Didn't know you'd be rescuing a foal and a cowboy today, did you Emerson?" Roe asked with a smile as he headed his boat away from the swim area.

Moore grinned. "No, I'm more used to rescuing damsels in

distress," he kidded.

On the way back to Curtis Merritt Harbor, Roe turned to Moore. "I was thinking about something."

"What?" Moore asked.

"These reporters know me. I was the Fire Company spokesperson before Denise. They could end up at my house to ask me questions and discover you there."

"I don't want any of that," Moore sighed. "I need to get out of Dodge! Maybe I'll head down to Cape Charles. I've wanted to check out that area."

"Nice little town. It's on the Chesapeake Bay side of the peninsula," Roe offered.

"Yeah. That's what I'll do," Moore confirmed.

They entered the harbor and docked Roe's boat. Shortly afterward, they were on the way back to Roe's house where Moore changed out of his wet clothes and jumped into the Jeep to get out of town.

# CHAPTER 11

## Early Afternoon
## Cape Charles, Virginia

After a little more than an hour drive, Moore entered Cape Charles. As he turned left onto Fig Street, he spotted Rayfield's Pharmacy and decided to buy some aspirin to relieve a hammering migraine headache that had developed during the drive. He pulled into the parking lot and shut off his engine.

When he walked into the pharmacy, he was surprised to see it had an old-fashioned soda fountain bar. It was crowded with patrons. The tables and booths were also filled. What a nice set up, Moore thought to himself as he turned and walked down the aisle to find the aspirin.

After paying for the aspirin and getting a cup of water, he downed two and headed outside to his Jeep. Starting it, he continued driving the short distance down Fig Street and turned right onto Mason Street.

At the intersection with Peach Street, he spotted an old gas station that had been converted to a book store and coffee shop. Moore couldn't resist and pulled into the parking lot of Peach Street Books. He loved repurposed old gas stations.

Moore entered the area that had once been the service bay where vehicles were repaired. He walked up a couple of steps to the counter where he placed his order for a cup of coffee.

After paying for the coffee, Moore purposefully wandered around the store. He was curious and interested in its history as he followed a narrow hallway to the front area, which long ago had served as the lobby for gas station customers. He loved the store's ambience as he viewed its construction style and imagined the lasting memories it created for so many customers through its years.

In returning to the bay area, Moore briefly examined a collage of old photographs and framed newspaper clippings he saw mounted on a wall that celebrated the history of the building through the decades. He finished his coffee and decided to explore the quaint town that was lined with old buildings along Mason Street.

After walking a few blocks in quiet solitude and stopping in several of the stores randomly to browse, Moore spotted Watson's Hardware store just ahead. The front of the store had merchandise, including a bright red kayak, displayed on the sidewalk. Three white rockers beckoned passersby to sit a spell. There was also a large Pepsi vending machine next to the rockers.

He couldn't resist and walked inside, stepping into a store that time had forgotten. It was like the stores that one's grandfather would have visited many years ago. It was jammed with all kinds of hardware and merchandise like fishing, hunting and rain gear, bicycles, knives, plumbing fixtures—just about everything imaginable that one might need for a do-it-yourself home repair. There was a potbelly stove with old upholstered chairs around where locals would sit and talk.

When he finished filling his mind with old memories and browsing through the store, Moore reluctantly left and returned to the car. He looked at the Cape Charles map he had picked up and decided to head to the beach on the western side of town. It was a short two-minute drive, and he parked along the side of the road.

He walked across the street and on a path through a sand dune to the expansive beach. It was small in comparison to Assateague Beach, but he liked it. Assateague Beach had been more crowded that week because of all the people on the island for the Pony Swim. Moore decided to take a seat and mindlessly watch the nearby shipping traffic on Chesapeake Bay.

No more than ten minutes went by before Moore's solitude was interrupted by someone calling him on his cell phone. He reluctantly answered.

"This is Emerson."

"Emerson, it's Nick Relle from the Accomack Sheriff's Department. We met when you accompanied Billy Joe and us on the drug raid."

"Yes, Nick. I remember."

"Are you busy? Can you talk?"

"I'm free. I'm just taking in the sites in Cape Charles. What's up?"

"I thought you'd be interested in knowing what we found at that trailer."

"I am," Moore said as he directed his full attention to the call.

"We found over $5,000 in cash, two pounds of cocaine, two pounds of marijuana and seven grams of heroin."

"Sounds like a good haul."

"It was."

"I'm curious. Did you find any weapons?"

"No. Not with these boys. They're just locals trying to make some extra money. They're not violent like the gang headquartered where you are, right now."

"Here in the sleepy town of Cape Charles?" Moore asked, stunned.

"Yes. Max Steiner heads up their trafficking business."

"Billy Joe had mentioned Steiner," Moore recalled out loud.

"Steiner has a huge estate just north of Cape Charles on Antebellum Lane. We believe Steiner is the head honcho for all of the drug trafficking on the Eastern Shore, but Steiner is a hard one to catch. It's difficult to tie anything directly to this drug lord."

Moore was fully alert now. "Maybe I'll take a drive up there and poke around."

"I would advise against that," Relle warned. "Otherwise I may find myself and my men poking around the ground, trying to find out where you're buried."

"I'll be careful. Maybe I'll do a drive by. Moore-style," he grinned before ending the call.

A few minutes later, Moore was sitting in his Jeep and using Google Maps to find Antebellum Lane. He started his vehicle and followed the directions to the lane, which was about ten minutes away.

As he turned off Hermitage Road onto Antebellum Lane, he saw a "No Trespassing" sign, but ignored it. It didn't matter. He had to stop his vehicle anyway. He couldn't drive any farther because a private security vehicle was blocking the lane. A red-uniformed security guard approached Moore's vehicle.

"Can I help you?" he asked as he looked first at Moore and then inside the vehicle to see if anyone else was there. Seeing no one, his eyes turned back to Moore.

"I'm just sightseeing," Moore answered as he peered past the officer. He could barely see a large home back from the lane.

"No sightseeing here. This is private property," the guard explained.

"That sure does look like a huge house down there," Moore said as he pointed.

"None of your business, sir. You need to turn around, or I'll have to call the police on you for trespassing. This is a private road," the guard said with a stern look.

"There's no need to do that," Moore said, putting his Jeep into reverse. "You have a nice day."

He made a mental note of the name of the security service so that he could check them out to see if they were the real deal. He would learn later that they were legitimate. The owner of the estate hired them to keep everyone away from the nefarious goings-on at the house.

Moore looked at his map and decided to head over to the Oyster Farm Marina and Resort which sat on a small peninsula with Chesapeake Bay on one side and Kings Creek Inlet on the other. He soon found a parking spot in the lot and walked up to the aqua blue building that dominated the property. The resort encompassed thirty-nine acres and had luxury villas and suites, a year-round bayfront restaurant named the Seafood Eatery and a marina with 124 slips on the inlet.

Moore elected to pass on the full-service restaurant and instead headed for the less formal C Pier Dock Bar.

A smiling bartender greeted Moore. "Beautiful day isn't it?" he asked as Moore perched atop a barstool.

"It sure is."

"First time here?"

"Yes. This is beautiful," Moore said as he allowed his eyes to wander from the bar out to the four piers and the inlet. "Absolutely beautiful."

"You be taking an Absolut then?" the bartender joked.

"No. I'll take a Malibu coconut rum with Coke," Moore answered. He picked up the bar menu as he realized that he hadn't eaten since breakfast.

"We have craft beers, too."

"The rum will be fine."

Within a minute, the bartender returned with Moore's drink. "Are you having lunch today?"

"I think I will. I'll try one of your all-beef hot dogs."

"Would you like it smothered with onions?"

"No way. I'm allergic to them," Moore answered quickly.

"Anything to go with it? Fries? Onion rings? Oops. I forgot you're allergic to onions," the bartender recounted.

"Funny thing is that I can eat onion rings as long as I don't overdo it."

"That's weird!" the bartender remarked with a puzzled look on his face.

"It is. But, nothing else. The hot dog is enough."

"I'll get it right in," he said as he walked over to enter the order.

He returned to Moore and slid a bowl of pretzels across the bar. "Thought you might like some of these," he offered.

"Thanks," Moore commented. "I bet you get some panoramic sunsets here," he said as he swiveled on his stool to look toward Chesapeake Bay.

"Gorgeous. We get pretty crowded in here at sunset time," he said before walking to the other end of the bar to serve some new arrivals.

Moore looked over the bar area, thinking back to his recent undercover tour of duty at Booger Blake's Bar in Key West. He was glad that gig was behind him. After Moore finished his lunch, he wandered outside to look at the various watercraft moored in their slips.

As he approached the fueling station, he spotted a grizzled-looking, weather-beaten man wearing a stained work shirt and equally stained ball cap. The cap read "Baltimore Orioles" in faded colors. The man was waiting while his charter fishing boat was refueled.

"Catch anything today?" Moore asked as he stopped near the man.

"Shark."

"Out in the bay?" Moore asked.

"Yep. Don't forget that bay is connected to the ocean," the man said with a sly smile and a twinkle in his eyes.

Moore could tell he was ornery. "Of course," Moore smiled.

"Them sharks are smart. Did you know they teach the youngsters how to eat humans?"

"I never gave it a thought."

"Yeah. It's usually the father shark. He tells them that the first thing you have to do is to swim around one time so that the human can see you. Then you make another swim-by, but closer. Then on the third time, you attack and eat the human," the man said nonchalantly. He'd set up Moore and Moore bit.

"Why do they teach them to swim by two times? It'd just be easier to attack and swallow the first time."

"They could, but they'd be eating a human with the shit still inside of them," he snickered.

Moore laughed. He liked the charter boat captain.

"Life's a funny thing. Take my pal, Carl, here." He pointed to the guy who was refueling the boat.

"Yes?" Moore asked.

"He told me that he's thinking about divorcing his wife.

Isn't that right Carl?"

Carl nodded and looked at Moore. "Captain Jerry likes to tell stories."

Moore shook his head knowingly.

"Yeah. He told me that she hasn't spoken to him in two months. I told him that he better think twice about divorcing her. Women like that are hard to come by."

"I bet they are," Moore agreed light-heartedly.

Captain Jerry then leaned toward Moore. "If he goes through with it, I'm going to ask him for her number," he chuckled.

Moore did likewise and then asked, "You been around these parts long?"

Captain Jerry lifted his ball cap and scratched his balding head. "Now let me see. Yes, I've been here a long time. I still remember the day that Noah and his ark floated by."

"Long time I gather," Moore smiled.

"I guess if that's how's you interpret my answer. Why do you ask?"

"I was admiring that huge estate over there." Moore pointed across the inlet where a seaplane was floating next to the estate's dock. "I believe someone by the name of Steiner owns it."

Captain Jerry's eyes lost their twinkle and his face clouded over. "They friends of yours?"

"No. I haven't met them."

"Stay clear of them people. They're nothing but trouble. People who go poking around over there end up disappearing."

"Do they have guards on the inlet side of the property?" Moore asked.

"Guards, hell. You wish that's what they were. They're some of the toughest bullies I've run into, and I've had my share."

"You've had a run-in with them?"

"Only because I once had a problem with my steering and the incoming tide carried my boat over there," Captain Jerry explained.

"You thought I was leading an invasion landing at Normandy Beach the way they acted. Came out of nowhere with AK-47s. Screaming and shouting. I explained what happened, and finally one of them got into one of the boats they have over there and pulled me back here where I got my steering fixed. I'm telling you that you don't want to mess with them people."

As Captain Jerry narrated the tale, his face became red. What he didn't reveal to Moore was that one of Steiner's henchmen took a shot at and killed Jerry's dog.

"Serious stuff," Moore said as Captain Jerry took a deep breath and exhaled. His color returned to normal.

"You seem like a nice feller. I'd suggest you take my words to heart," he advised.

"Thank you, Captain Jerry. I will." As Moore turned to leave, he said, "I enjoyed chatting with you."

"One more thing."

Moore turned back to look at the Captain. He saw the mischievous glint had returned to his eyes.

"I was married until three months ago."

Moore tried to guess where this was going, but couldn't.

"Yep. When we first got married, she had big boobs and long legs. When we got divorced, she had long boobs and big legs. Such is life," he said as he turned away to pay Carl.

"Have a good day," Moore said as he walked away. His farewell fell on deaf ears since Captain Jerry's attention was focused on Carl.

An hour later, Moore pulled into Roe's driveway and parked the Jeep. He walked up the steps and entered the workshop where Roe was carving another decoy.

Roe looked up when he heard the door open. He sat back in his chair. "How did your visit go to Cape Charles?"

"Uneventful," Moore replied as he decided not to mention anything about his interest in Max Steiner. "I did find the best little hardware store."

"Watson's?"

"Yes. You've been there?"

"Yep. It's a throwback to days long gone," Roe said with a bit of nostalgia. "Sounds like you enjoyed the store."

"I did. It was like a dusty museum. I bet you could spend a week there and not see everything."

"Probably right," Roe agreed.

"Any reporters show up here?" Moore asked.

"Two. They wanted to know about the guy in my boat who saved the saltwater cowboy. I told him you wished to remain unnamed," Roe answered. "We'll have to see if you're on the Salisbury TV news at 6:00. I'm sure some of the TV cameras captured you."

"It's almost six," Moore said as he looked at the clock on the wall.

"Might as well head in the house. Monnie is cooking up a storm," Roe said. "I've got a real treat in store for you tomorrow," he added.

"What's that?"

"The Redeye Club," he answered with an air of mystery and intrigue.

Moore looked at his friend, who had a devilish look upon his face. "Huh. You taking me to a strip club?" Moore inquired.

"It's a club alright, and you might find some nudes when they skinny dip," Roe chuckled. "But unfortunately, they're male nudes."

"Whatever are you talking about?"

"Some of the boys and I built a fishing and hunting cabin up the bay on the other side of Cords Marshes. It's a great little place to spend the night after a long day of fishing or hunting and have a few beers. A few years ago, we built a couple of duck blinds nearby. I've got one blind that completely hides my boat when you pull in."

"I'd like to see that."

"You're going to more than see it. We're going fishing, and maybe you'll spend the night there."

"Okay, but no skinny dipping," Moore teased.

"You can count on that," Roe retorted.

"How did the club's name originate?"

"The boys would have too much to drink at night and sleep in until 9:00 the next morning. They usually had red eyes when they got up," Roe laughed as the two headed for the house.

Over dinner, they watched the TV news and saw the clip of Moore saving the saltwater cowboy. Moore was relieved that he hadn't been identified.

"We have a real celebrity staying with us, Roe," Monnie teased Moore.

"Want my autograph?" Moore teased back.

# CHAPTER 12

## Next Day
## Curtis Merritt Harbor

Parking his truck on the far left end of the harbor, Roe walked around the vehicle, followed by Moore who exited through the passenger door.

"I always keep her at the far end. A little quicker to get out," Roe explained as he walked down to the dock and dropped the bait bucket that he was carrying into his Carolina skiff.

"How far away are we from the Redeye Club?" Moore asked. He then stepped aboard and settled on the seat in front of the center console.

"It's about a twenty-minute fast ride," Roe explained as he untied the lines and jumped into the boat.

Within a few minutes, they were speeding up Chincoteague Bay to the club, which was a half-mile north of Chincoteague Island and across the channel from Wildcat Point.

"There she is," Roe said as he eased back on the throttle. They calmly approached a one-story, white-sided building set on pilings in Cherry Tree Hill Bay.

"Over there, you can see two duck blinds. The one on the far right is big enough for me to pull my boat in. You'd never know it was there."

"Are there a lot of ducks out here?" Moore asked.

Roe grinned. He was going to enjoy answering Moore's question. "Not after I'm done shooting them."

"Okay. Okay. I get it," Moore laughed.

As they neared the clubhouse, Moore moved to the bow and jumped onto the dock when the boat bumped up next to it. He quickly secured the lines as Roe shut off the outboard.

"Come on in. I'll show you around," Roe invited Moore as he produced a key and unlocked the door.

Moore followed him into the cabin and observed unfinished walls that revealed bare studs. He also noticed it was sparsely furnished with a small kitchen table and three chairs, plus one stool. There were also a couple of worn overstuffed chairs and two sofas.

"Those are sofa beds," Roe explained. "If we have too many beers after fishing or hunting, we can sleep here. Over there in the corner, we've got a couple of sleeping bags in case we have a couple of guests with us."

Roe pointed to an area to the right of the door. "That's the kitchen area. We've got a propane stove there to cook on or to boil water to drink, although I can assure you, we do not drink a lot of water when we are out here."

"No electricity, right?" Moore asked.

"Not really. We've got kerosene lanterns and a propane heater. We do have some electricity when we crank up a generator in the attached shed outside."

Moore looked around. "No bathroom?"

Roe's face cracked a quick smile. "Right here," he said as he opened up a trap door in the floor. "You just squat right here in front of everyone in the cabin and drop your load," he grinned.

"What?" Moore asked with a look of astonishment.

"No, I'm joshing you. That's where we can keep fish fresh.

Look here. You'll see there's a big fenced in area here. We just drop our catch down there and don't have to worry about any varmints getting them. It's also a good place for us to stow our beer. Keeps it real cold," he said as he closed the door and stood.

"And your outhouse is where?" Moore asked.

Smiling, Roe said, "Follow me."

The two men walked out of the cabin and to the back of the building to an area with a three-foot high wooden wall around it and a shed roof. There was a portable toilet sitting there.

"If you need to drop a load, you do it here. The last one to drop a load has to empty it and wash it out before we leave. If you need to take a whizz, you just walk up to the end of the dock here and point and fire," he grinned.

Moore chuckled at the explanation. He really liked his down-to-earth friend. No pretenses about him at all.

"Are we still spending the night here?" Moore asked.

"Not tonight. Looks like we've got a storm moving in. We'll do that another night. You have to experience it."

"Sounds good to me."

The men locked up the cabin and spent the rest of the day catching fish before returning to Chincoteague. After securing Roe's boat, they were driving back to Roe's house when Moore's phone rang.

"Hello?"

"Emerson?"

"Yes."

"It's Nick Relle."

"Hello, Nick. What can I do for you?" Moore asked.

"It's not so much what you can do for me as it's more about what I can do for you."

"Okay?"

"We're going on a raid tomorrow, and I thought you might like to join us."

"Sure would!" Moore said as he sat up straight in the passenger seat. "Where do I meet you?"

"Come on over to the Sheriff's Office around 2:00 p.m. and we'll get you set up."

"I'll be there. Is Billy Joe going with us?" Moore asked.

"No. It'll just be a few of my team. Still interested?"

"I am. I'll be there. Thank you, Nick," Moore said as he ended the call.

"Going on another raid?" Roe asked as they drove past Captain Bob's Marina on South Main Street.

"Yep. Can't wait," Moore replied enthusiastically.

# CHAPTER 13

## Early Afternoon
## Kings Creek Inlet, Virginia

Kings Creek Inlet's water depth ranges from three to five feet. The entrance channel, which is 300 feet wide and 11.5 feet deep, starts two miles southwest of Cape Charles in Chesapeake Bay. Boaters pick up the Old Plantation Light, then target red buoys and green cans toward Cape Charles Harbor. They follow the channel past Cape Charles and turn right into the entrance to Kings Creek while avoiding the area's shoals.

Worrying about shoals was far from the minds of the three occupants of a seaplane flying overhead. The plane dropped altitude as it flew over the Oyster Farm Marina and Resort, its last visual reference point.

The pilot expertly landed the plane on the glassy smooth surface of the inlet as water splashed over the floats. He pointed its nose toward the massive waterfront home, and the plane coasted toward the adjacent dock where a man waited. As the plane slowed, it nudged up against the dock where the man secured it by tying lines to the float cleats.

"Another nice landing," Steiner said.

"Thanks, Max," the lanky pilot, named Henley, replied.

"It's good to be home," Steiner said.

"Always," Clawson added from his seat behind Steiner.

Reefer Clawson was Steiner's right-hand man. The powerfully-built forty-year-old could be counted on to follow Steiner's directives and carry them out violently. He had thick black hair and an equally thick beard. His eyes were the color of anthracite. He had a deadly air about him.

The plane's occupants exited, and Steiner and Clawson boarded a waiting golf cart for the short ride to the main house.

Max Steiner had amassed a huge fortune by trafficking drugs, a business which Steiner's father had started ten years ago. When he was gunned down by another drug lord, Max took over the family business and grew it – and soon killed the other drug lord.

Before his death, the elder Steiner built his massive estate on the banks of Kings Creek. The thirty-acre estate was near the end of Hermitage Road and off of Antebellum Lane. The 18,000-square-foot main house had twelve bedrooms and twelve baths. It was at the end of a limestone driveway lined with trees and a white fence. The driveway turned to concrete as it circled in front of the house and continued to the left side to a four-car garage.

The three-story white brick mansion featured a pillared entrance with a waterfront view to the rear foyer. A sunroom was at the end of the front hall foyer and its curved walls maximized the panoramic views. The elegant home showcased customized Carrara white marble floors and was decorated in modern French.

There was a large pool and pool area accentuated with a fireplace and pergola-covered seating area and a tidal pond. There were paths, walkways and sidewalks flanked with a variety of flowers, shrubs and trees among a well-manicured lawn.

To the right side, there was a caretaker's cottage and garage that matched the main residence's style. It housed some of the staff and gang members. To the left side of the mansion, a guest-house with water views connected to the main home through a newly constructed breezeway. Some of the gang members also resided there.

The rest of the estate offered a four-stall barn, airplane hangar, 2,000-foot grass runway, two-bedroom farmhouse, large equipment barn and a private dock with electric boat and jet ski lifts.

When the golf cart reached the main house, Steiner and Clawson stepped out and walked into the main house. They immediately went to the library where Steiner conducted business.

"Welcome back," Wolf Graber greeted the two as he entered the library.

Graber was in charge of security and managed the estate for Steiner. He was fifty years old and had thinning salt-and-pepper hair. A former Army Ranger, he had a medium build and, like Clawson, worked out to stay in fighting shape.

Ignoring the greeting, Steiner got down to business. "When was this room last swept?"

"This morning," Graber answered. "We did the entire house."

"Good," Steiner replied. "Anything I should be aware of?"

"No. No intruders, although we did get a report from the security guards that a car tried to drive down Antebellum Lane yesterday."

"Anything to be concerned of?" Steiner asked with narrowed eyes.

"No. Just a tourist who made a wrong turn," Graber replied. "But there is one thing I should make you aware of."

"Yes?"

"The Shaka gang in Norfolk has brought in a couple of Jamaican shooters."

"What for?"

"Getting ready to make another run at your business?" Graber guessed. "Maybe arming their trucks as they run up the peninsula."

Steiner bristled. "Reefer, I want you to deal with it. Eliminate these guys."

"I'm on it," Clawson said as he walked out of the library to make a call on his cell phone.

Steiner looked directly at Graber. "And there's nothing on the estate that I need to worry about, right?"

Graber knew that there was no way that Steiner wanted any drugs there. That rule was carved in stone. Drugs on the estate would cause a problem if, for some reason, law enforcement would show up with a search warrant. All drugs were housed at off-site stash houses or the Norfolk warehouse, which was not leased in Steiner's name.

"Right," Graber answered.

Clawson returned to the room. "I just talked to Zimo and found out two pieces of information."

"What are they?" Steiner asked impatiently.

"He said the Shaka gang has a card game tonight and his guy is one of the players."

"There is? Who's going to be there?"

Clawson rattled off the names of a couple of the leaders of the Shaka gang.

"Have Zimo deliver a letter to his guy."

"I'll call him and get it handled," Clawson assured his boss. "And he's learned that there's a truck headed north tonight with a full load. He's getting me the details and license plate number."

"Good," Steiner said. "I want that truck. I don't care what you do with the driver, but bring the truck to the warehouse."

"We'll take care of that," Clawson responded.

"It's even more important now that we secure more product since El Patrón's operations are in disarray and Baudin's been killed. I want you to set up a meeting with the Colombians here. We're going to have their ships come up the coast and offload to us at sea."

"I'll call them."

"It's such a mess down there. Baudin blew it. Big time," Steiner groused, recalling what had recently happened in Cuba. "Find out what happened to that nosy reporter, Emerson Moore. I want to know if he made it out alive," Steiner ordered.

"I'll check our sources there and see what we can learn," Clawson said quickly.

"Be sure to check with that guy in Cuban intelligence. I think his name is Fuentes. I know he and Baudin were involved in getting behind Moore's alias, Manny Elias. He might know what happened to Moore," Steiner fumed.

"I'll call him right away."

Steiner's attention was focused on the laptop on the desk. Opening a program, Steiner quickly went through encrypted emails.

Thirty minutes later, Clawson walked back into the library.

"I found Fuentes. He's the chief of the Intelligence Directorate in Havana. He wasn't excited about talking about Baudin with me until I told him that we worked with Baudin and knew he was getting payoffs from him. I had to wire him $20,000 to get information from him," Clawson explained.

"And what did he tell you? Is Moore alive or dead?" Steiner

asked, leaning with both hands on the desk. Steiner's eyes were filled with fury.

"He didn't know. They couldn't find him. They did have a report from one of the Cuban guard towers at Guantanamo that the Americans had a helicopter pull a body out of the river."

"That could have been Moore. Did he say who it was?" Steiner growled.

"No. The body swept into the American zone before they could get to it."

"Maybe he's dead, then. But keep an eye out. If he comes snooping around our business, I want him dead. What about the Colombians?"

"Rojas is flying into Norfolk tomorrow. We'll pick him up and take him to the dock to catch one of our boats. He'll then be taken to the cove to catch your seaplane for a flight back here. We'll be sure he's not followed."

"Be absolutely sure," Steiner warned with a lethal look.

"We will," Clawson assured Steiner.

"Good."

Later that evening, a black Cadillac Escalade parked next to one of the buildings the Shaka gang used in Norfolk. Zimo and the driver exited the car and walked up to the door where two burly men guarded the door.

"What do you want here?" one asked.

"I want to talk to Abarra," Zimo instructed.

"Wait," the guard said as he called on his cell phone into the card game.

"What do you want? Don't you know we're playing cards here?" Abarra asked, irritated that his concentration was interrupted.

"Zimo is here. He wants to come in," the guard answered.

"He is? What does he want?"

"To talk to you."

"Frisk him and send him in."

"He's got a homeboy with him."

"The homeboy stays outside," Abarra instructed as he hung up.

"I need to frisk you," the guard said as he placed his cell phone in his pocket.

"Do your stuff," Zimo said as the other guard pointed his AK-47 at Zimo while keeping a wary eye on Zimo's companion.

The guard quickly ran his hands over Zimo and didn't find any weapons. Stepping back from Zimo, he said, "You can go in. They're up the stairs and to the right," he instructed. "Your bang buddy stays here," he said with an evil glint in his eyes.

"No sweat, man," Zimo replied as he walked to the door, opened it and entered the building which was in need of repair. He climbed the creaky stairs, noting the gangsta words written on the stairway walls. When he arrived on the second floor, he turned right into a smoke-filled room.

To one side there was a table that held a variety of liquor bottles and beer. Two shotguns were leaned against the wall in the corner. In the center of the room, four men were seated at a well-worn table that held a pile of cash from their poker game. They each had glasses of liquor in front of them. One was smoking marijuana. The mean-faced one, facing the door, smoked a cigar. His name was Abarra.

"Dawg, what's crackin? Why you gotta come down here and interrupt my card game with my posse?" Abarra asked.

"Steiner sent me."

"Steiner sends the roll dog down here to bother me?"

Zimo's eyes had taken attendance. He didn't see the head of the Shaka gang in the room. "Is Obasi here?"

"No, dawg. He left. He's spending time with his chica. I'm the man in charge here. What you want?" Abarra asked as he sat back in his chair and exhaled cigar smoke.

"Steiner wanted to make him an offer," Zimo replied, disappointed that Obasi had left earlier. "But I was to make it to him," he said.

"Make it to me," Abarra said in a firm voice.

"Can't do that. You know how Steiner is about following instructions."

"You tell your cheese muffin that I'll tell Obasi about your visit. Steiner can give him a call."

"I'll do that," Zimo said as he turned and started out the door.

As he did, the player with his back to the door stood.

"Where you going, Mosi?" Abarra growled, irritated about the delay in the card game.

"I need to release the firehose," Mosi said as he followed Zimo out the door. When they reached the hallway, Zimo pulled an envelope out of his pocket and furtively handed it to Mosi, who quickly stuffed it in his pocket before walking to the bathroom at the end of the hall.

It was a good thing that the envelope handoff happened quickly because Abarra unexpectedly walked out of the room. He saw that Zimo had reached the bottom of the steps. Abarra walked back inside the room. He stepped over to the window and watched as Zimo and his companion walked over to the Escalade and drove away. Satisfied, he returned to his seat at the table and emptied his glass.

Meanwhile, Mosi had entered the second-floor bathroom.

He withdrew the envelope from Zimo, who had been buying information from him over the last six months. Opening the envelope, he read it. It said: *Kill them all.*

Mosi smiled. He knew that this day would come and Zimo had promised him a big payday. He flushed the envelope and note down the toilet and calmly washed his hands at the sink.

Opening the door, he walked down the hall and paused at the door to the room.

"I'm going to catch some fresh air. I'll be right back."

"You hurry. I'm takin every one of you suckas' money," Abarra beamed as he won another hand.

Mosi walked down the steps and out the front door.

"Break time," he said as he walked past the two guards at the front and over to his car. He reached into the back seat and pulled back a blanket. He picked up a .22 caliber pistol with a silencer and stuffed it behind his back, inside his waistband. He then walked back over to the two guards.

"What's that over there?" he asked as he pointed.

When the two guards looked to their right, Mosi pulled out the .22 and fired four times, quietly killing the two guards.

Mosi returned to his car and reached for the sawed-off shotgun. The pump-action Mossberg 500 held seven shells in the magazine and one in the chamber, giving him eight rounds for the three card players. He closed the car door and returned to the building.

When he neared the top of the stairs, he heard Abarra laughing as he won another hand. When Mosi walked through the doorway, he leveled the shotgun at the man to his right and fired. The man was knocked off his chair to the floor where his blood-splattered body convulsed twice before becoming still.

Seeing movement to the left, Mosi swung around and saw the other card player scrambling out of his chair for one of the shotguns stacked in the corner. Mosi fired twice, and the man crumpled to the floor.

When Mosi moved to face Abarra, he was met by two rounds fired from Abarra's .45 which Abarra had pulled from the waistband of his slacks. Before falling to the floor, Mosi shot off two blasts to Abarra's head, instantly killing him.

Mosi groaned as he lay on the floor bloodied with a wound to his left arm and one to his abdomen. He heard footsteps pounding up the stairs as he painfully brought the shotgun around and aimed it at the doorway.

He sighed with relief and lowered the weapon when he saw that it was Zimo.

"They're dead?" Zimo asked as he quickly looked around the room and pointed his own shotgun at each of the bodies.

"Yes. You have to help me."

"We were parked around the corner and headed right back when we heard the first shot," Zimo explained quickly as he returned to stand over the bleeding Mosi.

"You have to help me," Mosi repeated as he struggled to raise his body.

"That's why I'm here," Zimo said as he fired two rounds into Mosi, killing him. Zimo turned around quickly and raced down the steps to the waiting Escalade, and they drove off as sirens announced the approaching police cars.

As they drove off, Zimo called Clawson on his cell phone.

"Hello?" Clawson answered.

"The packages have been distributed," Zimo answered cryptically.

"Understand. And what about the guest of honor?" Clawson asked, referring to the Shaka gang leader Obasi.

Zimo paused. He didn't want to share the bad news that Obasi had escaped unharmed, but there was no way to avoid telling them. There were deadly consequences for not being truthful to Clawson or Steiner, and he had witnessed them. "He had to leave early and missed the end of the party."

Clawson frowned at hearing the news.

"What about the package giver?"

"Gone to the North Pole," Zimo answered sinisterly as he thought how he iced Mosi.

"Good. Thanks," Clawson said as he ended the call and turned to Steiner. "Zimo's successfully completed his mission, although there was a small problem."

"What's that?" Steiner asked with a dark cloud of concern.

"Everything went well other than Obasi leaving early. He's still alive," Clawson explained.

Steiner erupted angrily and started swearing profusely. After a few minutes, Steiner's rage subsided a bit. "I want Obasi dead. Find him and take him out. Do you understand?"

"I do. We'll find him. He doesn't stray too far from his business. We'll get him," Clawson said as he walked out of the room to escape Steiner's wrath.

Meanwhile, a white box truck with signage identifying it as Best Bay Seafood crossed the Chesapeake Bay Bridge and headed north on Route 13. Shortly, it drove past the combination visitors center and rest area.

The occupants of a white Ford Explorer, which was parked to the side of the entranceway to Route 13 from the center, watched as the box truck drove by. Using the lights from the visitors center, they could easily read the truck's signage.

"That's it," the driver said. "Get the lights ready," he said to his companion who grabbed the set of blue lights and stepped out of the vehicle. He affixed the magnetic base of the lights to the roof of the vehicle and placed the trailing wire into the SUV as he jumped back inside. He plugged them into the cigarette lighter outlet and sat back. Once he turned them on, they would appear to be a police vehicle.

The driver put the vehicle in gear and drove down the ramp to catch up to the truck. Within a half a mile, he had closed in on the box truck.

"Hit the lights and put your cap on," he instructed his companion, who placed his cap on top of his head to complete the stolen state trooper uniform.

Inside the box truck, reggae music filled the air. The driver and his gun-toting Jamaican guard were jamming to the beat.

"Hey, we've got trouble," the truck driver exclaimed as he looked at the outside mirror and saw the blue flashing lights behind them. He began to slow the vehicle.

"Whassup?'" the Jamaican asked as he gripped the shotgun tighter.

"Police. Looks like we're being pulled over," he replied as he slowed and parked the truck next to the highway. He turned off the CD player.

The Jamaican whipped his head around and looked out his side mirror. He saw that the vehicle had parked behind them.

"You weren't speeding, man, wuz you?" he asked hurriedly.

"No."

"I don't get it. Why de want to pull over poor old us in the middle of the night?" he worried.

"Probably just a routine traffic stop. Be cool," the driver warned his nervous passenger. "And put that shotgun down."

The Jamaican lowered his weapon and watched as one of

the uniformed men walked up along his side of the truck.

On the other side, the driver rolled down his window and waited for the other uniformed officer. He spoke as the officer stopped below his window and looked up at him.

"Evening officer."

"Out of the truck," the officer ordered.

"But we weren't doing anything wrong," the driver protested.

"Out," the officer repeated.

"You too," the other officer said to the Jamaican.

"Be cool, now. And we will be back on the road in a few minutes," the driver whispered quickly to the Jamaican, who complied and placed his shotgun on the floor.

Both men exited the vehicle, closing the doors behind them. The officers ordered them around to the rear of the truck.

"Either one of you armed?" the officer asked.

"No," the driver responded.

"Open the doors," he instructed as he nodded at the rear doors to the truck.

"But why? We didn't do anything."

"Do as I say."

"You don't have my approval to search my truck. You guys need that or reasonable cause," the driver smirked at the officers. He knew the law.

"Do I have your approval now?" the officer asked as he withdrew his weapon from his holster and pointed it at the man. His partner did likewise and pointed his .45 at the Jamaican.

"Just be cool. Yeah, dat's no good now," the Jamaican said in a hushed sarcastic tone to the driver, who returned his comment with a glare.

"It's illegal. I'm telling you, it's illegal. You can't search my truck without my permission," he said as the driver swung open the doors to reveal thirty-one large plastic bags filled with marijuana. There was over 3,000 pounds of it.

"Payday!'" the first officer said as he fired three shots into the truck driver and killed him.

The Jamaican began to sprint around the rear of the truck toward the cab and his shotgun. He was dead before he had taken five steps, crumbling to the ground.

"Nice haul," the second officer said as he returned his .45 to his holster.

"Oh yeah. This is a big haul," he said as he headed back to the vehicle and tossed his cap into it. He then turned off the flashing blue lights and removed them from the roof of the SUV before tossing them inside.

The other officer walked around the truck and climbed up into the cab and smiled when he saw the keys were still in the ignition. He started the truck and pulled away from the dead bodies as the SUV followed him.

Twenty minutes later, they had pulled off Route 13 and headed for a safe house where they parked the truck in the barn. The driver of the SUV had called Clawson to let him know that they had accomplished their deadly assignment.

# CHAPTER 14

## The Next Day
## Kings Creek, Virginia

The seaplane swooped low over Kings Creek so that the pilot could take a closer look at water conditions. The wind had picked up speed and the inlet was choppy. The pilot decided the grass landing strip would be a wiser choice and circled around to set up his approach.

"Not landing on the water?" the swarthy Colombian asked in heavily accented English.

"Too rough," Hensley the pilot replied.

Sitting next to Hensley was a leader from the Cali cartel in Colombia. He had a pock-marked face and his black hair was slicked back. He had dark eyes that hinted of the evil inside. His name was Ricardo Rojas. He was better known by his nickname Packo.

The pilot expertly landed the plane through a tough crosswind, and the plane taxied up to a waiting golf cart. As the pilot switched off the engine, Rojas climbed down from the plane.

"Packo, I trust you had a good flight," Graber said as he welcomed Rojas.

"It was okay. Where's Steiner?" he asked, miffed by Steiner's lack of courtesy in greeting him personally. He didn't realize that it was contrived to show that Steiner was the more important of the two drug runners.

"Inside. Waiting for you," Graber answered.

As a perturbed Rojas began to climb into the golf cart for the ride to the main house, Graber stopped him. "I need you to step out of the cart."

"What for? I thought you were driving me to the house."

"I am. I need to make sure you're unarmed."

Annoyed, Rojas snapped, "I was already searched before I was allowed on your plane, *Cabrón*."

Graber ignored the insult. "My boss is very careful. So, if you don't mind, I need to do this."

Reluctantly Rojas stepped out of the golf cart and stood still as Graber ran his hands expertly over Rojas. He was pleased that he didn't find any weapons.

"We're good."

The two men settled into the golf cart for the ride to the house. Five minutes later, they had parked in front of the main entrance, and the two men walked to the door.

"Have you ever been here before?" Graber asked, even though he knew the answer.

"No."

Graber smiled as he saw Rojas' eyes widen as he took in the grandiose home. Steiner's plan was to demonstrate success through the house's opulence.

"Very nice," Rojas said as he walked into the foyer which was lined with gold-framed mirrors. He couldn't resist commenting on the home's grandeur.

"We're back here," Graber said as he escorted Rojas down the main hallway to Steiner's library.

As they entered, Rojas took in the elegantly furnished room which contained a large cherry desk with striking book-matched panels and a matching computer credenza with a storage hutch. Several matching open and four-doored cherry bookcases lined the cherry-paneled walls.

A burgundy leather high-backed chair sat behind the desk, and two matching leather chairs were in front of the desk. Several expensive oil paintings of ships at sea hung on the walls.

In front of the large window, facing Kings Creek, was a table which held a decanter filled with coffee. Next to several coffee cups was a bowl of fresh fruit.

Graber walked Rojas to the table.

"Coffee? Fruit?" he asked as he pointed to the items.

"Or maybe something stronger, Packo?" a voice asked from the doorway.

Rojas turned and saw Steiner enter the room. He quickly walked over to Steiner and shook hands as Graber left the room. "You read my mind."

"People say that I'm very good at reading minds," Steiner smirked before opening one of the cherry doors on the liquor cabinet. "Tequila?"

"Perfect."

"I take it that your flights went with no problems?" Steiner asked while pouring the tequila into tall shot glasses and handing one to Rojas.

"They did," he said as he raised his shot glass to Steiner and they downed their shots.

"Another?" Steiner asked.

"Yes."

Steiner refilled the glasses. After they tossed them down, they settled in the chairs. Steiner opted to sit next to Rojas in front of the desk.

"We need to figure out how you're going to supply me on a

direct basis since Baudin's operation in Cuba no longer exists," Steiner said to open the discussion.

"He's dead, right?" Rojas asked.

"He is. Thanks to a nosy reporter's involvement," Steiner fumed.

"And do you need us to take care of him?"

"No. That pleasure I want to have all to myself. We're trying to track him down although we suspect he died in the jungle trying to escape. We're working on it."

"Did you check with Cuban intelligence?"

"They're working on it, too," Steiner replied.

"We have some contacts on the island, too. I'll have them see if they can find the reporter. Do you have a name?"

"His real name is Emerson Moore, but he used an alias on the island. It was Manny Elias."

"I've heard the Elias name," said Rojas. "He had a run-in with some of our Miami connections in a deal that went bust in Key West."

"Probably the same guy."

"The boys in Miami would like to get their hands on him, too," Rojas commented.

"No. He's mine. You tell them to hand him over to me if they get him before I do. I have something wicked in mind for him."

"Aw, revenge. Nothing like sweet revenge."

Steiner's eyes narrowed. "I owe him for what he did to my supply channel."

"Not so fast. He may have done you a favor. This could work out better for you by dealing with me directly. No middleman. A better price for you." Rojas smiled.

"But more risk. I work hard to keep myself distanced from

the buying and selling. We've got too many law enforcement agencies trying to pin a connection on me. So far, I've been able to keep them at bay," Steiner boasted. "And I want to keep it that way."

"We can still do this and protect you. You have people you can trust?"

"I do. The ones I can't trust aren't around anymore." There was something sinister in Steiner's tone.

"I understand that."

"So how do we get your drugs here?"

"In the past," Rojas explained, "our ships offloaded near Cuba and Baudin used his ships and go-fast boats to deliver our shipments. Now for you, we'll have our ships sail up the coast. Can we have them come into Chesapeake Bay?"

"Not anymore. The Customs agents are all over any ship coming into the Bay, especially from Colombia," Steiner noted.

"That may not be such a big problem. We use non-Colombian ships, too. And we've become more sophisticated in how we use containers. We've hired hackers to trick container company employees to install our malware. They use a phishing attack through emails."

"You've got hackers?" Steiner asked, surprised.

"Yes. And if the container company discovered a breach in their system, we've had our people break into their facility to install keystroke-logging devices on their computer keyboards. That gives us wireless access to their keystrokes and allows us to grab screenshots, too," Rojas bragged.

"Sometimes our people install their own hardware inside the hard drive so they can access and remotely control data on the shipping companies' computers. It helps our drivers when they break into the premises to steal the right containers."

"That's amazing," Steiner smiled at the news.

"And we don't always have to steal the containers. By hacking into their systems, we know when the container is going to be moved from the shipyard and on what truck, then we simply highjack the truck."

"How do you find the truck on the road?" Steiner asked.

"Easy. On some of the containers, we install a GPS transmitter when we load the cocaine inside to make it easy to track down the truck. We can move a ton of cocaine very easily."

"Still sounds risky. We're hearing that the police have scanners that they can use on vehicles that will alert them to drugs hidden in a vehicle. The only thing helping us is they must have either the driver's permission to search the vehicle or have probable cause," Steiner explained.

"I'm aware. They are also scanning the containers, but they can't scan them all," Rojas beamed.

Steiner stood and walked over to the computer. After hitting a few keys, Steiner beckoned Rojas to look at a map on the monitor screen.

"I'm concerned about the success rate you have with your approach."

"It's very successful," Rojas protested.

Ignoring the comment, Steiner continued. "The Chesapeake Bay is filled with Customs agents and Coast Guardsmen. I'd rather do something more quietly to get our shipments."

Steiner's finger pointed to Assateague Island and Chincoteague Bay.

"This is a much quieter area. Not so much traffic or law enforcement presence. If your ships could offload to our boats off Assateague Island in the Atlantic, we could run our boats up Chincoteague Bay to the end to make deliveries for Berlin,

Salisbury and Ocean City. We could also truck it from there up the East Coast. And we could do it very quietly."

Steiner's finger moved up the coastline. "And we could also run our boats up the coast to make deliveries to our dealers in Atlantic City and Philadelphia."

"I really do think you should try our shipping container approach," Rojas urged.

"Let me think about it. Maybe in the future, but I want to do this. Trust me. It will work." Steiner said forcefully.

The two spent the rest of the time discussing the quantity, pricing and timing of the shipments before adjourning for lunch. Later that afternoon, Rojas flew out on Steiner's plane to Miami where he caught a commercial flight to Colombia.

# CHAPTER 15

## Sheriff's Office
## Accomac, Virginia

After a morning run and some time helping Roe around the workshop, Moore drove down to Accomac. He parked the Jeep in the parking lot and walked into the Sheriff's Department where he was quickly cleared and then escorted to Relle's office.

"Emerson, come join me in the conference room," Relle said when Moore walked into his office.

They walked into the adjoining room, and Moore saw Zak Sherman who he had met on the last raid. He couldn't help but notice the wildly-colored socks Sherman was wearing. "Nice socks," Moore teased as he greeted Sherman.

"Yeah. You're just jealous because you don't have any like these," Sherman cracked back.

"Is that part of the approved wear?" Moore asked even though he knew the answer.

"It is in my case," Sherman shot back with a grin.

"You let him get away with wearing those?" Moore asked Relle.

"I do. I have to be careful with him," Relle answered.

"How's that?"

"His father is my dentist. I want to be sure that I don't make his dad angry for the next time I get work done."

Moore laughed.

Relle introduced Moore to another man in the room. He was tall, thirty-nine years old and lean with a shaven head. "This is Matt Lemke. He runs our counter-intelligence team."

"Glad to meet you, Matt," Moore said as they shook hands.

"You're that award-winning newspaper reporter I've read so much about," Lemke said.

"You have done your homework," Moore countered with a grin as the men took a seat at the table.

"Always," Lemke smiled. "Remember, I'm in intel!" he grinned.

"Okay. Enough chatter. Emerson, we're going to give you a little insight into the drug-running operations here in the lower Delmarva Peninsula. Matt, it's your show," Relle said as he sat and focused the team on the business at hand.

Lemke sat at the keyboard and entered several keystrokes, which resulted in the contents of his computer monitor being displayed on a large screen at the end of the room. The screen showed the Sheriff's Department logo.

"Let's start with the biggest drug lord in these parts," he said as he began to depress several keys.

"Max Steiner," Moore volunteered to show he knew who they were going to talk about.

"Right," Lemke said as he hit enter and Max Steiner's face appeared on the screen.

Moore's eyes widened, and a gasp escaped from between his lips.

"Are you okay?" Relle asked the distraught Moore.

"That's not Max!" Moore said with disbelief.

"Yes, it is," Lemke shot back. "That's Maxine Steiner."

"No, that's Peaches Babbit!" Moore exclaimed as he grabbed the table's edge to steady himself from the shock of seeing her.

"What are you talking about?" Relle asked, confused.

"That's the woman I met in Cuba. She worked for Henri Baudin, aka El Patrón."

"Go on. We've heard about him."

Moore quickly gave them a brief recap of what recently had transpired in Cuba, including Baudin's death and Peaches' disappearance.

"So, she left Cuba and ends up here? This is unbelievable," Moore said as his eyes returned to stare at her picture on the screen.

"Sounds like she really worked you," Relle noted after hearing Moore's recount of his Cuban adventure. "Obviously, Peaches Babbit was an alias she used just like Manny Elias was yours."

"I would never have thought of her being from here," a shaken Moore offered. His mind raced as he thought about confronting her for misleading him and leading him on in Cuba. He was overwhelmed by stumbling upon her here.

"Baudin's death created a void in drug trafficking in Cuba and it disrupted shipments up the East Coast," Lemke added.

"Right," Relle agreed. "And who wants to bet that Steiner wants to step in to close that gap?"

"At least until the Cubans get it all worked out," Sherman suggested.

"I don't know. She can be ruthless. She will do her best to hang on to any market share she can grab," Relle said.

"We might see the Colombians shipping up here," Sherman proposed.

"I agree," Relle said as he turned to look at Moore who was still staring at Steiner. "You okay there, Emerson?"

"I'm just stunned. What a schmuck I can be. I'm an absolute

proctologist's dream, I am!" Moore proclaimed as he looked at Relle. "She just reeled me right in. I was such a sucker!"

"And we still don't have solid evidence on Steiner. Even though Baudin may have told you that she worked for him, he's dead," Relle added.

"We'll need to work hard to build the case," Lemke said. "She's very difficult to catch."

"Like Teflon. Any time we think we have her, she slips away. Nothing sticks to her. She's very clever about keeping her hands clean. Matt, go on with your presentation," Relle said as the men returned their attention to the screen.

For the next thirty minutes, the officers focused on updating Moore about the drug trafficking in the peninsula region. They were interrupted by a knock on the conference room door. A number of officers walked in to be briefed on the late afternoon raid.

Relle introduced Moore and updated the rest of the team about the raid. Afterward, everyone geared up prior to meeting outside in the parking lot. Relle tossed Moore a bullet-proof vest.

"Better wear this."

Moore frowned. "I don't like these things. Besides, I didn't need one last time."

"The day you don't wear one could be the last day of your life," Relle warned.

"All right," Moore said as he reluctantly pulled on the vest.

Twenty minutes later, four police vehicles pulled out of the parking lot.

"Where are we headed?" Moore asked.

"We're raiding a safe house outside of Onley," Relle replied. "They use it as a drug stash and sell to distributors in the county.

"Expecting trouble on this one?"

"Maybe. These guys are more violent than the guys we encountered on the last raid."

"I take it you have a search warrant?" Moore asked.

"We do. We used several investigative techniques to gather information about what was going on at the house. We also had two of the neighbors come to us about suspected drug traffic at the house. We then put some covert surveillance tools in place and saw some known sellers going in to buy. Built our case from there."

"A lot of work."

"Well, it helped that the two guys who live there have been convicted in the past for selling drugs," Relle added.

Within ten minutes, the four police vehicles approached the house.

Relle radioed the other officers. "Looks like things may be a bit complicated. There's a large RV parked in the drive. Might be buying a ton of illegal drugs. Keep alert, men."

Relle parked his vehicle in front of the one-story house while the others parked on both sides of him. The fourth vehicle parked in front of the RV to block any potential escape.

As the men exited the vehicles, someone closed the front window drapes, and an armed man bolted out of the front door and headed for the RV.

"Freeze! Police!" the nearest officer yelled.

Instead, the man turned and began firing. Two officers returned fire, killing the man as their bullets found their target.

Meanwhile, Moore and Relle ran behind their vehicle for cover.

"What do you have there?" Relle asked Moore in surprise.

Moore had grabbed the shotgun from its rack on the vehicle's passenger side. "Just in case," he smiled.

Relle shook his head. "You be careful."

Moore nodded. "I know how to use these."

Relle turned his attention back to the house and spoke on the loudspeaker. "Police! We have a search warrant!"

Before he could say anything more, the door to the house opened, and a man fired two rounds from his shotgun at Relle's vehicle.

Relle and Moore ducked.

"Out back!" a deputy in the car behind Relle's car yelled. He gunned the engine and drove into the side yard where he and his partner exchanged shots with a man trying to escape through the backyard.

One officer was struck in the shoulder as he crouched outside of his open SUV door. The other officer fired three more times and killed the suspect.

With that, a fog of silence settled over the house. The men waited for a couple of minutes, and then cautiously moved toward the house. Relle had instructed Moore to stay at the vehicle until the house was secure.

When the officers entered, Moore suddenly heard an engine start. It was the RV parked in the driveway. Apparently, someone had been hiding undiscovered inside the RV. The driver gunned the RV and crashed into the police vehicle blocking it. It shoved the vehicle into a small ditch on the other side of the street. The RV backed up, and the driver opened the window. He pointed a .45 semi-automatic handgun at Moore, who didn't wait for it to be fired.

Moore fired two rounds from the shotgun at the driver, striking him with both shots as the RV accelerated. It careened into the ditch on the side of the road and struck a telephone pole.

Moore slowly approached the vehicle with his weapon aimed at the driver's window. When he heard the sound of approaching footsteps, he turned and saw two officers running from the house to support him. Quickly he turned his eyes back to his target and stopped.

"We got this," one of the officers said as he ran by Moore.

The two officers ran around the vehicle with their weapons drawn and carefully opened the passenger door where they saw the driver slumped over the steering wheel. They cautiously entered the vehicle and made sure it was empty before returning to the driver. He was dead.

"Can't leave you unattended," Relle commented as he walked over to Moore to make sure he was unharmed.

"Some say I need adult supervision," Moore quipped.

Relle took a quick report from the two officers who had joined them. Afterward, he turned to Moore. "Let's head for the house."

"Did you get the two guys that lived here?" Moore asked as they walked up the front steps.

"Yes." Relle pointed to the man who had run from the front of the house. "That's one of them. The other was the one who ran out back."

He turned to one of the officers. "Call that ambulance again. I want them here now." Relle was concerned for his officer who had been wounded during the exchange of gunfire.

For the next hour, the officers searched the house for the drug stash, but couldn't find anything.

"This doesn't make sense. There should be drugs here," Relle said in frustration as he stood with Moore at the side of the house. He turned to one of the men. "Check that RV."

The officer ran over to the wrecked RV and began to search it. Within minutes, he was back. In his hand, he held a small suitcase. "I found this. Looks like cocaine," he suggested.

Relle nodded. "There's got to be more."

"Is there a basement?" Moore asked.

"Not in these parts. Too wet. Besides, we checked the house plans yesterday, and it didn't show one."

"Then why is that water being pumped out?" Moore asked as he pointed to a plastic drain hose that protruded from the concrete block upon which the house was set.

Relle turned and looked. "That is interesting."

"I know some homes back in Ohio where people dug out a basement by hand after the house was built for extra storage," Moore explained.

"Boys, let's see if we can't find a hidden trap door somewhere," Relle said as he led two of his men back into the house. Moore followed.

The men began searching the floor as they looked for a trap door, but couldn't find anything.

"I'd bet they wouldn't put it somewhere obvious," Moore quipped.

"It would have to be where people wouldn't expect it, especially if they were concerned about some users breaking in and stealing their drugs."

Moore walked into the kitchen area to conduct his own investigation. It was his nature to be curious, particularly at a crime scene. Suddenly, he noticed that the refrigerator was on aluminum appliance rollers.

"Check this out," Moore said as he approached the fridge and grabbed hold with his hands. He pulled, and it moved out easily over the worn tile floor. It had been covering the trap door to the basement.

"Here's the door," Moore said, proud of his observation skills.

"Nice job, Emerson. Stand clear," Relle said as he reached down and threw open the door. "Anyone down there?" he called.

Not getting a response, Relle nodded to Sherman who approached it and threw a flash grenade down the opening. It went off with a brilliant flash and bang.

"You go first," Moore said to Sherman, who looked at him for a second. He saw that Moore was grinning.

"If nothing happens, I'll follow you down," Moore teased.

"That's a bit of wicked humor at a time like this," Sherman said sternly.

"Stepping out of my comfort zone," Moore said. He was surprised at himself for the uncharacteristic comment.

Quickly, Sherman and another officer descended the flight of steps into the dark hole with flashlights and guns drawn. Within seconds, Sherman found a light switch and turned on the lights.

"All clear," he shouted.

Relle and Moore descended the stairs and examined the twenty-by-twenty room that had been shorn up with cinder block. It was dank and musty. Its wet floor was slanted to a corner where a sump pump was located.

"There's your sump pump and the hose that we saw outside," Moore pointed to the corner.

"You're right," Relle remarked, but he was looking at several metal briefcases that were stacked on three steel shelving units. "And I bet that's what we were looking for."

Sherman walked over and jimmied the lock on one of the briefcases. He opened it to find several packages of cocaine inside.

"Nice haul," Sherman said.

"The forensics team is here," a voice shouted down the stairs.

"We'll be right up. Zak, leave those there, and we'll let the forensics team take care of it," Relle instructed.

"Right," Sherman replied as he turned and followed Relle and Moore up the stairs where they greeted the arriving DEA agents and the forensics team.

Thirty minutes later, Moore asked, "Anything here tie all of this to Steiner?"

"Not yet. They're still going through everything," Relle replied.

"I just can't get over Steiner and Peaches being the same person," Moore said as the two walked back to their vehicle.

"Life is full of surprises, isn't it?" Relle responded.

"I guess so. I'm just stunned," Moore commented. The two men entered the SUV and returned to Accomac where Moore was debriefed about killing the RV driver. Once the interview and corresponding paperwork were complete, he retrieved the Jeep and headed back to Chincoteague.

When he returned to Roe's house, he found Roe and Monnie relaxing in their family room.

"You're not going to believe this!" Moore started.

"Give us a try, son," Roe suggested.

Moore quickly recounted his surprise at learning that Peaches Babbit and Max Steiner were the same person. He then gave a brief overview of the raid, including how he ended up killing the RV driver.

"Lucky you were armed," Roe commented in a serious tone.

"I'll say. I just had a feeling that I better tote that shotgun."

"And that's something about Max and Peaches being the same person," Monnie added.

"You have plans to meet up with her?" Roe asked with a concerned look.

"Probably. I need to think on it more," Moore said.

"I don't need to tell you about being careful," Roe cautioned.

"No. Everyone under the sun tells me that," Moore smiled. "I think I'm going to call it a night."

"Did you have dinner?" Monnie asked.

"No."

"Come on into the kitchen with me, and I'll make you a sandwich. You like turkey?"

"Sure," Moore replied as he stood up from the chair and started to follow her.

"Emerson," Roe called.

"Yes?"

"Billy Joe stopped by today."

"He did?"

"Yes. It's about the Kronsky boy." Roe had a troubled tone in his voice.

"What about him?"

"He's been spotted hanging out with the wrong people down in Northampton County."

"Oh, no!"

"Yeah. I'm going to have a man-to-man talk with him when he shows up again. You might want to encourage him, too. He's come a long way and doesn't need to be sliding back into his bad habits."

"I think he wants to do the right thing. There's something about him that I like and I want to support him. You can count on me," Moore assured Roe.

"I knew that," Roe smiled.

Moore headed to the kitchen where Monnie fixed his sandwich. After he gobbled it down, he headed for bed. It had been a long day and his mind was reeling.

# CHAPTER 16

## Two Nights Later
## Offshore Assateague Island

Ten miles off the coast, a freighter and fishing trawler rocked gently together in relatively calm seas under a moonless night. The freighter's crane lowered a plastic wrapped pallet onto the deck of the fishing trawler.

Two crew members aboard the trawler freed the line as the pallet settled on the deck. When they finished, they signaled the freighter, and the crane operator retrieved its line. The two ships separated and continued their voyages.

The trawler, named *Cathy's Pony*, was forty feet long with a fifteen-foot beam. She had a 300 HP, six-cylinder Cummins diesel engine and could operate in depths as shallow as four feet—perfect for traveling the north end of Chincoteague Bay.

The trawler pointed her bow toward the entrance to Chincoteague Bay as two crew members worked quickly to remove the plastic wrapping. A bearded man stepped out from the wheelhouse to check on the progress of the crew.

"You don't have all night," he shouted. "Get the lead out!"

"On it, Captain," one of the crew members yelled back as they finished removing the last piece of plastic to reveal the pallet contents. There were stacks of plastic-wrapped cocaine bricks piled high.

The men began transporting the bricks inside the cabin where they stacked them out of sight. They were still at risk if stopped by the Coast Guard and boarded.

When the two men finished stacking the cocaine bricks inside, they returned to the empty pallet. Picking it up, they simply tossed it and the plastic wrapping overboard.

Within hours, the trawler entered Chincoteague Bay and motored past Chincoteague Island's Coast Guard station. It continued up the bay to a secluded inlet edged by tall trees in Maryland. It was a few miles south of busy Ocean City and provided a quiet dock for unloading the clandestine cargo.

After the trawler was secured, drivers in a rented white box truck and Cadillac Escalade started their engines and drove from where they had been waiting in the darkness. The Escalade parked near the dock while the box truck backed up as close as it could to the trawler. The armed occupants stepped out of their vehicles and walked over to the dock. They were led by Zimo who had driven up from Norfolk to oversee the operation.

Zimo stepped onto the dock and walked to the trawler. He greeted the captain who descended from the wheelhouse.

"Any trouble?"

"None."

"Good," Zimo remarked. He motioned to two of the men from the box truck. "Set up the lights. We've got an hour until dawn. Let's get this loaded."

The men scurried to the back of the truck where they opened it and unloaded two portable lighting systems. They quickly set them up to illuminate the area between the truck and the trawler.

Four men walked over, each with handcarts, and began

helping the ship's crew offload the drugs. When a handcart was fully loaded, one of Zimo's men would wheel it to the truck where he used the hydraulic lift to raise the drugs to the truck's bed. He then helped another man unload the bricks onto a pallet situated inside the truck.

When the men finished loading the truck, Zimo handed a cash-filled envelope to the captain. "Good job! See you in a couple of days."

"Thanks. This was a piece of cake," the captain answered as he returned to his trawler.

Zimo walked over to the truck where he spoke to the driver.

"Give me a couple of minutes head start, then follow the route that we laid out."

"Got it," the driver replied.

"And no speeding," Zimo reminded the driver.

"Right."

"You don't want to be pulled over with this load."

Zimo joined his other men in the Escalade, and they pulled away from the dock. They were running interference in front of their precious cargo to spot any potential police checkpoints. Zimo and the rental truck driver had portable two-way radios so that Zimo could alert him if he spotted any trouble.

They didn't need the radios on this run to Ocean City as it went smoothly with no disruptions. They pulled onto a side street and approached a dimly lit warehouse.

Zimo picked up his phone and called a number. The call was answered on the second ring by the buyer who went by the nickname of Charcoal due to the color of his skin. His real name was Dave Cropper.

"Yeah?" Charcoal asked.

"We're thirty seconds away. You want to open the door?"

Zimo asked.

"Yeah," the man said as he hung up and turned to one of his gangbangers. "They're here. Open it."

The man ran to operate the garage door opener which slid the massive door up.

At the same time, Charcoal barked orders to his heavily armed gangbangers. "Take your places."

Charcoal wasn't taking any chances. He had done business with Zimo in the past with no problems. He liked that Zimo had been up front with him in explaining about the temporary interruption in their supply of cocaine from Cuba. This was going to be an exceptionally large delivery to make up for the shortage.

Charcoal wanted to be extra careful since Zimo had told him that they were implementing a new delivery system with shipments straight from Colombia. Sometimes, new processes had a few problems, and he didn't want to be surprised. That was another reason he had gunmen stationed along the street to the warehouse. If anything looked suspicious, they were prepared to resolve it lethally.

The Escalade pulled into the warehouse and parked. It was followed shortly by the white box truck and the garage door closed behind them.

The armed passengers departed their vehicles and suspiciously looked around at Charcoal's equally well-armed men.

"Expecting trouble?" Zimo laughed it off bravely.

"Can't be too careful, my man," Charcoal answered. "What do you have for me?" Charcoal asked as he followed Zimo to the back of the truck.

The truck driver opened the back of the truck to reveal the pallet full of cocaine bricks.

"Nice," Charcoal said as he eyed the delivery. He nodded his head, and one of his gangbangers jumped aboard a tow motor and eased it up to the truck. He maneuvered it so that the front prongs went under the pallet. He then lifted the pallet and backed up.

After setting the pallet on the floor, Charcoal nodded to another of his gangbangers, who walked over to the pallet. He took one of the bricks and carefully cut open the plastic.

Charcoal walked over and inspected the brick. "Nice and white," he said, knowing the color indicated the coke's purity. He then dipped his finger in and placed it in his mouth where he rubbed the powdery substance across his gums and tongue to gauge its numbing effect.

"Good," he said after a few seconds. "Test it."

The tow motor driver withdrew a cocaine purity test kit from his pocket. He took the transparent ampoule and added about 20 mg of the white powder. After capping the ampoule, he gently shook it. The contents of the ampoule changed color.

When Charcoal saw the white contents change to dark red, he smiled. "Very high quality!"

"Of course," Zimo smiled.

Charcoal reached into his pocket and pulled out a key fob. He depressed it, and the trunk of his Mercedes, which was parked in front of Zimo's vehicles, popped open. "You held up your end of the deal like always, and I've held up my end. There's your payment," Charcoal smiled as they walked over to his car.

Zimo opened each of the four suitcases and quickly examined the cash. Satisfied, he smiled. "Nice doing business with you," Zimo said as he nodded for his men to grab the suitcases.

His men knew the drill. They picked up the cases and placed

them in the Escalade.

"When is my next shipment?" Charcoal asked.

"Three days from now."

"Good. You confirm, and we'll set up the meet."

The two men shook hands, and Zimo and his men returned to their vehicles. The garage door opened and they drove out, heading back to Norfolk.

On the way back, Zimo called Clawson and let him know that everything had gone well. They made arrangements to meet to pick up the cash-filled suitcases before Zimo drove across the Chesapeake Bay Bridge. After ending the call, Clawson reported the night's successful transaction to Steiner, who was equally pleased.

# CHAPTER 17

**Roe Terry's Workshop**
**Chincoteague Island, Virginia**

"You've been moping around here these last couple of days like somebody who lost their best duck hunting dog," Roe commented as Moore brought in a few pieces of cottonwood.

"Sorry, Roe, but this whole thing with Maxine Steiner and Peaches Babbit being the same person has hit me like a ton of bricks," a melancholy Moore replied. "I feel like I should go over there and confront her."

"Why? Whatever is that going to do for you? Give you some silly-assed satisfaction?" Roe asked as he paused carving the decoy in his hand and looked at Moore.

"It just might," Moore commented.

"And you don't think that would be dangerous?" Roe asked, exasperated.

"Not really," Moore replied, although he had to agree that Roe was raising some good points.

"To my way of thinking, son, I'd say that woman sounds like she's so mean that she makes a hornet look cuddly," Roe said half-teasing.

"That's not the experience I had with her," Moore countered.

"That might have been because she was setting you up, son.

You did tell me that, right?"

"I did," Moore agreed, unenthusiastically.

"I told Billy Joe on the phone the other day about Max and Peaches being the same person. He said the rumor was that Steiner was behind a lot of the violence that was going on among drug gangs between Norfolk and Ocean City. They were having territory battles," Roe explained.

"And she's probably pissed off that you interrupted her drug supply from Cuba. I'd say it's a dangerous time to be sticking your neck out with her. You'll get your head chopped off like a chicken!" he added.

"I hear you," Moore agreed unconvincingly.

Roe noted Moore's reaction. "I'm serious, son. If you try to reconnect with her, I'm going to slap you so hard that even Google Maps won't be able to find you."

Moore knew that Roe had good intentions with his advice, but Moore didn't always heed good advice. That was one of his character flaws. He didn't always follow good advice.

"Go get me some more cottonwood," Roe said. "And I'm going to have a straight talk with Louie whenever that boy shows up. He's supposed to be here helping," Roe groused.

Moore walked out of the workshop and spent the next hour working on the tasks that Roe assigned him.

When Roe was ready for a lunch break, Moore begged off.

"I'm going for a run on Assateague," Moore explained.

"Another run? I thought you already went out this morning," Roe said as they left the workshop.

"I did, but I need some solitude."

"Go ahead. Take your time," Roe said as he walked into the kitchen. Moore hurried down the hallway to his room to change into running gear.

Twenty-five minutes later, Moore had parked the Jeep next to the beach and stepped out to stretch. He alternated placing his feet on the vehicle's bumper as he stretched his leg muscles. Looking around, he was stunned by how full the parking lot was

Physically, he was feeling much better. He had regained his strength and was healing well from the wounds in his shoulder and abdomen. On the other hand, his mental healing was lagging. He still had qualms about his future as an investigative reporter.

When he walked through the gap between the sand dunes, he saw that the beach was equally as crowded as the parking lot. Beachgoers had spread south into the area where he liked to jog. This was a reminder to him as to why he liked coming to the unoccupied beach for an early morning jog.

But he didn't care this afternoon. He was on a mission which he didn't want to share with Roe. He jogged down to the southernmost point and sat down at the water's edge. He had decided that he wouldn't leave the beach until he planned his next move to meet Steiner.

The fresh ocean breeze and sounds of waves breaking on the beach were joined by some boisterous seagulls that were loudly squawking nearby. It was, to Moore, nothing but ambient noise. He instead was intently processing his thoughts on how best to confront Steiner. Not a one did he embrace as a viable option.

After an hour of allowing his mind to drift in and out of focus, he decided on a specific approach. Pleased with his decision, he stood and jogged back to the car. He had a new perspective.

When he returned to Roe's, he showered and changed into

a pair of khaki slacks and a crisp white shirt. He logged onto his laptop and looked up a phone number in Cape Charles. He initiated the first step in his plan by calling the number. Logging off his laptop, he made his way down the hallway. As he exited the house, he saw Roe walking out of the workshop.

"Roe, I'm running out for a while."

Roe couldn't help noticing how dressed-up Moore looked. "Got a date?"

"Maybe. Just maybe," Moore answered as he headed to the Jeep.

"Anybody I know?" Roe asked with a sly grin.

"No. But I'd like you to meet her one day," Moore replied honestly.

"If she's got your attention, she must be something else," Roe commented.

Moore chuckled. "Oh, she's definitely something else," he agreed, although he felt uneasy in not being completely truthful with Roe.

"Well, have fun then," Roe said as he walked into the house.

Within minutes, Moore turned right onto the causeway and drove to Cape Charles. He had a large smile on his face as he thought about his evening plans.

When he reached Cape Charles, he drove to the Steiner Estate where he again was stopped by the private security team as he had been during his earlier reconnaissance visit.

"You back again?" the guard asked as he recognized Moore from his previous visit.

"Yes, but I have an urgent message for Max Steiner," Moore replied.

The guard shook his head. "Nope. I still can't let you in."

"I figured you'd say that," Moore said as he held up a sealed envelope. Before leaving Roe's house, he asked Monnie for an envelope and a sheet of paper. He had written an invitation to Steiner and sealed it inside the envelope.

"Could you have this note delivered to Max?" Moore asked as he handed the envelope to the guard.

The guard had a skeptical look on his face. "Are you a friend of Ms. Steiner's?"

"In a manner of speaking, you could say that," Moore answered.

"Do you want me to call the house and see if they will allow you in?"

Moore shook his head. "No. I'd appreciate you getting this delivered for me."

Reluctantly the guard took the envelope. "I'll see what we can do."

"I appreciate it," Moore said as he put his car in reverse and drove the short distance to Cape Charles where he parked in front of Peach Street Books. He had some time to kill and decided to browse the book selection and have a cup of coffee.

Two hours later, Moore drove his car three blocks down Mason Street and found parking near the restaurant he had picked.

Lange's Café was in an older two-story brick building. The remodeled interior was a mixture of cherry wood and brick and was filled with antiques. The ceiling light fixtures came from a closed hotel in Virginia Beach. The wooden booths were refinished pews from an 1800's church in Richmond. There was a stained-glass dome light over the pub-style bar.

Moore entered the café and was immediately greeted by the pretty blonde hostess, Barbie Lange.

"Can I help you?" she asked with a glowing smile.

"Yes. I had dinner reservations for two under the name of Moore."

Barbie looked around for the other party, and Moore noticed. "I'm early. My guest should be here shortly," he explained.

"All I have left is this window table," Barbie said. "We're all booked up for tonight."

"That will be fine," Moore said as he followed her to the table next to the window overlooking Mason Street. He selected the chair that faced the entranceway so that he could see his guest when she arrived.

He took the menu Barbie handed him as he looked around the empty restaurant, "Did you say you were booked up?"

"Yes. We got a call from a tour bus company informing us they have two busloads of tourists arriving in about fifteen minutes."

"I'm glad that I made my reservation for when I did," Moore smiled as she walked away. He looked at the uniquely designed menu. Its graphics were award-winning in Moore's mind.

Within a minute, a tall man with thick graying hair and an equally thick mustache appeared next to Moore's table. "Welcome to our café," he said.

Moore looked up at the gentle giant. "This is yours?"

"Yes, I'm Denis. I believe you met my wife, Barbie," Lange replied.

"I did. I love your décor," Moore said with admiration.

"Thank you. We're very pleased with the way it turned out."

"And I love the graphic work on this menu. It's outstanding," Moore added, in further complimenting the owner.

"Thank you. I designed it," Lange proudly shared.

"You did?"

"I was a graphics designer before I opened this restaurant."

"Nice. Very nice," Moore repeated.

"Could I take a drink order for you?"

"Yes. I'll take a Sailor Jerry's rum with Seven-Up."

"Not Coke?" Lange asked.

"No. The caffeine will keep me up," Moore replied.

"I understand. I'll get it right away," Lange said as he walked away.

Moore thought back to Barbie's comment about the two busloads of tourists booking out the restaurant. There was something about that comment that was unsettling.

"Here you go," Lange said when he returned and handed Moore his rum. "Let me know how it is," he said before walking away.

Moore sipped on his rum, thinking again about the two busloads of tourists. His gut was talking to him. There was something wrong. He knew it, but could not specify the uneasiness he was feeling.

The door opened, and a young man walked in. He was carrying a vase with flowers and walked past Barbie. He went directly to Moore's table.

"Are you Emerson Moore?"

"Yes."

"I have a present for you," he said as he handed the flowers to Moore.

"What are these for?" Moore asked

The man didn't reply. Instead, he turned and walked quickly out of the café as a motorcycle slowed in front of it. The rider watched the delivery man as he returned to his vehicle. The rider then directed his attention to the café and saw Moore seated at the window before he revved his motorcycle and sped away.

This is really strange, Moore thought suspiciously as he

looked at the flower arrangement, then outside at the flower delivery man's car. He casually noticed the motorcycle as he turned his attention back to the flowers. The arrangement included a small attached envelope.

He retrieved the envelope and withdrew a small card. It read: *I'm not that easy!*

The returning sound of the noisy motorcycle instantly grabbed Moore's attention. He knew what came next. Moore stood up and raced across the room to the hostess stand. As he ran, he yelled to Lange who had been walking toward him. "Hit the floor! Now!"

Moore launched himself in the air and tackled Barbie to the wooden floor as the motorcycle rode up onto the sidewalk in front of the restaurant. The helmeted rider, who was outfitted in black, swung up an Uzi submachine gun and fired a stream of bullets through the window where Moore had been sitting seconds earlier.

The window shattered as shards of broken glass flew through the air. Bullets peppered the area like a shotgun blast and struck one of the ceiling light fixtures, breaking the bulbs. Several bullets hit the stained-glass dome over the bar and broke several of the panes, dropping the glass to the floor.

Then the shooter revved up the motorcycle and sped down the street, disappearing around the corner on his way out of town.

"That was close," Moore said as he rolled off of Barbie and stood, shaking several shards of glass off his clothes. He reached down and helped a visibly shaken Barbie to her feet.

"What was that all about?" she asked as she stood weakly.

Lange, who had also jumped back on his feet, walked over to his wife, put his arm around her and echoed her question.

"Why did that happen? We've never had any trouble like this in the past."

Moore's quick wit tempted to quip that maybe someone had a bad meal there, but he thought better of saying it. "I'd say that someone had it in for me."

"I'll say," Lange commented as he rubbed his wife's shoulder. "Are you both okay?"

"I am," Moore said promptly.

"I am, too, thanks to his quick thinking," Barbie said. "How did you know?" she asked with a wrinkled brow.

"I had a feeling that something was amiss, and when I heard that motorcycle coming, I thought it would be better to be safe than sorry." Moore looked at Barbie. "I hope I didn't hurt you when I tackled you."

"Oh, no. I owe you my life," she said sweetly.

Lange had a question for Moore. "Does this type of thing happen to you often?"

"No. This is my first drive-by," Moore replied with a slight touch of humor. "Obviously, I was set up. It all makes sense. There are no two busloads of tourists coming tonight. It was a ploy to make sure that the restaurant was empty. At least they didn't want to take out innocent bystanders."

"That was thoughtful," Lange said, perplexed as he surveyed the broken glass and the bullet holes in the wall and ceiling.

"I'm sure they didn't want the bad press or any additional heat from law enforcement if a bunch of people were killed here," Moore added.

"Things like this just don't happen in Cape Charles," Barbie stammered.

"I'm sure they don't," Moore acknowledged.

"Good thing your friend wasn't here," Lange said.

"Yeah," Moore replied, figuring she was the one behind the assassination attempt. "She couldn't make it, and I'm sure she sent me the flowers."

"Those came close to being flowers for your funeral," Lange commented seriously.

"They could have been," Moore agreed as the door opened and several area business owners walked in to see if the Langes were okay. Two police cars pulled in front of the building. Two officers exited the cars and walked inside to conduct an investigation.

Meanwhile, the assassin had pushed his motorcycle into the back of a trailer that was parked two miles out of town. He tossed his helmet inside and dropped the Uzi on the trailer floor before he closed the trailer's doors. He went around the trailer, entered his Escalade and headed for Norfolk.

As he drove, he placed a call on his cell phone.

"Zimo?"

"Yes," Zimo answered.

"How did it go?"

"The package was delivered. No problems," Zimo said, confident that he had killed Moore with his fusillade of bullets.

"Are you sure?"

"I know my business. That front table area was destroyed," he said confidently.

"Good job," Clawson said as he ended the call and turned to Steiner. "He's dead."

"Good." She was still fuming over the fact that Moore was alive. She had hoped he died in Cuba. She was even more upset that somehow, he had traced her to Cape Charles. Maxine Steiner was relieved by Moore's stupidity in thinking for one second that she would show up at the restaurant. His apparent audacity made her temper boil.

"I won't have to worry about him anymore," she stormed.

Two hours later, Moore rolled into Roe's driveway. He parked the Jeep and walked inside.

"How did your mysterious date go tonight?" Roe asked with a sly look in his eyes.

Moore hesitated. He knew that Roe would be displeased with what he tried to do. He thought for a moment and decided to tell Roe.

When he was done, Roe sat back in his chair.

"You're in trouble now," Roe said with an air of exasperation.

"What are you going to do? Send me to the principal's office? Maybe take me out back of the woodshed for a beating?" Moore asked in a half-serious tone.

"That's not a bad idea, the woodshed," Roe said. He then turned sideways in his chair and called, "Monnie, you better come in here and set this boy straight. He's not listening to me."

Monnie walked down the hallway into the family room. "Why do you think I'm going to get him to listen to me when I can't get you to listen to me?" she asked half-jokingly. "What's the boy gone and done now?" she asked as she dropped into a chair next to her husband.

Moore related his close call to Monnie who shook her head. "My momma used to tell us kids not to go out and dig up more snakes than we can kill. Otherwise, one of them is going to get you. You know what I mean?"

Moore nodded, ambivalently. "I do, Monnie."

"Emerson, for someone who I'd think was a smart guy, you baffle me with some of the things you do. If I didn't know better,

I'd say that you're as sharp as a bowl of jello," Roe said as he wiggled his body a bit in jest.

"Don't we all make mistakes at times?" Moore offered.

"But from what you've told me about your narrow escapes, you have a dangerous habit of using bad judgement. You need to be more careful, or people won't be sending you flowers for your dinner date. They'll be for your funeral," Roe warned.

"I know," Moore agreed, hesitantly.

"What's next? What are you going to do stupid next?" Roe asked.

Before Moore could answer, there was a knock at the door.

"You want to get that since you're standing?" Roe suggested.

Moore turned and opened the door.

"Hello, Carleton," Moore greeted the owner of Daisy Island Cruises. "Come on in. We were just having a party," Moore said as he stepped aside to allow Leonard to enter.

"Yeah. It was going to be a lynching party, and Emerson was going to be the guest of honor," Roe said quickly.

"What?" Leonard asked as he turned to look back at Moore.

"You don't want to know," Moore hastily assured him.

"Okay," Leonard said as he turned back to Roe. "I was on my way home and thought I'd drop in, Roe."

"You know you're welcome here any time. Just bring beer next time," Roe kidded his friend.

Leonard had a serious look on his face. "You know anything about a red fishing trawler going up the bay before dawn?"

"No. That's strange," Roe answered with a wrinkled brow. "You'd think they were headed down the bay to go out fishing before dawn. Besides, there're no fisheries up there. The only one hereabouts is the Chincoteague Fisheries on South Main

Street. That's near the Clam Shells Pub that burnt to the ground when you were here last time, Emerson."

"I remember seeing it," Moore nodded.

"It's not one of the trawlers that we usually see around here. It just seems suspicious."

"Did you see it?" Roe asked.

"I did. I took out the *Martha Lou* for an all-night fishing trip for some out-of-town fishermen, and we saw it go by before dawn today. It's been bugging me all day."

Roe thought for a moment. "There's nothing up there unless it was following the bay up to Ocean City for some reason."

"I don't know. Seems awful strange to me," Leonard said. "Think about it and let me know if you have any ideas. I need to get home."

"I will, and I'll let you know if I come up with anything," Roe said as Leonard walked out of the house.

"That was interesting. What do you think is going on with that trawler?" Moore asked, relieved that the conversation shifted from a focus on him to the trawler.

"Maybe nothing. Who knows?" Roe replied.

Moore's curiosity was piqued. His inner investigative sense told him there was more to this wayward trawler. "I'd like to see if there's more to it."

Roe thought a second, then pointed to a pair of binoculars on the gun cabinet. "You can use them to find out," he suggested.

"I can't see all the way up to Ocean City with those," Moore protested.

"You're right, son. But you can use them if you climb up to the top of the crow's nest and see if you can spot that trawler heading up the bay again. And you'll lose some sleep if you do that," Roe said helpfully.

Roe was referring to the structure that he had built to the back of his house. It was a three-story-high deck. The top level provided an unrestricted view of the water traffic on the bay. It would be easy for Moore to spot the trawler.

"There're some comfy chairs up there, and you can take one of the thermoses I use during hunting season, fill it with coffee and take it up there with you."

"That's an idea," Moore smiled.

"If you spot it there tonight, you can wake me, and we'll run down to get my boat. Then we'll follow it to see where it's going. That work for you?" Roe asked.

"Sounds like a plan," Moore agreed.

"Why is it that this is going to cost me some interrupted sleep?" Roe asked half-joking.

"Thanks for putting up with me," Moore said appreciatively.

"Son, sometimes I think you're more trouble than you're worth," Roe kidded.

"I'm going to try to grab some sleep before I have to go up there," Moore said as he headed to his bedroom.

"I'll put a thermos full of coffee on the kitchen table for you," Monnie called to Moore.

"Thank you," he said as he walked into his room. He set his alarm for 1:00 a.m. and got ready for bed.

# CHAPTER 18

## Steiner Estate
## Kings Creek

When the TV reporter finished his story on the 11:00 p.m. news about the drive-by shooting in Cape Charles, he mentioned there had been no casualties. Steiner exploded and unleashed a series of expletives as she stormed around her office.

"Didn't Zimo tell you that he took out Moore?" she screamed angrily at Clawson. Her fingers curled around a pencil that she picked up from her desktop. She snapped the pencil as if she was snapping Zimo's neck for not doing his job. It felt good. If Zimo was in front of her, she could imagine smashing his face with a sledge hammer. She was furious.

"He did. I don't understand," Clawson answered. He was also stunned by the news report.

"You get him on the phone. I want to know what's going on!" she raged as she threw the broken pencil across the room. She leaned on her desk. Her knuckles were white from tightly clenching her fist. She gritted her teeth as she tried to calm down so she could hear Clawson and Zimo talk.

Clawson hurriedly called Zimo on his cell phone and placed it on speaker mode.

"Hey my man, how are you doing?" Zimo was in a celebratory mood from the successful completion of his mission.

He had been drinking since he had arrived at the warehouse in Norfolk.

"Moore isn't dead," Clawson spoke sternly as he announced the news to Zimo.

"What?" Zimo asked as he heard the sobering revelation. "How do you know that? No one could have lived through that," he said quickly.

"Listen *Cabrón*," Steiner started as she let lose a torrent of foul language at Zimo.

Zimo sat straight up in his chair as he weathered Steiner's blistering verbal attack. He had never been the recipient of Steiner's ferocious temper, although he had witnessed it in the past.

Finally, Steiner paused, and Zimo responded urgently, "It's impossible for him to have lived through that. I drove by slow on my first pass and saw him sitting there. Then, I turned around and drove up onto the sidewalk right in front of that window. I shot the hell out of it."

"Did you see Moore then?" Steiner snapped.

"I did," Zimo lied, now realizing that he didn't recall seeing Moore at the table. In his hurry to complete the task and make a clean getaway, he had been rushed. "That's why I don't understand how he lived!" Zimo continued with his lie.

"I don't either. I don't know how he got out of Cuba alive!" she stormed. "What bothers me is how he was able to figure out who I was and where I lived. He's dangerous to me, and he's dangerous to you. I want him found. I don't know if he's close by or where he is. Find him. You both understand me?" Steiner walked over to the liquor cabinet and poured herself a strong drink of whiskey.

"I'm on it," he replied rapidly.

"I am too," Clawson said. Just being in Steiner's presence, he was feeling the brunt of her wrath.

"Just get it done," she bellowed as Zimo hung up and Clawson scurried out of the room.

# CHAPTER 19

## The Crow's Nest
## Roe's House

Stifling a yawn, Moore applied more bug repellant to his exposed skin. The mosquitoes were out in force, and Moore was a favorite target of theirs. Moore was glad that Monnie had left the repellant on the table next to the thermos. He had brought both of them up to the crow's nest.

Moore had been sitting in his perch surveying the bay for two hours and hadn't spotted any watercraft. He was thankful that the moon was out and providing light that shimmered on the water.

He reached for the thermos and poured himself a cup of coffee, then replaced the cork. It was going to be a long night, he thought as he sipped the coffee.

Suddenly, a movement down the bay caught his attention. He stood and grabbed the binoculars. When he looked through them, he saw a trawler slowly making its way up the bay. That had to be the trawler, he thought as his adrenaline coursed through him, making him wide awake.

He picked up the thermos and bug spray and raced down the two flights of stairs to the rear of the house. He entered it and ran down the hallway to Roe's bedroom where he knocked on the door.

"Sleeping beauty. Time to get up," he announced.

"You see the trawler?" a muffled voice called through the door.

"Yes. Let's go."

"Okay. Let me get dressed. I'll be there in a jiffy," Roe said as he rolled out of bed.

Moore returned to the kitchen where he poured a cup of coffee for Roe. When Roe appeared, he handed it to him.

"Thanks. Now, are you sure it's the trawler?"

"Absolutely positive," Moore replied. He was anxious to get moving.

"Okay then, let's hit the road," Roe said after he finished his coffee.

The two men left the house and drove down to Curtis Merritt Harbor where they boarded Roe's boat. Within minutes they were heading up the moonlit bay to catch up with the trawler. They flew past the Coast Guard Station and under the causeway bridge.

After a while, Roe commented to Moore who was standing next to him at the Carolina skiff's center console, "I'm shutting off the running lights. No sense in alerting them that we're back here."

"What about your outboard's noise?" Moore asked.

"I doubt very much that they would hear it over the diesel engines they're running," Roe responded.

Ten minutes later, Roe squinted his eyes. "I think that might be them," he said as he slowed the boat. "I don't want to run up on them," he cautioned.

Moore nodded in agreement as the two men focused their attention on the trawler's faint silhouette.

As the trawler neared Ocean City, she turned left into the

same small inlet that she had been using on past trips.

"You see that?" Moore asked excitedly.

"Yeah. I'm going to pull a little closer to shore. It's going to be shallower over there, and we're going to need to be careful," Roe said as he throttled back to slow his watercraft.

"I know where they're heading. That inlet is small and has a dock, but we can't go in there," he added.

"Can we go ashore?" Moore asked.

"Yes," Roe responded, and he eased his boat from the deeper bay water into the shallow marsh. A few minutes later, Roe ran his boat up on a small beach.

"We're in luck. Sand, not muck," he said as he turned off the motor and the two men stepped off the bow of the boat.

"What do you think they're doing?" Moore asked excitedly.

"Running illegal immigrants or drugs," Roe guessed. "We'll know in a few minutes," he said as he led Moore through the forest.

They walked as quietly as they could toward the dock which was lit up by an Escalade's headlights, portable work lights and the lights on the trawler.

"You bring those binoculars?" Roe asked.

"Got them right here," Moore said as he clenched them in his hand.

"Take a looksee over yonder and tell me what they're doing. I don't think they've got a load of illegal immigrants," Roe said confidently.

Moore held the binoculars up to his eyes and looked. He saw several men wheeling stacks of white blocks over to a box truck. Something about the blocks looked familiar to Moore. He then remembered, they looked like the packaged bricks of cocaine he'd seen at Baudin's operation is Cuba. This was a drug deal they were witnessing.

"Cocaine is my guess," Moore said as he handed the binoculars to Roe.

"Probably so," Roe agreed as he studied the men's movement through the glasses.

"What do we do now?" Moore asked.

"We certainly can't go in unarmed and yell *'citizen's arrest!'* now can we?" Roe asked sarcastically, but seriously.

Not to be shaken, Moore replied, "But there must be something we can do."

"There is. We're going to get our butts safely out of here and report it. We'll let the big boys handle this before we go full-boat ugly on them." Roe knew his limitations, although he wasn't one to back away from a good fight, especially if he was armed.

"You're absolutely right," Moore concurred.

"You bet your sweet ass I'm right. Now let's get moving before we're discovered," Roe said as he moved from a kneeling position to a crouch and began to hastily return to the boat. Moore followed him, and the two scurried away in the boat. They didn't accelerate the boat until they were five minutes down the bay and then they flew at full throttle.

After they returned to the harbor and secured Roe's boat, they headed back to Roe's house. Once they arrived, Roe told Moore to catch up on his sleep because that's what he was going to do. Afterward, he promised they would figure out their next steps.

# CHAPTER 20

## Midday
## Roe's House

The loud conversations drifting down the hallway to Moore's room woke him up. He peered through sleepy eyes at the clock on his bed stand. It read noon. Moore couldn't believe that he had slept in that late and ran to the bathroom to get cleaned up.

When he emerged in the kitchen fifteen minutes later, his jaw dropped open as he recognized the people sitting at the table with Roe.

"What in the world are you two doing here?" Moore asked "Big Daddy" Chuck Meier and his old friend Sam Duncan. "Chuck, I thought you were up in Baltimore area working. And Sam, I had no idea that you were around."

"We wouldn't be here right now if our mutual buddy, Roe, hadn't called me before he went lights out this morning. Sounds like you two buckaroos had an interesting night," Meier answered.

"We did," Moore admitted as he looked from Meier to Duncan. "I didn't know that you two knew each other."

"It's a small world, Emerson," Duncan offered.

"And getting smaller," Meier chipped in.

"We've known each other from our private contracting days.

Even worked on some assignments together," Duncan smiled.

"Like we are now," Meier said. "We are on a special task force for the DEA and have a lot of latitude in how we can get things done."

"What are you working on?" Moore asked without hesitation.

"Let me give you one little guess there, partner. Why do you think we're sitting across from you?" Meier asked.

"You're after Steiner, too?" Moore asked with widened eyes.

Meier turned to glance at Duncan. "If I didn't know better, Sam, I'd say Emerson forgot to pay his brain bill this month. What do you think?" the quick-witted Meier asked as he turned back to Moore.

"He can be a little slow on the draw," Duncan agreed. He couldn't resist jabbing his friend.

Ignoring them, Moore continued, "This is great. We can work on this together."

"I'm not sure where you're getting this together shit," Meier paused as he looked around the room. "But it does appear to me that we have the Pro Bowl team here," he smiled.

"Are we going to bust them tonight?" Moore asked, excited about working with them.

"More than likely. But we want to see who they're selling to. We'll tail them into Ocean City or Salisbury or wherever they're going and do some serious damage to their operations," Meier said.

"And once we have the drop on them, we'll radio the Coast Guard so they can detain the trawler as she comes back down the bay," Duncan added.

"For this operation, I want to make one thing perfectly clear to everyone in this room," Meier said in a serious tone.

"What's that?" Moore asked.

"I'm the rooster in this chicken coop. You all have to do what I tell you, and I'll be bringing in some of the other boys who Sam and I have been working with for extra fire power. *Comprende*?"

"Got it," Moore said.

"Who else, but you?" Roe asked as he acknowledged Meier's leadership.

"Good." Meier smiled.

"I need to step outside to make a call," Duncan said as he headed toward the door.

"Are you going to call who I think you're going to call?" Meier asked cryptically.

"Yes."

Moore had a puzzled look on his face.

"Patience. You'll soon find out," Meier said when he saw Moore's face.

As Duncan stepped outside, Meier asked, "Anyone have a laptop here?"

Moore and Roe responded together, "Yes."

"Do either of them work?" Meier couldn't refrain from his quips.

Roe responded first, "Chuck, mine's right here, but let me check one thing first." Roe looked behind the laptop and back at Meier. "Yep. Mine is working. It's plugged in," he teased Meier.

"Okay ladies, let's gather around and check out this inlet. Roe, can you get her up?"

Roe cast a sly look at Meier. "Of course," he smiled. He turned his attention to the keyboard, and within seconds, he had the map of the upper bay displayed. He zoomed in so they could see the area in more detail.

As the men studied the map and discussed it, Duncan returned inside and joined in the conversation.

Fifteen minutes later, the doorbell rang.

"I'll get it," Duncan said as he walked to the door and opened it. "Glad you could join us on short notice."

"I wouldn't miss this for the world," the bearded man said as he walked in. "Thanks for giving me a call."

"Wait! I know you," Moore said as he recognized the owner of Sundial Books. With a perplexed look on his face, Moore turned to Duncan. "What gives? Why is he here?"

"Let me explain. This is Jon Richstein. Jon and I did some black ops together over the years before he got out of the business. He's really good with weapons and somebody you want next to you during a firefight. He's willing to come out of retirement this one time to help us out. Right, Jon?"

"One time only," Richstein beamed as he looked at the group.

Duncan introduced him to everyone, and the men spent the next few hours making their plans for following the drug shipment.

# CHAPTER 21

**Steiner Estate**
**Kings Creek, Virginia**

Wheeling over the calm inlet, a number of seagulls gracefully skimmed the water, searching for prey. Several swooped down in daring dives to pounce on their unsuspecting targets, then beat the air with their white wings as they departed with their catch firmly gripped in their beaks.

Steiner stood at the window, watching the seagulls. She likened herself to them as far as being daring. She liked to take risks, albeit she weighed the odds of success carefully. But then again, there were times where she had to bull her way through issues.

The elimination of Emerson Moore weighed heavily upon her thoughts. It remained an unsuccessful quest and that troubled her deeply. Moore tasked her. She was frustrated by her apparent inability to see the pesky reporter dead once and for all. Her thoughts were interrupted when Clawson entered the room.

"I've got some good news about Emerson Moore," he said.

"It's about time somebody gave me some good news," she said as she turned from the massive window that overlooked the inlet and faced Clawson. "Tell me."

"We've had people spending a lot of time tracking down

Moore," he added.

"Good."

"And we've pushed our contacts for information."

Steiner was getting weary of the build-up. "Get to the point. What did you find out for me?" she stormed.

"Moore has two homes. One is on an island in western Lake Erie. He lives there with his aunt. The other is a houseboat on the Potomac River in Alexandria."

Steiner thought a moment as her mind went through a quick calculation. "Alexandria is about four hours from here."

"That's about right," Clawson agreed.

"Did you send Zimo up to the houseboat to finish the job?" she asked

"I've got a guy in Alexandria checking to see if Moore's there before we send Zimo up. He's going to stake out the houseboat and let us know," Clawson answered. "We are also checking out his Lake Erie home."

"Good," she said as she turned back to watch a few seagulls squawking at each other as they stole fish from another seagull on the dock.

"One more thing," Clawson said, holding back the best news for last.

"What?" Steiner inquired, exasperated how this conversation was dragging on.

"We learned that Moore was involved with some incidents on Chincoteague Island some time ago."

"What?" she asked as she whirled around to face him again.

"We're trying to find out if he's there and where he might be staying. We've got a good source up there who could help us."

"Tell them not to waste any time," she said firmly.

"Right. He could be there. That would explain him poking

into the estate here and being in Cape Charles since we're so close to Chincoteague."

"If he is there, I don't like it. Especially with the trawler going up Chincoteague Bay with our cocaine. It would be just my luck for him to snoop that out and screw up our business, just like he did for Baudin in Cuba."

"If he's there, we'll find him," Clawson assured her.

"And bring him to me. I want to see him. Then I want to see him die," she said as hatred filled her heart. "I want to destroy him."

"We will deliver him to you. I promise," Clawson said as he turned and walked to the door.

"I want him alive," she reminded Clawson as he left.

Steiner swung around and returned her attention to the seagulls. They were tenacious in their search for food. Steiner laughed softly as she thought how tenacious she was in driving the search for Moore. She couldn't wait to have him in front of her and hear him squawk in pain.

# CHAPTER 22

## That Night
## Berlin, Maryland

Moore, Roe and Richstein drove up Route 113 to the rendezvous point near Berlin to meet Meier and his team. When they pulled into the Sonny Frazier storage facility's parking lot, they saw two black Chevy Suburbans.

Meier stepped out of one and walked over to them. "You can park it here and ride with us," he said. Roe shut off the engine and the three men exited Roe's vehicle.

"That will help protect your vehicle from being identified by the bad boys," Meier added.

"As well as protecting my vehicle from getting shot up tonight, right?" Roe retorted.

"That, too," Meier chuckled as Duncan and three other men walked over to greet them. One of the men was a dwarf.

Roe couldn't help himself. "We going to the circus or what?" He knew that he was with a group who didn't care about being politically correct.

"You must mean my little buddy, Peter Payne," Meier roared.

"Sorry, I made a mistake. We're not going to the circus. We're going to Neverland. You have Tinkerbell around here, too?" Roe teased as he pretended to look around for her.

The group laughed, including the good-natured Payne.

Meier joined right in. "I've brought him along so we'd have a little Payne relief." But then Meier became semi-serious. "Peter specializes in little problems. Tell them about the House of Payne, Peter."

When the dark-haired Payne started to talk, he caught the others off guard with his deep voice, not what they had expected.

"I'm an explosives expert. I can defuse any device you encounter. And with me being so close to the ground, I'll spot a tripwire faster than you," Payne said.

"Except for one time when an explosive detonated prematurely. It took Peter from being six-foot tall down to where he is now," Meier joked as everyone snickered.

"Peter is also very good with technology. He's our drone expert, and you'll see what he's going to do for us later," Meier added before introducing the other two men, Russ Brode and Charlie Hardman.

"Russ and Charlie legitimize what we are doing tonight. They're official DEA agents although pretty much out there on the edge at times. That's why we get along so well."

Both men looked dangerous and experienced in the manner which they carried themselves. Brode was five-feet-eight inches tall, medium build and with a clean-shaven head. The blond Hardman was six-feet tall, medium build and had a confident smile on his face.

After everyone shook hands and talked a bit more, Meier said, "Ladies, it's time to gear up." He led the group to the back of the Suburbans and opened the rear hatches. "Take what you need."

While the group began sorting through the equipment, Moore spoke to Meier. "Looks like you have quite a group of experts with special skills here."

"They like to say they have special skills. But to my way of thinking, it's more like they have special needs," Meier countered as only he could.

Moore smiled and turned his attention to the weapons. "You've got some heavy-duty weapons here," he said as he looked at the array of artillery.

There were three M4's with 30-round box magazines, three Remington 870 DM pump-action shotguns with a 6+1 capacity, a Remington 700P, bolt-action sniper rifle and an array of handguns including .45 caliber Glocks and SIG Sauers. He also had other tactical aids like flash bang and tear gas grenades.

"You gotta go in with heavy firepower. They're going to have it, too. You'll see," Meier warned. "Hey Roe, what kind of handgun can I get you?"

"Don't need one. I have my own," Roe said as he pulled out a Kimber .45. "This baby will take care of me," he grinned.

As the men put on bullet-proof vests and began choosing weapons, Meier noticed that Moore hadn't selected a vest.

"What's wrong here? We don't have a vest in the color you like?" he asked.

"I don't need one."

"Emerson, you should wear one of these. They're lightweight," Meier urged. "Everyone is going to wear one."

"No thanks."

"Okay Superman, you think bullets are going to bounce off your chest?" Meier asked, annoyed at Moore's reluctance.

"I don't expect to be in the thick of it, especially with the team you've assembled."

"Don't say I didn't warn you. It's your funeral that I'll be arranging," Meier said in a miffed tone.

When the men had finished getting ready, Meier looked them over. "Okay ladies, let's saddle up," he directed as they got into the two vehicles. "Emerson and Roe, you two can ride with Peter and me," he said as he opened the driver's door and settled in. Roe sat next to him since he knew the area and could provide directions.

When Moore climbed in the seat behind Roe, he was stunned by the technical equipment he saw. "You playing video games back here, Peter?"

Payne laughed softly. "No, but be patient. You'll see what we're up to in a bit."

Roe guided Meier down Route 376 to Route 611 where they turned left. After a mile, Roe cautioned Meier. "The road leading to the dock should be about half a mile ahead of us."

"Alrighty then. We'll pull over here for a little recon," Meier said, and they pulled to the side of the road and parked. The SUV following him did the same.

"Benjamin Franklin once said that there are no gains without pain. So, Mr. Payne, you are up. Work your magic and help us gain some intel," Meier requested as he stepped out of the vehicle and walked to the back.

Payne grabbed his laptop, and everyone exited the vehicle to walk to the rear where Payne set up his laptop.

"What's up?" Moore asked as he saw Payne powering up his laptop.

"Big Daddy is getting ready to launch a surveillance drone. We're going to have it gather intel for us," Payne said proudly. "That way, we don't risk our lives."

"Sounds good to me," Roe cracked as he saw Meier holding

a drone that he had taken out of the rear of his vehicle.

"We ready, *compadre*?" Meier asked.

"Go ahead," Payne said as he took control and Meier released the drone. Payne navigated the drone up the street while the three men watched the laptop's screen.

"This one has night vision which should make it easier on us," Payne said.

"I'd guess you'd turn right there," Roe said when he spotted the road that led to the dock. "I checked on the map and you should have a turn coming up."

"There it is, and we have a watcher. Just picked him up," Payne said.

"Look at that stupid dumbass. He's smoking a cigarette while watching for someone to come down the road," Meier said as he reveled in the man's stupidity.

"That glow from the cigarette is hard to miss, isn't it?" Moore asked.

"Good thing we didn't drive down there, Roe. They would have had us," Meier snapped.

"Yessiree. Nothing like a little caution," Roe remarked.

The drone turned down the road and headed for the dock.

"Would you look at that? That dock is lit up brighter than a Walmart parking lot at night. Better turn off your night vision, Peter," Meier said as Payne slowed the drone's flight speed.

Payne kept the drone at a safe distance so that it wouldn't be spotted. It was unlikely, however as the thugs were focused on unloading the drug shipment and transferring it to the truck.

"You're recording this for evidence, right?" Meier asked.

"Yes," Payne said as he had the drone gain altitude and circle the activity below. He captured images of the Escalade, the box truck and trawler.

"Are you able to zoom in the camera lens and get license plate numbers?" Moore asked.

"Just about to do it. And I'll get the trawler's name. I'll also try to zoom in and get the best close ups of everyone there," Payne said as he worked the controls.

An hour later, the box truck was loaded. The men had climbed into the truck and Escalade while the crew of the trawler reboarded. As the Escalade and truck drove away and the trawler left the dock, Meier said, "Emerson, watch what Peter does next."

Payne expertly dropped the drone over the truck which was following the Escalade.

"Is the drone going to stay in that position until the truck reaches its destination?" Moore asked.

"Oh, no. Peter has a gift for them. Don't you?" Meier asked all-knowingly.

"Right. Emerson, I'm going to set the drone on the roof of the truck and place a magnetic tracker on its roof. Then I'll recall the drone," Payne explained.

"That way we can follow at a safe distance with no fear of losing them," Meier added.

"Cool," Moore commented.

"That Escalade will run interference for them like a lead blocker and let the boys in the truck know if they encounter any police checkpoints," Duncan commented.

"I would have thought you guys would have made sure there wouldn't be any tonight," Moore said.

"Already taken care of, my friend. This isn't my first rodeo, you know?" Meier replied. "Okay ladies, time to saddle up," he said as he led the group back to their vehicles and prepared to follow the box truck.

"They've pulled out on this road and turned right for Ocean City," Payne said as he looked at his laptop screen.

"Okay, then. We'll go ahead and follow them," Meier explained as he started his vehicle and pulled back on the road with the other Suburban following.

Twenty minutes later, the Escalade turned onto Ocean Gateway and drove a mile west to a vacant car lot. It stopped briefly to allow one of the armed passengers to step out. The man walked over to the side of a brick building where he set his Uzi on the ground. He pulled out a cigarette, lit it and went around the corner to lean against the front of the building to act as a lookout. It would be easy for him to grab the Uzi if trouble appeared.

The Escalade drove down the driveway to the side of the car dealership where it pulled up in front of the entrance to the body shop. The garage doors opened as Zimo depressed the opener.

Zimo was very happy with how the transaction had gone so far. As he drove into the partially-lit body shop, he saw several damaged cars parked inside. He spotted Charcoal's Mercedes and a dark blue van. Zimo parked in front of them, and the four men stepped out of Zimo's Escalade.

"Everything good?" Charcoal asked as he and three of his men appeared from the shadows.

"No problems at all," Zimo said as he placed the radio to his lips. "Bring her in."

"Be there in two minutes," the radio crackled as the box truck driver responded.

When the truck pulled in, the garage door closed behind it. The truck parked next to the Escalade, and the men followed their routine of testing the quality of the cocaine. Charcoal didn't do any deals until he knew the quality was right.

Meanwhile, Payne saw on his laptop that the truck had stopped. "Looks like they are at their rendezvous point."

Meier wheeled the Suburban into an empty parking lot and parked. The following Suburban pulled up next to him, and its windows rolled down as they waited for instructions.

Payne was identifying where the truck was. "It's a vacant car dealership. Looks like the truck is in the back."

"I'll get the drone out for a quick looksee," Meier said as he jumped out of the driver's seat and quickly retrieved the drone. Within seconds, it was airborne and flying for the dealership.

"We've got one tango in front of a building next to the dealership," Payne said as he watched the laptop's screen.

"Can we get to him?"

Payne flew the drone around the area to recon. "Yeah. We'll have to go down an alley behind some buildings. Then we can ease up on the other side of where he is."

"Can you check the access to the body shop?" Meier asked.

"Flying there now. Looks good. Don't see anyone. A couple of lights are on inside."

"Okay. Bring the drone back."

As Payne flew the drone back, Meier outlined his plan of attack.

"Boys, we've got a bit of problem here, but I have the short answer to fix it," Meier said.

"What's that?" Moore asked.

"My man, Peter Payne!" Meier smiled as he explained what he had in mind.

When the drone returned, Payne placed it in the rear of the SUV, and they drove the two vehicles down to the alley that Payne had found. Once they pulled into the alley, they turned off their lights and proceeded carefully to get near the brick building.

In the meantime, the man in front of the building had just finished his second cigarette. He was grinding its remains into the sidewalk under his heel when Payne walked around the building. He was unarmed and wobbled as if he were drunk. The man was surprised in seeing a dwarf, especially an apparently drunk one.

"I'm lost," Payne said as he neared the man. "Can you help me?" he asked as he slurred his words.

"No. You get out of here. You shouldn't be around here," the man said nervously as his eyes darted around, looking for any trouble.

Payne didn't stop. He kept up his charade. "Is your name David?"

"It don't matter what my name is. You git out of here," the man said as he reached around the corner and grabbed his Uzi. "Now git!" He pointed the Uzi at Payne.

"David, I've got to piss," Payne said as he wobbled around the corner.

As the man followed Payne to make him leave, he walked around the corner. Unexpectedly, a large hand reached out and grabbed him by the neck.

"Hello, David. My name is Goliath and this time I win," Meier said before he knocked the man unconscious. "Let's get him secured and we'll come back for him later," Meier said as Hardman and Brode bound him with plastic ties.

"That was a pretty brave move," Moore praised Payne.

"Yeah, for a little fellow he's got the *cajones* of a fighting bull," Meier chuckled.

Payne hadn't been paying attention as he was focused on

his laptop. "It's a buy. They just exchanged cash for cocaine," Payne said.

"How do you know that?" Moore asked.

"That little tracking device on top of the truck had a microphone. We just taped the buy," Payne replied proudly.

"Let's get moving ladies," Meier said urgently. "You know the drill."

The men returned to their vehicles, and they drove around the brick building. The vehicles split with Meier driving to the side of the showroom and parking there. Hardman's vehicle with Duncan, Brode and Richstein drove down the other side and parked. They immediately exited the vehicle and made their way along the side of the building to the entrance to the body shop.

Meier's team moved quickly down their side of the building. When they arrived at the side door, Payne slipped a small spy camera with a flexible neck through a crack in the door.

As he twisted the camera around, he said, "Chuck, we've got seven that I can see. Four have Uzis. I assume the others are armed, too."

"You copy that, Sam?" Meier radioed to Duncan and his team.

"Roger that. We've got an explosive attached to the door and flash bangers ready to go. Give me the word, and we'll start the party to distract them from your end."

Meier looked down and saw that Payne had attached an explosive charge to the entrance door. "Ready there, Peter?"

"All set."

"Sam, execute," Meier ordered.

Duncan set off the explosive and kicked in the door on the other side of the building. They threw in several flash bangs through the broken doorway and quickly entered the building yelling, "Police! Drop your weapons!"

Before the gangbangers could react, the main entrance door exploded, and Meier and his team charged in. They also shouted, "Police! Drop your weapons!" as they took cover.

The gangbangers reacted by firing furiously at the intruders. They knew that they had been caught red-handed and were determined to escape. The two teams returned fire and the firefight exploded.

Zimo and Charcoal watched while they lost men as slugs pinpointed skull and flesh. Charcoal dove into his car and started the engine. The car's tires were peppered with rounds, flattening them. Charcoal made the mistake of sticking his head up at the wrong moment, and a round from Roe's Kimber struck his head, killing him.

Moore made the mistake of seeking cover behind an upright steel beam and had dropped his shotgun when a round from one of Charcoal's men struck it. As shots ricocheted off the beam, he knew he had to immediately move. He was angry for choosing poor cover and wasn't sure that he could run twenty feet safely across the garage floor for better protection behind one of the junk cars. He decided to confront it head on.

He withdrew the two .45s he had selected and stepped out from behind the beam, firing both guns as he advanced on the gunman who had been firing at him. Two rounds from the gunman caught Moore in the chest, and he fell.

"Moore's down!" Payne yelled from behind a stack of wooden crates.

"Crap!" Meier yelled as he looked at the fallen Moore. He was amazed when he saw Moore stand to his feet and begin firing again as he advanced. This time two rounds connected, killing the gunman.

Meanwhile, Brode and Hardman each were wounded. Another gangbanger dropped as Duncan and Richstein advanced with weapons blazing. Roe and Meier were firing away, and more bodies dropped to the ground.

When the firing stopped, Meier asked, "Did we get them all?"

Roe counted quickly. "Missing one."

Just then, the garage doors on both sides of the building began to open. The team spun around with their weapons pointed, expecting trouble. They heard the Escalade's engine start. Before anyone could react, it accelerated across the garage and outside.

Zimo's square jaw was set, determined to make good his escape. He turned right and drove fast down the side lane.

The team started firing at the Escalade and raced out of the garage after it. When they ran outside, they saw the vehicle careen through a turn onto Ocean Gateway and speed away. They didn't have a chance to go after it as their vehicles were parked down the side of the building.

"Not bad. Only one got away," Payne said, disappointed.

"That's one too many, Peter," Meier growled. "Everyone okay?"

"Charlie and Russ are wounded. Nothing serious. I've got the first aid kit and I'm taking care of them," Richstein shouted.

"Just find some dirty rags and use them for band aids," Meier teased.

"Yep, that's what I'd expect you to do," Brode joked back.

"I checked the van, and it has the coke loaded in it," Duncan said as he walked towards Meier.

"And the cash was probably in the Escalade," Roe guessed.

"Probably," Meier agreed, and turned to Moore. "Did you all see what our buddy Emerson did?"

He didn't wait for a reply, but continued. "He walks around the beam, firing a pair of .45s with both hands. He's firing away like he's the Lone Ranger. Are you related to Clayton Moore, the guy who played the Lone Ranger? What's wrong with you, son? You have a death wish?"

"It was the adrenaline," Moore answered quickly.

"Adrenaline my ass. That was pure stupidity!" Meier was irritated with Moore's foolish action, and he wanted to make a point of it. "It was a good thing that you changed your mind back there and put on that vest. It saved your life," Meier said firmly.

"I do listen," Moore said.

"Half listen is more like it," Meier retorted.

"Peter, can you call this in? We're going to need some help here with sorting everything out," Meier asked.

"I already did. The local police are on the way," Payne replied.

Ten miles down the road, Zimo was driving slightly over the speed limit. He wanted to avoid any unwarranted attention from law enforcement officers after the mess back at the dealership. He reached for his phone and called Clawson.

"Zimo, we were expecting your call. How did it go?" Clawson asked, anticipating good news. He and Steiner were sitting in her office.

"Busted."

"What?"

When Steiner saw a concerned look appear on Clawson's face, she stormed, "Put him on speaker!"

Clawson complied, and she asked quickly, "What happened, Zimo?"

"The deal was busted. Must have been the DEA. They busted in. Shot up the place. I think I'm the only one who made it out," Zimo said nervously, knowing that Steiner's wrath would be coming.

"And Charcoal?" she asked.

"Took one in the face. He's gone."

"Where's the coke?" she asked as her face reddened in anger.

"They got it."

"And the cash? Who has it?" she seethed.

"I've got it," he said.

"At least one thing went well. Where are you?"

"I'm heading for the meeting spot. I can let Clawson know when I'm closer. I wanted to call in right away and let you know what went down," Zimo explained.

"Okay. Don't get pulled over," she warned.

"That's on my mind, too," Zimo said slowly. He paused and added, "There's one more thing."

"Yes?"

"That Emerson Moore guy that we were trying to find."

"What about him?"

"He was there," Zimo said.

That's all Steiner needed to hear as she became intoxicated with anger. Her rage was like a wildfire and its flames were about to go out of control. She erupted with a string of obscenities for the next two minutes. It only ended with her gasping to catch her breath. The glowing embers from her rage would not die until Moore was dead.

Clawson's eyes were cast downward. He bore the brunt of her vehement outburst. "Was Moore killed?" Clawson asked, hopefully.

"No," Zimo answered as quickly as he could.

"I want him dead," Steiner ordered. "You said you had a contact in Chincoteague. What did he tell you?" she bristled as she questioned Zimo.

"He said he'd nose around on the island and see what he could learn. I'll follow up with him and get back to you."

"Do that today!" she commanded sharply.

"I will," Zimo said.

"That's all for now," Steiner said as some of the color returned to her face and Clawson ended the phone call.

"We've got a couple of problems. We lost Charcoal and now we have to find a new buyer," she said as she paced the floor. "And I need to figure out what to tell Rojas because we need him to hold off on his shipments."

"Unless we receive them and store them in Norfolk," Clawson suggested, trying to be helpful.

"That might work. I'll have to work out a deal with Rojas to delay paying him. We'll see how persuasive I can get," she said.

The cell phone rang. Clawson looked at the caller ID. "It's Zimo," he said as he answered it, putting the call on speakerphone.

"What is it now?" she asked.

"I just got a call from our trawler. The Coast Guard was waiting for them as they came down Chincoteague Bay. They're ordering them to stop their engines and are going to board her." Zimo allowed the words to spurt out of his mouth.

"There are no drugs on board. We should be okay," Steiner said.

"Unless they test for residue. They may detain them," Zimo

said, not knowing that Meier's team had video evidence of the cocaine being taken off the ship.

"All right. Keep us advised," she fumed as she nodded to Clawson to end the call.

"I'll wait until morning, then we'll get Rojas on the phone," she said as she turned and looked out on the inlet. The morning sun was breaking, casting a warm glow on the water. Steiner was glowing too—like a volcano.

# CHAPTER 23

## The Next Day
## Roe Terry's House

Half the day had passed before Moore rolled out of bed. After the raid wrapped up, Meier drove them back to Roe's vehicle at the storage unit in Berlin and Roe, Richstein and Moore headed home. As they drove, the three men recaptured the events of the evening.

Once they dropped off Richstein at his house, they rolled into Roe's driveway at 8:00 in the morning. They were both bushed from the previous evening's adventure and headed straight to bed.

When Moore arose, he slowly walked along the hallway and entered the kitchen where he saw Roe seated, enjoying a cup of coffee.

"There's sleepyhead," Roe greeted.

"Morning, I mean afternoon, there brother," Moore greeted Roe.

Moore walked over to the coffeemaker and poured himself a cup of coffee. As he took a seat across the kitchen table from Roe, he said, "Last night was quite an adventure!"

"I haven't been involved in something like that since my SEAL days. And that's fine with me," Roe commented. "I'd rather go after ducks and alligators. They don't shoot back," he kidded.

"But the gators bite. You told me about that one that you shot in Louisiana and hauled in the boat. Then he came back to life and started gnawing at your boot."

Roe laughed as he recalled the dangerous incident. "Yep. And I put another round in his skull. That took care of him. But like I said, they don't shoot back."

"You can keep those gators. I've been out there and seen how big they are."

"Speaking of out there, look out the window. You see who showed up to work with us again?" Roe asked.

Moore glanced out the window and saw Kronsky carrying some cottonwood into Roe's workshop. "He's back," acknowledged Moore.

"Yep. I think he got here early. I heard his truck pull in and park behind the workshop like he always does. I just rolled over and went back to sleep."

"Have you had a chance to talk to him yet?"

"Not yet. I'll talk to him first and let you know how it goes. Then you can talk to him. It looked like you two were working up a good relationship."

"We are. You're right. He seems like a good kid who couldn't catch a break," Moore said, sharing his observation.

"Yep, and he gets pulled back into the old ways from time to time. We'll just keep loving him and making him feel at home," Roe said.

"You going for a run today?" Roe asked as he stood from the table and walked over to the sink to rinse out his coffee cup.

"No. I'm going to clean up, and I'll be out to help you and Louie," Moore confirmed as he joined Roe at the sink and washed out his cup, too. "I'll be out in a few," Moore added as he walked down the hall to his bedroom.

Twenty minutes later, Moore walked out of the house and over to the workshop. As he walked through the door, Roe looked up from his chair.

"You bringing me a present?" Roe asked.

"I've got a cold sweet tea for you."

"Thanks. You can set it right there." Roe pointed to the shelf above his cluttered workbench. "Who's the other one for?" Roe asked, seeing that Moore was holding another glass.

"Louie. Did you get a chance to talk with him?"

"I did. I give him credit for being honest with me. He was down in Cape Charles doing some carpentry work and got connected. So, he was off the wagon for a bit."

"You straightened him out?"

"As best as I could, but the boy needs to seriously want to be straightened out," Roe said. "And you're not going to believe where he was working."

"Where?"

"Your friend's place. The Steiner Estate."

"What?"

"He's been holding out on me. Apparently, his buddy has a small contracting business. When he needs help, he calls Louie to help him. This guy does a lot of work for Steiner."

"Think we have anything to worry about as far as him telling Steiner that I'm here?" Moore asked.

"I don't think so. He likes you. I don't think he'd rat you out," Roe suggested.

"You never know. That craving for drugs makes people do things they don't normally do," Moore said with a look of concern.

"I know. But I think we're good. We'll just have to keep an

eye on it. When his buddy and he are finished with their jobs there, they get high together."

"Sad."

"It is."

"I'll have a chat with him and try to encourage him to break out of this whirlpool of trouble that he gets into," Moore said as he left the workshop.

When he walked around back, he spotted Kronsky sweating up a storm. "Hey, Louie. Would you like a sweet tea?" Moore called as he walked over to a shaded area.

Wiping his wet brow with the back of his hand, Kronsky answered, "I sure would. Thanks, Emerson."

"No problem," Moore said as he gave him the tea. Kronsky took it and held the glass against his brow for a moment.

"Roe told me that you've been using while you've been gone," Moore said, getting down to business.

A sheepish look appeared on Kronsky's face. "Yeah. I messed up."

"You've had it rough, Louie. Growing up, you had your father abusing you emotionally and physically. I can't imagine how the beatings felt."

Kronsky interrupted Moore. "The beatings ended when I grew bigger than him," he said firmly with an all-knowing smile.

"Then you had your brothers pressuring you to join them in doing drugs and petty theft," Moore added.

Kronsky nodded his head in agreement.

"The drugs were your escape from the reality you lived in."

"I try to quit, but I get these uncontrollable cravings," Kronsky explained. "And when I take them, my mood changes. I'm happy and excited. It seems like I can concentrate better."

"But you can't forget the downside to taking it. It's coke, right?"

"Yeah."

"How do you take it?"

"I usually smoke it. I'll snort it, too."

"When you use, do you notice yourself being angry or anxious? Maybe a little aggressive?"

"I have," Kronsky agreed as he thought about it.

"Coke can raise your heart rate. It can cause strokes and heart attacks as well as death."

"Yeah. I know about that stuff," Kronsky countered.

"Ever have memory loss or suicidal thoughts? Maybe panic attacks when you're using?" Moore asked.

"I have."

"You can overcome this, Louie."

Kronsky lowered his head and stared at the ground. "I'm just a failure," he admitted as he relived his personal shortcomings.

"Get that head up, Louie. You've got a lot going for you," Moore said in an encouraging tone. "It's not a failure of your will or character. What you have is a chemical dependency. It's a medical issue."

"I never thought of it being a medical issue," Kronsky commented.

"It is. You're playing Russian roulette if you don't get real help. I'd be glad to help you go to a detox facility, if you're willing," Moore offered.

Kronsky's eyes widened at Moore's kind offer. "You'd do that for me?"

"I would. Nothing like helping someone out of the cesspool of life they are wallowing in," Moore smiled. He felt bad for the young man who had been dealt a rough start to life.

"But you don't really know me other than these last couple of weeks," Kronsky said. He was stunned by Moore's gracious offer.

"I'm glad to help. And speaking of helping, we need to get this cottonwood moved for Roe," Moore said as he playfully punched Kronsky's shoulder before moving out of the shade and heading to the wood pile.

Kronsky finished his tea and joined Moore. Maybe he did have a chance to change his life, he thought. He joined Moore and spoke.

"Emerson?"

"Yes?"

"I'd like to do something nice for you."

Moore stopped and looked at Kronsky. "And what would that be?"

"I'm a pretty good carpenter. At least when I'm thinking straight. I'd like to build you something," he offered.

"You don't have to do that," Moore protested. He didn't expect anything for helping Kronsky.

"No. Really. Something special."

"I don't need anything," Moore said.

"You think about it and let me know. I just want to do that for you. No one has offered to help me like you have."

"Think nothing about it," Moore said. "I enjoy helping people."

"Just let me know," Kronsky repeated himself, and he started helping Moore with the cottonwood.

Two hours later, Moore took a break in the workshop.

"It's warm out there," he said as he sat on an empty chair.

"Grab yourself a beer or pop out of that old fridge. There

might be a few bottles of water in there, too," Roe said as he continued carving a decoy.

Moore walked over to the fridge and selected a bottle of water. He twisted off the cap and took a long sip before plopping back in the chair.

"I had a good talk with Louie."

"You did?"

"I offered to take him to a detox facility."

"What did he say about it?" Roe asked as he continued working.

"He's going to think about it."

"That's a good first step." Roe looked up from his work. "I think that boy admires you, Emerson."

Moore shook his head. "I don't know about that. I'm just interested in his welfare. I think he's a good kid at heart."

"He is," Roe agreed.

The door swung open, and Kronsky entered. "You guys in here where it's nice and cool, and I'm out there in the heat, working away?" he asked wryly.

"Join us. Sit for a spell and grab a cold one before you do," Roe said as he pointed to the fridge.

Kronsky opened the fridge and grabbed a can of beer. He pulled the tab and took a swig before sitting on a nearby bench.

"What are you guys talking about?" he asked as he relaxed.

"Your future and how bright it is," Roe answered quickly.

"I hope so," he said. He cast his head downward and a frown appeared on his face.

"What's wrong, son?" Roe asked, seeing the expression.

"I've been holding back something from you two," he replied without lifting his head.

"By the look on your face, I guess it's not news like you're going to get married," Roe said lightheartedly as he tried to lift Kronsky.

"No. It concerns Emerson."

"Me? How's that, Louie?" It was Moore's turn to ask a question.

"I've been doing some work for my buddy down in Cape Charles. We've been working at the Steiner Estate."

Roe and Moore exchanged knowing glances and continued to listen.

"One day, one of their people showed us a picture of Emerson on their cell phone and asked if we knew him. They said he owed them money."

"I don't owe them money," Moore interrupted.

"Just a ploy. I'm sure they got your picture off the internet," Roe suggested. "Go on, Louie."

"They think he's on the Delmarva Peninsula and want to find him real bad. They said they'd make it worth our while if we saw him and let them know."

"Did you tell them that he's staying at my place?" Roe asked.

"No. I didn't."

"Good," Roe said, relieved.

"I got a phone call today from a guy I bought drugs from in Norfolk. His name is Zimo. I've seen him around when I worked at the Steiner Estate. He was pretty stressed out. They want to find Emerson in a real bad way."

"You didn't say anything, right?" Roe asked again.

"I didn't."

"Good," Roe said. "Louie, would you mind excusing Emerson and me for a bit. I need to talk to him privately."

"Oh, sure." Kronsky stood and walked back outside to return to work.

"This is not good," Roe said to Moore after Kronsky left.

"I know," Moore agreed.

"Let's get Meier on the phone and get his advice," Roe suggested as he reached for his cell and punched in Meier's number.

"That's a good idea. He'll like to help on this."

"Calling him about this is like throwing raw meat in a lion's cage. He'll tear right into it," Roe said as he waited for Meier to answer.

"Hello, Roe," Meier answered on the second ring.

"Hey, buddy. How are you doing?"

"I've got a splitting headache. I was so drunk when I finally made it home that I called 911 and ordered pizza. The police showed up at my door."

"What happened?" Roe asked.

"Hell, I asked them if they brought my pizza. They didn't think that was funny. I got a lecture. Well, at least I think I did. I was too drunk to remember clearly."

"You must have been really drunk. Where could you order pizza in the morning?" Roe asked.

"I never gave that a thought. What's cracking?"

"Emerson and I were sitting here talking about Steiner wanting him dead."

"I don't think that's any big revelation," Meier groaned.

"There's been a development that could work in our favor."

"What's that?" Meier asked as he perked up.

"Go ahead, Emerson. Tell him what you heard," Roe urged Moore.

Moore quickly related what they learned from Kronsky. He then added, "And I have an idea that hatched while you two were talking."

"What's that?" Meier asked.

"The Redeye Club."

"Stop. I know you guys can't see my eyes. You're not close enough. Why are you making fun of me?" Meier interjected.

"No, buddy. That's my fishing and hunting cabin up the bay," Roe explained.

"Okay."

Moore continued. "What if we set up a trap to entice Steiner and her cronies to come there and we capture them?"

"You've been watching too many cowboy movies, *compadre*," Meier said.

"No. I'm serious."

"It's out in the middle of nowhere and there's little risk that any innocent bystanders would get hurt," Moore suggested.

"That's for sure," Roe agreed.

"And what are you going to use to lure her out there? Drugs? That won't work because she stays away from any direct connection with it. Keeps her hands clean," Meier said.

"I've got the perfect bait," Moore said confidently.

"Oh crap, I see where this is going," Meier reacted.

"Me."

"I knew it," Meier groaned.

"She couldn't resist coming for me. We can get Kronsky to tip them off that I'm hiding out there. Then they come up to snoop around, and we ambush them."

"It might work. I need to come down and see the site. We can then figure out if this is viable or not. Roe, are you willing to risk some damage to your cabin?"

"A few bullets holes won't hurt anything. I've had visitors discharge weapons there accidently. It's no big deal to me."

"Where are you now?" Moore asked.

"I'm in Salisbury with my guys. Give me a couple of hours and we'll come down. Roe, you have a boat big enough to take us all out? I'd like to do a recon of the area."

"No, but I'll call Carleton Leonard. I'm sure I can get him to bring one of his pontoon boats over to the bay behind my house. We all can board it and take a run up the bay."

"Good. And don't say a word to Kronsky until I know this is a go," Meier added.

"Mum's the word," Roe said.

"If this goes the way I think it can go, Max Steiner's shelf life is about to expire," Meier added before hanging up.

"I'll give Carleton a call and get the pontoon boat over here," Roe said.

The workshop door opened, and Kronsky walked in. "I think I'm done for the day." He was sweaty and looked tired.

"You did good, Louie. I appreciate how hard you work for me," Roe said.

"Thank you, Roe."

"You're coming back tomorrow morning, right?" Roe asked with an intent look on his face.

"I'll be here. Just staying home tonight. Might go out and catch a few fish for dinner."

"Nothing like fresh fish," Moore agreed.

"I'll be going then," Kronsky said as he turned and left the workshop.

"See you tomorrow,' Roe called after him.

"Bye," Moore chipped in.

Roe picked up his cell phone and called Leonard. While he waited for Leonard to answer, Roe leaned toward Moore and offered, "Carleton was in Special Forces. He knows all that black ops stuff, but he doesn't want folks to know."

"Yes, Roe?" Leonard answered his cell phone.

"I got a big favor to ask you, buddy."

"What's that?"

"I've got some black ops stuff going over the next 24 hours that would be a perfect fit for you and the *Martha Lou*." Roe raised his eyebrows expectantly as he waited for Leonard's response.

"You're not going to get my boat blown up, are you?"

"No, because you'll be at the helm." Roe allowed a low chuckle to escape from his lips.

"Sounds like fun. When do you need her?" Leonard asked.

"In about an hour for a walk through. Is she available?"

"Let me check the schedule. I've got it right here. Yes, she's available tonight. Is that the only time you need her?"

"Probably tomorrow, too," Roe guessed.

"I can do that. I'll have to switch out a tour to one of the other boats, but I can make that work."

"Great. Can you bring her over in about an hour and we'll do that recon? I'm waiting for my team to get here," Roe explained.

"Sure. See you then. I'll call when I'm there."

"Thanks, Carleton."

"Now, let's go in and grab a quick dinner before the guys get here," Roe suggested.

"You sure got this pulled together fast," Moore said admirably.

"I don't like to waste time," Roe said as the two walked out of the workshop and headed for the house.

After a while, a black SUV pulled into Roe's driveway and parked. Meier, Duncan, Brode and Hardman exited the vehicle and were greeted by Roe and Moore.

"Let's get this party rolling," Meier said as he walked over to Roe.

"Hey, where's your little buddy?" Roe asked.

"Peter Payne? He and Tinkerbell are off on an assignment. That gives us a bit of Payne relief," Meier teased.

Moore looked past Meier and asked Brode and Hardman, "You two good to go despite your wounds from the other day?"

Brode answered, "I am."

Hardman followed, "Nothing but a little nick."

"That's good to hear," Moore said.

Roe answered his buzzing cell phone and had a brief conversation with Leonard before ending the call.

"You guys follow me down this path to the bay. My buddy Carleton just called, and he's waiting to take us up the bay," Roe said.

Moore walked next to his friend. "Sam, this is like old times. You and me working together," Moore said with a smile.

"Yeah. But this time we have a small army to protect you from getting killed, my friend."

"We've been through a lot of scrapes together," Moore added as he thought about some of their close encounters with death.

"We have."

"Where's your buddy Richstein? Is he coming along for this adventure?"

"Tomorrow. He had plans for tonight. But he said to count him in for the action tomorrow," Duncan replied as the men walked aboard the pontoon boat and were introduced to Leonard.

"I like the overhead cover," Meier said as he looked at the boat's aluminum roof. "Especially if we get that plane flying in."

The men talked amongst themselves while Leonard navigated the boat away from shore and up the bay to the fishing cabin.

As they neared the cabin, Meier said, "Sure is wide open out here. No one can sneak up on you. You could see them coming from a mile away."

"Pristine and calm," Moore offered.

"Not tomorrow, I bet," Meier countered. "Not a good place for us to conceal ourselves. Too open," Meier said as he surveyed the area.

"There's a big duck blind that I built over there," Roe said as Leonard headed to the blind and circled it. "It's got a couple of gun platforms."

"Excellent," Meier said as the pontoon boat headed to the cabin and circled it. "And you two will be here, right?"

"Right. I'm thinking of taking the Redeye Club sign down and replacing it with a sign in Emerson's honor," Roe said with a wicked glint in his eyes.

"And what, pray tell, will that sign say?" Meier asked.

"Bait House," Roe laughed as the others joined in.

"Roe, I'm surprised at you," Meier said.

"Why, Chuck?"

"You keep calling Emerson bait. I'd think someone in your line of work, Duc-Man, would be calling him a decoy," Meier roared.

"Good one," Roe said. "You had me there for a moment, Chuck" he commented as the team chuckled.

"I don't care if you call me bait or decoy, I just want to get Steiner," Moore spoke in a serious tone.

"Oh, we'll get her, alright. As long as our plan works," Meier said confidently. "Okay, ladies. Let's get down to business."

The men worked over the next thirty minutes in devising a plan for luring Steiner to the cabin and capturing her and her henchmen. When they returned to Roe's house, the visitors departed to spend the night at the Waterside Inn.

# CHAPTER 24

## The Next Morning
## Roe's Workshop

The door to the workshop opened, and Kronsky walked in. He knew right away that something was up when he saw the faces of Roe and Moore. They weren't smiling the way they usually did when he arrived for work. They had a grim look that spelled trouble to Kronsky.

"What's wrong?" he asked.

Moore spoke first. "We have a huge favor to ask you."

"A really big one that would help us and you," Roe added.

"Shoot. What is it?" Kronsky asked, not knowing what they were going to propose.

"You mentioned that you were shown my picture when you were working on the Steiner Estate and some guy called you the other day to follow up with you to see if you'd seen me up here," Moore said.

"Yeah. A guy named Zimo in Norfolk. Tough dude."

"We'd like you to tell him that you did see me," Moore said.

"What? Are you serious?" Kronsky asked, confused.

"I'm very serious," Moore replied.

"He is, Louie," Roe chimed in.

"Are you sure about that? Zimo scares me. He's not someone you want to mess with. I can tell. He's dangerous," Kronsky argued. He couldn't understand why Moore would want Zimo to know his whereabouts.

"It's okay. There's a good reason for all of this," Roe assured Kronsky.

"I don't know," Kronsky said warily.

"It's fine. We've got this under control," Moore added.

Kronsky was skeptical. "Listen, I've heard stories about this guy. He can get really violent. He's not someone you want to mess with."

"How do you know him, Louie?" Moore asked, although he remembered Kronsky telling them the previous day.

"I've seen him at the Steiner Estate, and he's hooked me up with drugs in Norfolk."

Moore and Roe exchanged glances.

"You know where he lives?" Roe asked.

"No. But I go to the warehouse they have in Norfolk. I've done some carpentry work for them in exchange for drugs," Kronsky answered.

"Louie, I need you to do this for me," Roe said. "All you're going to do is tell Zimo that you saw Moore at the Island Foods grocery last night."

"Right. And you saw me in the checkout line and heard me telling the cashier that I was going to the Redeye Club cabin the next day to do some fishing," Moore urged.

"Are you really okay with this, Emerson?" Kronsky drilled in. He was concerned for his newfound friend.

"Louie, I wouldn't ask you if I wasn't."

"Neither would I," Roe threw in.

Kronsky hesitantly agreed. "I'll give him a call. But let me step in the other room to do it, okay?" He reached into his pocket for his cell phone.

"Sure, son. Go ahead and close the door behind you for some privacy," Roe said. He was pleased that Kronsky was going to take the first step in the plan for the day.

Within minutes, Kronsky was back. "All set, and that was lucrative. He's going to give me a bundle of cash next time I see him for the tip."

"Good. Better cash than drugs," Roe said.

Moore watched Kronsky's reaction to the comment and knew better. "He's giving you drugs, too. Isn't he?" Moore probed.

Kronsky didn't reply right away. He had a sheepish look on his face at Moore catching on so fast. "I won't take the drugs. I'll just take the cash," he said, although his delivery wasn't convincing.

"Louie, you're making such good progress. Don't take the drugs." Moore wanted to help him and not be the cause of a setback in the progress Kronsky had been making.

"I'll do my best," Kronsky said.

"Louie, you want to head out back and start working on that cottonwood again?" Roe asked. He needed Kronsky to leave so that he and Moore could call Meier.

Kronsky started for the door, then paused. "Can I ask you why you want Zimo to know that information I passed along to him?" Kronsky asked.

Roe answered, "We can't. If we tell you, it could jeopardize your safety. The less you know, the better."

Kronsky wrinkled his brow in frustration.

"Like I said, I can't tell you. But I can tell you that the cottonwood isn't going to get cut with you standing in here, son."

"I'll get right on it," Kronsky said, and walked out of the workshop.

Roe picked up his cell phone and called Meier at the Waterside Inn.

"Good morning, Roe. You're talking to your big ray of sarcastic sunshine. I hope you have good news because I slept like crap last night from all of those drinks yesterday morning. This is not a good day to piss me off," Meier greeted Roe.

"Then it sounds like you're all psyched up and ready to go," Roe chuckled.

"Are we on?"

"Kronsky made the call. We should be good to go."

"Good. He's our huckleberry. Today I'm ready to kick ass and make nightmares come true," Meier growled. "I'll get the boys and we'll head over."

"We'll get ahold of Carleton and get the *Martha Lou* here," Roe said. "He's going to tow my boat over since they're both down at Curtis Merritt Harbor."

Thirty minutes later, Meier parked his SUV in Roe's drive. The doors opened and Meier, Duncan, Hardman, Brode and Richstein exited the vehicle. They had stopped at the bookstore along the way to pick up Richstein. The men walked around to the back of the truck to gear up and select their weapons.

Hearing the SUV, Moore and Roe walked out of the workshop. Roe was carrying a cup of coffee.

"Morning, boys," Roe greeted them as they all exchanged salutations.

Meier noticed Roe's coffee cup. "You need to get yourself a different cup, Roe."

"Why's that?" Roe asked with a perplexed look on his face.

"I started drinking my morning coffee out of a clear mug so that people know what my tolerance level is. If I haven't drunk most of it, they can see right away to be careful how they approach me."

"I'd think anyone would be careful how they approach you any time," Moore cracked.

Meier didn't hesitate as he fired back. "The stupid ones aren't. Stupid people are like glow sticks. I want to snap them and shake the crap out of them until the light comes on."

The men roared at the giant's unbridled quick wit.

Meier looked around, "Where's that Kronsky boy?"

"He took off," Roe said.

"You spook him?"

"I'd guess he's a little nervous. Probably wants to lay low," Moore guessed.

"By the way, we checked out that Zimo. He's meaner than a mad momma wasp. He's probably behind a dozen brutal murders in Norfolk and the Delmarva Peninsula, but no one can nail him," Meier said.

"Like Steiner, Teflon-coated. Nothing sticks to them," Moore commented.

"Zimo's the kind of guy that I'd like to send a picture of my rectum to," Meier said grimly.

"Why?" Moore asked.

"So he knows what I think he is!" Meier said. "We're wasting time jawing. Let's get moving."

"I was about to say that," Roe said. "You have gear for Carleton?"

"Oh yeah. We're all going to be geared up except for our live bait," Meier said as he looked at Moore.

"After everyone telling me to wear a vest, now you don't want me to wear one!" Moore moaned half-jokingly.

"You take one, but you can't put it on until they bite. They see a vest on you and they'll scatter," Meier smiled. "Keep it inside the cabin door where you can grab it quick."

Moore nodded.

The men grabbed their tactical gear, weapons and ammo, then headed for Leonard's boat.

As they walked, they heard the sound of a duck call.

"Okay. Who's being funny?" Roe asked as he looked at the group.

He didn't have to look far as Meier turned to face him. He had a Duck Commander duck call between his lips.

"I wanted to make sure we had all of our ducks in a row," Meier laughed as he took the device out of his mouth.

"Okay there, you wise quacker," Roe shot back. "I can throw them out, too," he countered.

When they approached the pontoon boat, Roe noticed that the side rails had sheets of metal attached to the interior sides of the rails. "Carleton, whatever have you done to your boat?" Roe asked.

"You like?" Leonard asked in return. "I've got both sides covered."

"Protection, huh?"

"Yep. If this is going to be a gun platform, I thought a little protection would be helpful," Leonard smiled.

"That's good of you. We appreciate it," Duncan said as he boarded. He knew that his assigned location was on board the *Martha Lou*.

As the men boarded the pontoon boat, Roe spoke to Leonard. "Carleton, we brought an extra tactical vest for you and an M16. It's probably been awhile since you wore one of these."

"Thanks, Roe. It has," he said as he saw the men stacking their equipment on the deck. "Brings back memories of my Special Forces days."

"I knew it would," Roe grinned as he watched the men settle in.

"From tourist boat yesterday to a floating gunship today," Leonard commented.

"Twenty-four hours ago, who would have thunk it?" Roe smiled at his friend.

Leonard drove the *Martha Lou* away from the dock. He was looking forward to being involved with these dangerous professionals. He couldn't wait to see the look on Meier's face when he saw the surprise that he and Roe had cooked up earlier in the day.

Leonard and one of his captains had delivered a sleek Baja 24 Outlaw go-fast boat with 450 HP to the duck blind near the cabin for Meier to use. He thought it would be helpful to have in the event of a boat chase.

# CHAPTER 25

## Steiner Estate
## Kings Creek, Virginia

A nor'easter storm was brewing and would be blowing in that afternoon. Even the local seagulls knew it was coming. They were like a barometer, sensing the small changes in air pressure that signaled a storm was on its way. They had been flying in low, tight circles for the past five hours.

There was another storm, but it had already arrived. It was inside the Steiner mansion. Maxine Steiner was standing with her hands on her hips and was watching the seagulls as she tried to regain her composure. Steiner was more than angry; she was livid.

Her furious diatribe was heard throughout much of the first floor and echoed off the wall of the stairwell to the second floor. It was a good warning to the staff. They were avoiding any contact with her in fear of being verbally assaulted.

Steiner had finished a phone call with Rojas. He hadn't liked the idea about delaying future shipments until she could work out a safer delivery operation. It was no surprise to her when he revealed that he had been in discussions with Obasi in Norfolk. She was further incensed after Rojas told her he was going to significantly increase his cocaine sales to Obasi's Shaka gang.

Steiner realized that Obasi would gain market share and

could potentially knock her from her position as the biggest seller in the area. She couldn't let him get a bigger foothold.

She wouldn't have any of these problems, except for one person disrupting her illicit business. His name was Emerson Moore. She would make him pay dearly when she finally got her hands on him.

Thirty minutes later, Steiner was still seething, almost uncontrollably, when Clawson walked in. He was carrying his cell phone.

"Max," he started as he entered the library.

"What?" She spun around angrily from the window.

One look showed Clawson that while her fury had barely diminished, it was seething just below the surface, ready to again erupt. "I've got Zimo on the line. He's got good news."

"Somebody needs to do something right around here. And this better be good," she snapped. "What is it, Zimo?"

"We found Emerson Moore," Zimo said hurriedly.

"Where?" she demanded.

"He's at a fishing cabin in Chincoteague Bay," Zimo explained.

"How do you know?"

"My snitch told me. Louie Kronsky."

"Are you sure Kronsky's information can be relied on?" Steiner asked skeptically. She wanted to release her pent-up exuberance at hearing that Moore had been found, but she was skeptical that the information was correct.

"He knows I don't screw around. If he sent me on a wild goose chase, there'd be hell to pay," Zimo said arrogantly. "The kid is afraid of me. Those are the best kind," he smiled although she couldn't see it.

"Kronsky's been here," Clawson started.

"He's been here!" Steiner exploded. "What is he doing here on the estate?" she demanded as her face turned red with rage. "I've told you guys that I don't want any transactions taking place here. This is to be a clean site!" She wasn't in a listening mood as her anger boiled over and she let loose a torrent of obscenities.

Clawson and Zimo waited. When she finally stopped, Clawson spoke.

"Max, he was here as part of the construction crew. The kid has a lot of talent. He can build furniture and do fine finish work along with the regular construction gig," Clawson explained.

"Any transaction that occurred took place off the grounds or in Norfolk. Some of them involved some of our distributors. He's not a dealer. He's a user and only in small quantities, too," Zimo elaborated.

"Zimo, I want you to get that Kronsky on a three-way call with Henley. Have him tell Henley where that cabin is located. Then Reefer, I want Henley to fly you up to the cabin and see if you can spot Moore there. You know what he looks like from the pictures, right?"

"Yes," Clawson answered.

"Max, I'm sure that he is there. Kronsky wouldn't lie to me," Zimo interjected.

"Shut up, Zimo. I'm going to handle this one myself. It's going to get done right," she said defiantly. "Reefer, I want you to radio me when you confirm he's there. And make sure that the area is deserted. We don't need any witnesses."

"Right."

"Then you fly back and get me. I don't want to waste my time if this is a wild goose chase."

"Understand," Clawson confirmed.

"Zimo, if you're so sure about this. I want you to get some of the boys and whatever else you're going to need. Then take one of your go-fast boats and run up to Chincoteague Bay. Stay south of the causeway until I'm there and we'll coordinate catching him."

"Got it," Zimo said.

"And we don't have a lot of time. There's a nor'easter heading our way," she warned.

They ended the call, and the two men ran off to carry out their assignments.

# CHAPTER 26

## The Redeye Club Cabin
## Up Chincoteague Bay

"Catching some rays before the storm hits?" Roe asked Moore, who sat on a bench on the front deck of the cabin. He held a fishing pole in one hand.

"I guess so. I'm certainly not catching any fish," Moore said as he cast an alert eye toward the northeast. He could see the thick, dark, low-level clouds on the horizon.

"Maybe we should have waited," Moore suggested, although they had seen some recent reports that the brunt of the storm would miss them.

"I don't think our buddy Big Daddy knows what that word means. He's driven," Roe said from inside the cabin where he stood next to the open window. "We've got a few hours before she hits."

"Who? The storm or Steiner?" Moore couldn't resist kidding his friend.

"Both. One is dangerous. The other is deadly, and I'm sure you know which one I mean," Roe answered. "Besides, if she's as hopped up about getting you, I'm sure she won't waste any time either," he added as he looked across the bay to the duck blind.

Meier, Hardman and Brode were concealed in the duck

blind with the hidden Baja go-fast boat. Camouflage netting and marsh grass helped protect the craft from being spotted from the air.

Meier had thanked Leonard several times for loaning them the Baja. It would be a fast and dangerous gunboat for them to use.

About one hundred yards west of the cabin was the *Martha Lou* with Leonard, Duncan and Richstein on board. Their gear was covered by canvas, and they looked like harmless fishermen as they dangled their poles over the sides of the pontoon boat.

Back at the cabin, Roe turned to Moore. "You know if this goes well, Emerson, I'm going to consider carving a new line of decoys."

"What do you mean, Roe? You've kind of lost me." Moore had no clue where the conversation was headed.

"The Emerson Moore line," Roe teased.

"Funny," Moore cracked back. "And who's going to buy those?"

"Anyone interested in a whittle danger," Roe teased.

Moore groaned at the weak joke.

Over the next two hours, the men waited.

"This is taking so long," Moore grumbled. He was impatient. He wanted to get it over with and capture Steiner.

"Good things take time, buddy," Roe said. "I'm not used to sitting in the cabin waiting for my prey. I'm more comfortable being out there in the duck blind. But even there, you have to wait. The prey will get here when they're ready."

Roe continued. "Then you start hearing the geese squawking as they approach. Next, you can hear the flapping of their wings. They'll start to land by some of the decoys. Then you pop up, take aim and start firing. Then their goose is cooked."

"I know. Good things take time," Moore agreed reluctantly as he repeated Roe.

"You just keep listening. It's going to be that seaplane you mentioned or by boat. Either way, we'll get them," Roe said positively.

Suddenly, the conversation took a turn to a more serious note.

"Hear that?" Moore asked.

"The plane?"

"Yes. I'll bet you anything that's the seaplane I saw at Steiner's dock," Moore said as he looked to the southwest and scanned the sky.

"Is that the plane?" Roe asked as he picked up the radio to contact the other two groups.

"I can't tell yet."

Roe spoke into his radio. "Guys. Standby. That might be the seaplane that Emerson told us about."

"We're ready," Meier said as he gripped his weapon, ready to spring into action.

"Standing by," Duncan replied as he tensed for a possible firefight.

"Sam, do you see any boat traffic?" Meier radioed Duncan, who grabbed a pair of binoculars and looked up and down the bay.

"Nothing," he said.

"Might be a recon," Meier radioed.

"Or a fly-by shooting," Roe offered.

"That would not help us," Meier said. "I'm sure they want Moore alive or his body as proof that he was killed," he added.

"That's the plane. At least, it's the same color as the one I saw," Moore said as he watched it near them.

"Emerson just confirmed the plane as Steiner's. Everybody stay frosty," Roe spoke as he lowered the radio.

Overhead, the plane dropped altitude and circled the cabin.

"Henley, take her lower. That might be Moore on the deck," Clawson said eagerly. He had half a mind to take Moore out himself, but that would shortchange Steiner from taking her revenge.

"Waggle your wings at them like we're just saying hello," Clawson said as he looked at the picture of Moore in his hand and the man staring up at the plane.

Henley did as he was told while he dropped the plane dangerously low over the cabin.

"That's him," Clawson said excitedly as he recognized Moore. "We've got him," he smiled with evil glee as he stared at his target. "Now, take us around, I want to be sure there's nothing out here to worry us.

The pilot took the plane slightly higher, and they buzzed the pontoon boat with the three men fishing. The fishermen waved at the plane as it flew by.

"Looks pretty good to me. Take us back to get Max," Clawson said to Henley as he reached for the radio to alert Steiner so she could make sure Zimo and his team were on their way.

"We'll see if they take the bait. I only saw the pilot and someone in the co-pilot's seat," Moore said.

"That one who grinned like a gator before he attacks? Yeah, I saw him, too. That was no joy ride they were on," Roe said as he reached for the radio. "I didn't see a female. Was your lady friend in the plane?"

"I didn't see her," Moore replied.

"Looks like you were right, Chuck. Just a recon," Roe radioed.

"Right. Everyone stay alert. The next time will be the real deal," Meier warned.

They didn't have to wait more than an hour for action to develop.

"Boys, I've got eyes on a go-fast boat coming up the bay," Duncan radioed the team as he peered through his binoculars.

"She look suspicious?" Meier asked.

"I'd think so. You don't see many of them this far up the bay," Roe interjected on his radio.

"Sam," Meier called.

"Yes?"

"Have your boys gear up. Get those tactical jackets on," Meier urged as he peered out of the duck blind.

Duncan looked behind him and saw that Richstein and Leonard were a step ahead of him. "Got it," he replied as he set the radio down and slipped into his gear before looking down bay again.

"What about me?" Moore asked. "Shouldn't I gear up?"

Meier jumped on the question. "Isn't this funny. Mr. Smarty Pants, who doesn't like to wear protective gear, wants to know about putting on his gear. Not this time, bro. And this is a time you'd probably need it."

"There's a second go-fast boat," Duncan radioed as he interrupted their chatter.

"They're going to need a lot more than that to overcome our firepower," Meier said.

"And we have our plane returning," Roe broke in as the returning plane began a sweeping descent over the cabin.

"I'll make sure they see me," Moore said as he stood on the deck and waved at the approaching plane.

"Okay, Mr. Death Wish," Roe cracked. "It's about time you

get inside and take cover."

"Not yet. We need them to open fire first. Justifies our return fire," Moore cracked back.

"Okay, Mr. Decoy," Roe said as the plane dropped dangerously low to circle the cabin before landing down bay. "I'm covering you."

"Thanks," Moore said as he watched the plane. He smiled calmly when he spotted Steiner in the co-pilot's seat. "Steiner's on board," Moore called in to Roe.

Roe repeated the sighting on his radio. "Steiner's on board the seaplane. Things are going to get awful warm around here in a few minutes," he warned.

"Roger that," Meier radioed back as his face broke in a wide grin. He was ready for the action.

The two go-fast boats, with their heavily armed crews of four each, pulled up next to the seaplane, which shut down its engine.

Inside, Steiner's eyes had a red glow of anger to them at finally setting her eyes upon the elusive Emerson Moore. She couldn't wait for his capture and torture. Her face was filled with malice as she spoke. "Capture him alive if you can. If not, take him out. I'm going to enjoy this," she said as she sat back in her seat to watch the action.

"On it," Zimo said. "Ease up to that cabin," Zimo instructed the helmsman, who pushed forward gently on the throttle. "Keep your weapons out of sight, men."

Within thirty seconds, the two boats were just twenty feet away from Moore.

"Afternoon," Moore shouted nonchalantly as the boat neared.

"Nice day for fishing," Zimo said casually as he bought

time for the boats to get closer to the cabin.

"Depends on what you're fishing for," Moore commented, eyeing the crew cautiously.

Before Zimo could order Moore on board, one of his crew in the stern became too eager. He raised his AK47 and aimed it at Moore.

When Moore spotted the weapon being aimed at him, he yelled, "But you need the right bait." He dove through the open cabin door to relative safety.

With all pretense set aside, all of the men in the boats brandished their weapons, and Zimo yelled, "Come on out, Moore. You need to go with us."

"I don't think so," Moore yelled from inside as he hurriedly slipped into his vest.

Zimo looked back at the seaplane, then back to the cabin. He fired off a several rounds that peppered the structure's frame. "Come on out!"

In response, Roe appeared at the cabin's open window. "Drop your weapons!" he shouted as he shoved the barrel of his weapon through the window opening.

The boat crews quickly fired a fusillade of bullets into the structure. The rounds penetrated the soft wooden walls, sending splinters through the air and forcing the two occupants to duck to the floor.

As they fired, the team on the pontoon boat swung into action and began firing at the go-fast boats. Caught by surprise, Zimo screamed to the crew in the other boat. "Take care of them!"

The other go-fast boat broke away, accelerating to make a run at the pontoon boat and spraying it with a number of rounds which sent Duncan, Leonard and Richstein ducking for cover.

At the same time, Moore and Roe were exchanging gunfire with Zimo and his crew.

Suddenly, the Baja go-fast boat, with Hardman at the helm and Meier and Brode firing, broke out of the duck blind. Their boat accelerated quickly and raced over to aid the team on the pontoon boat, firing at Zimo's boat as they went flying by.

Inside the seaplane, Steiner had been watching the action unfold in front of her eyes. She was filled with uncontrollable rage. She was infuriated that they had been so stupidly lured into an ambush. Another black mark against Moore, she thought furiously.

With firepower from Meier and company concentrated on the second go-fast boat, its occupants were quickly dispatched and their bodies slumped onto the deck as the watercraft continued moving forward.

"Charlie, catch up to that boat. We can't let it run around here with dead men aboard and no one at the helm!" Meier yelled.

"I'm on it," Hardman said as he quickly shoved the throttle forward and they caught up to the runaway boat. Brode jumped aboard to take the helm and bring it to a controlled stop.

While Brode was checking to ensure the occupants were dead, Meier turned his weapon back to Zimo's boat. Zimo, his crew and the two in the cabin had been exchanging gunfire.

Zimo's radio suddenly caught his attention. It was Clawson. "Zimo, come over here. Now!"

Zimo ordered his helmsman to retreat back to the seaplane where Clawson opened the door and stepped out of the float.

"A little present for our friend, Moore," Steiner's hate-filled voice called out from inside the plane.

"Nice!" Zimo said as he took the RPG and prepared it for firing.

"Take him out!" Steiner screamed vehemently.

From inside the cabin, Roe and Moore had been watching from the windows once the gunfire from Zimo's boat had stopped.

"Son, looks like things are going to get real serious," Roe said as he spotted the RPG.

"We're not going to be able to take your boat," Moore said as he looked at Roe's boat tied to the dock.

"Nope. That'd really be suicide," Roe said. "Time for a little evasive action. Follow me and ditch the vest," he said as he dropped his vest on the floor. "Move fast."

"From one extreme to the other. You guys complain about me not wanting to wear a vest, and now you say to ditch it in the middle of a firefight."

"Oh, you can keep it on if you want. It might help you drown," Roe said as he opened the trap door in the floor.

"We're hiding down there?"

"Nope. It's our escape hatch," Roe said as he leaned down and quickly unhooked the fencing that was used to retain freshly caught fish. "Our whole world is about to come down on our heads. I hope you can hold your breath for a long time," he said hurriedly.

"I can," Moore said as he began taking deep breaths.

"Follow me and swim to the duck blind. Chuck should be on his way and be able to give us cover fire," Roe said. Then he dropped through the hatch and entered the water.

Moore followed, and the two began swimming. They had barely cleared the dock when the round from the RPG hit the cabin, exploding it in a fiery blaze.

Steiner laughed maniacally as she saw the destruction of the cabin. "No one could survive that!" she burst out triumphantly. "Climb aboard Zimo. Tell your men to take care of the rest of them," she declared, although she expected them to be killed by Moore's buddies. At least she could save Zimo's life in return for him killing Moore.

"Get us out of here," she ordered the pilot, who began to start the engine.

As he was climbing inside the plane, Zimo shouted to his men, "Finish them off."

His crew knew that their only chance to get away was by taking out Meier and his boat. They pulled their boat around in front of the seaplane and opened up the throttle as they headed directly for Meier.

Seeing them charging toward him, Meier yelled to Brode who was still in the other boat.

"Stay with it, Russ. Charlie and I'll handle them. Full speed ahead Charlie, and damn the torpedoes!" a wild-eyed Meier yelled as he brought his M249 SAW up and leveled it at the oncoming craft.

As he focused on his targets, Wagner's "The Ride of the Valkyries" music from the film *Apocalypse Now* played in his mind. Meier was in his true element as he went through another 30-round magazine.

The two boats were like two mounted knights on water with a gauntlet of bullets streaming toward each other as they rapidly narrowed the distance between them. Meier was like the Grim Reaper as he expertly mowed down the shooters in the other craft. Their bodies dropped to the deck as the boat slowed.

Hardman navigated his boat next to theirs so that Meier

could leap aboard and stop the boat's forward progress. When he stopped it and had made sure that everyone was dead, he looked toward the seaplane. It was gathering speed.

Meier pointed his SAW at the escaping plane. He was ready to take it out until his eyes focused on the plane's floats.

Meier couldn't contain himself as he saw in the distance what was happening. "Ah shit, Emerson. What in the hell are you doing?"

As he swam out from beneath the cabin a few minutes earlier, Moore hadn't followed Roe's instructions. Moore instead swam underwater toward the seaplane until he couldn't hold his breath any longer. His lungs were bursting. He emerged above the water surface and quickly looked around as he gasped for breath.

Between the burning cabin and the firefight going on with Meier, no one was paying attention to his head bobbing in the bay. He took several deep breaths of the cool air and went underwater, taking strong strokes toward the seaplane.

When he emerged from the water next to the float, Moore heard the seaplane engine starting. He grabbed one of the bars between the floats below the seaplane and held on tightly as the plane gathered speed. As the seaplane lifted off the water's surface and gained altitude, Moore perilously dangled above Chincoteague Bay.

He gripped the bar tightly and hoisted himself to the top of the float. His muscles ached as he focused his strength on securing a safe perch for himself next to the strut and float. The air tore at his body as the seaplane climbed steadily, banking to the southwest. He maneuvered his body so that his back faced the front of the plane and he hung on tighter than Spandex on a 350-pound heavyweight.

Twenty minutes later, the plane dropped altitude as it began a lazy turn over the bay for its approach into Kings Creek Inlet. It passed over Kings Creek Marina and Resort as it descended. Just before its pontoons made contact with the water, Moore rolled himself into a ball and dropped off the float. He hit the water after taking several deep breaths. His muscles had been burning from the dangerous ride.

When he hit the water, he bobbed back to the surface. Taking several deep breaths while he caught his bearings, he swam underwater toward shore. He was heading to a stand of trees and marsh near the edge of the Steiner Estate.

When the plane reached the dock, Graber greeted the occupants.

"How did it go?"

"Marvelous. Absolutely marvelous," a giddy Steiner responded as she stepped out of the plane onto the float. She had popped a bottle of champagne in the plane, and it had been passed around as they celebrated Moore's death.

As Clawson, Zimo and the pilot followed her out of the plane, Graber commented to the pilot, "You lost something back there." He pointed to the area where he had seen something fall off the seaplane's pontoon.

"From where?"

"Your pontoon."

"Shouldn't have been anything there, but that's interesting. The plane lifted a bit when we were around that point. I put it off to an air pocket or wind burst. But no, there shouldn't have been anything there."

Hearing the conversation, Steiner waved her hand. "Oh, just take one of the boats out and check it out. Maybe you picked up something on take off, and it just fell off. But go ahead and check it."

"Sure," Graber said as he turned to the pilot. "You want to come along?"

"I'd like to," he said as they walked over to one of the docked boats. Within thirty seconds, they were headed for the area where the plane touched down.

Meanwhile, Steiner had careened into Clawson. She had consumed most of the champagne. She was feeling no pain. "Let them go. You drive us back to the house, and I'm going to have a few more of these," she said as she swung the bottle around.

"And you can have one of the guys give Zimo a ride back to Norfolk," she tittered.

Back at the burning Redeye Club in Chincoteague, the team was gathered in the four boats as they stared at the smoking remains.

"Like I was saying, we can rebuild it," Roe said.

"I know, but that doesn't help us with our immediate problem," Meier fumed as he turned his head again to look in the direction that the seaplane had flown. "What was Emerson thinking?"

"Sometimes, I don't think he thinks. He just reacts," Roe tried to explain. "He'll probably hang on until that plane lands."

"Yeah and get himself killed," Meier groused as he turned to Duncan. "You know him better than any of us. Does he always do things like this?"

"Always. If there's one thing I can predict about Emerson, it's that he surprises you with his actions. He and I have been through so much."

"Sounds a bit like you and me a long time ago," Richstein interjected.

"Good comparison, Jon. But there was one big difference."

"What?"

"You were trained. He thinks he's trained because of that once in a lifetime training he got some time ago in Cedar Key, Florida. But he's prone to make mistakes," Duncan explained.

"Sounds like we need to bail him out," Richstein suggested.

"I'm going to hang out a sign. Bail Bondsman," Duncan teased.

"Enough chatter. We need to figure out where he's headed," Meier said.

"Probably Steiner's estate in Kings Creek," Roe suggested.

"Didn't Emerson tell us there was a marina nearby by?"

"Yep. I know that guy who runs it. It's called Kings Creek Marina," Roe answered.

"Why don't you call him up and ask him if they can see the Steiner Estate. Then ask if they can see if that seaplane is back there. If it is, then we can gear up and head down there. A little recon never hurt anyone," Meier smiled.

"I'm calling him as we speak."

Roe talked with his friend and ended the call. "Yep. The plane's there." Roe looked overhead. "We're going to catch the edge of that nor'easter," he said as lightning flashed and rain drops began falling.

"You think it will hit them at Kings Creek?" Meier asked.

"I don't think so. They're far enough south of here. We should head back to Chincoteague," Roe suggested.

"Carleton, I'll take all of the guys with me and you can head back as fast as you can in that gunship of yours. Thanks for all of your help and this nice Baja!" Meier smiled as he reached for the throttle.

"Glad to help," Leonard yelled. "It was nice to be a part of the action."

"Thank you, son," Roe shouted. "Chuck, I'll radio the Coast Guard and the police to come up for these bodies and two boats."

"Sounds like a plan," Meier said.

Hardman and Brode anchored Steiner's two boats and boarded the Baja with the rest of the team. Meier shoved the throttle forward and they raced for Chincoteague.

# CHAPTER 27

## Early Evening
## Steiner Estate

Hidden behind a half-sunken log next to the shore, Moore watched as the boat left the dock and the two men on board searched the area where he had dropped off the seaplane. When they didn't find anything, they returned to the dock and walked to one of the outbuildings.

Moore raised his head to survey the area between himself and the main house. It was too open for him to consider an attempt to cross it without being seen. He decided to wait in the water until twilight.

While he waited, he planned his next move. He would head to the guest house and make his way into the main house to capture Steiner. If that wasn't feasible, he decided he would swim over to the dock where two jet skis were tied. He'd steal one to make his escape.

When twilight arrived, he carefully eased his aching body out of the water and ran half-bent to the rear of the guest house. He heard music and men laughing in front of it. They were probably still celebrating his purported death, he thought. He tried the rear door and found it unlocked.

Carefully, he opened it and listened. Hearing nothing, he slowly entered the building and walked into the first room he found. It was an empty bedroom with an adjoining bath.

He made his way into the bath and stood in front of the mirror. He was a mess, soaking wet with his face, chest and arms bruised. He was surprised to see a wound over his eye, probably from one of the wood splinters at the cabin. It had opened up and blood was running down his face. He washed it off, and the blood ceased flowing.

He stripped down and grabbed a towel. After drying off, he tossed the wet towel and his clothes in a hamper. No sense in leaving it on the floor for someone to discover, he thought.

He walked back into the room and found some dry clothes to put on even though they were a size bigger than his normal size. They would do. He looked through the drawers and the closet in hopes of finding a weapon, but couldn't locate any.

When he left the room, he walked past a laundry room. He peeked inside and saw a wall phone. Taking one last look down the hallway, he stepped into the laundry room and reached for the phone. He quickly dialed Meier.

Meier saw his phone light up, but didn't recognize the number. He was too focused on leading his team in two SUVs to Cape Charles and wasn't going to answer it.

"You going to get that?" Roe asked.

"Probably a salesman," Meier grumbled.

"Or Emerson," Roe suggested.

Meier turned his head and stared briefly at Roe. He was irritated. "Alright. I can always hang up if it's a salesman, I guess. Hello," he said as he answered.

"Chuck?"

"You've got the Big Daddy. Who is this?"

"Emerson."

Meier caught Roe out of the corner of his eye. Roe was smiling because he had guessed right.

Meier peppered Moore with questions. "Where are you? Cape Charles? And why in the world did you fly the coop?"

"Yes, I'm at Steiner's. I'm going to capture her," Moore answered boldly.

"You and your lonesome are going to do that all by yourself?" Meier asked indignantly.

"Yes."

"And how many guns are there at her estate?"

"A lot," Moore answered.

"Are you armed?"

"No."

Meier couldn't help himself as he burst out into laughter. "You want to tell me how you are going to accomplish that mission, rookie?"

"I'm working on it. I just wanted you to know that I'm here," Moore explained.

"Good. We'll have a good start on where to look for your body," Meier countered. He did not like Moore going willy-nilly off the reservation.

"I have some bad news for you, Emerson," Meier added.

"What?"

"I'm out of magic dust. I can't spread it around and make this problem of you being there with no help simply go away."

Moore laughed softly. "That's okay. I'm usually good for a couple of rabbit out of the hat tricks," Moore countered.

"I shouldn't tell you this, but we guessed that you might be at Steiner's. We should be there shortly. Maybe, and I'm just saying maybe, we can pull your butt out of the fire."

"Thanks, Chuck. I better go."

Meier knew that there was no way anyone was going to talk

any sense into Moore to stay low and wait. "Okay. We'll see you on the other side. The dark side," he said in a serious tone.

They ended the call, and Moore stuck his head out to check the hallway. Cautiously, he made his way back down the hall and out the rear door.

Once outside, he looked around the property for any roving guards. He saw an armed man walking under the lights that illuminated the docks where the boats, jet skis and seaplane were tied. He'd have to keep him in mind if he used his jet ski escape plan.

He turned his attention to two French doors at the rear of the main house and planned a circuitous route to them. He then skirted shrubs and a low fence as he cautiously made his way there.

He bolted across the patio to the doors and tried them. They were unlocked. Carefully he opened one and eased himself into the room, closing the door behind him. It was Steiner's library.

His eyes quickly surveyed the room and he saw that the door to the hallway was closed. He turned his attention to her large desk. He walked to it and turned on the desk lamp. He began searching the drawers for any incriminating evidence that could be used against her.

He was frustrated when he didn't find anything of value. She was too smart to keep files here. He looked at her laptop, but hesitated to turn it on. It was probably password protected anyway. Maybe he'd steal it and take it with him when he captured her, he decided.

Her voice in the hallway caught his attention. He'd recognize that voice anywhere. He quickly turned off the desk lamp and looked for a hiding place. He spotted the floor-to-ceiling drapes on both sides of the French doors and headed for one.

He had barely slipped behind it when the library door opened.

"I haven't taken a nap like that in a long time," Steiner spoke to Clawson as she paused before walking in. "It was the champagne," she smiled. She was still in a very good mood after seeing Moore's death.

"And where's that Kronsky boy you were telling me about?"

"He's in Norfolk," Clawson answered. "Zimo convinced him to drive down so he could pay him."

"I want Zimo to talk to him. They were waiting for us when we landed at the fishing shack. I want to know if he set us up," she said sternly as she walked into the room, closing the door behind her and turning on the overhead lights.

She walked to her desk and turned on her laptop.

From behind the drapes, Moore peered around the edge. He spotted a large mirror on the wall that reflected Steiner. She was just as beautiful now as when he saw her the first time in Cuba. Her deep brown eyes were like dark chocolate. Her dark hair hung to her shoulders like the summer's shimmering last twilight.

Her lips were like two budded roses, and her cheeks looked as soft as peaches in July. Her teeth flashed white against her tanned face. She wore very little make-up. She looked fresh and clean.

"No more Peaches Babbit, right? Your real name is Maxine Steiner," Moore said as he stepped out from behind the drape.

In response, she whirled around in shock as she recognized the voice. Her face was contorted with disbelief as she stared at the man whose death, just hours ago, she had witnessed and celebrated.

"I thought you were dead!" she said as burning rage hissed through her body like a deathly poison. "I saw the explosion.

I saw you die, Emerson Moore." Fury swept over her face like ferocious waves. She was engulfed in wrath, demanding a violent release.

Not waiting for Moore's response, she turned and pulled open the right top desk drawer.

"Looking for this?" Moore asked as he pulled a Sig Sauer P238 Spartan II micro compact semi-automatic out of his pocket. "I found it when I searched your desk."

Her eyes narrowed as she turned and stared at the gun, then at Moore's face. "All I have to do is scream and my men will be in here," she said in a menacing tone.

"I know that, but I don't think you will," Moore said, confidently.

"Why?" she asked as her anger was overcome by curiosity.

"You want to know how I found you," Moore stated. "You probably have a lot of questions for me."

He felt like a cat in a room full of dogs and was simply trying to buy himself a little precious time. He wondered what was keeping his rescue team.

"Tell me then. You're in the driver's seat, Emerson Moore, the man who told me his real name was Manny Elias," Steiner calmly said. She relaxed her posture and slowly approached Moore.

"It was actually by accident, Max," Moore said as he purposely used her real name. "I was at the Sheriff's Office and I was surprised when I saw your picture there."

"I bet you were surprised," she laughed as she thought about his reaction.

"Stunned is more the word. I had no idea who you really were. It was pure coincidence that I ended up on Chincoteague and stumbled across you."

"Fate," she concluded emotionlessly.

"Maybe so, but our paths converged as they have now in this moment."

Steiner now stood directly in front of Moore with a completely different look in her eyes, one that momentarily confused him.

She slid her arms around him, extending her hands upward through the middle of his back and intimately leaned in close to his face. Their facial skin was nearly touching and he could feel her sweet breath exhaled upon his cheekbone.

Moore took her in, not only admiring her for her stunning beauty, but also noting that she was statuesque. He had a weakness for tall, beautiful women.

Steiner slightly turned her face so that it touched Moore's face just below the peak of his left cheekbone. Her slightly endowed lips were pursed together as she ever so slightly withdrew from Emerson's face. She then leaned again into him by placing her luscious lips next to his left ear and whispered, "Oh Manny, take me away from all this."

Moore slowly withdrew his face from her and slightly tilted it downward. At that precise moment, she barley lifted herself from her feet so that her lips reached his and then kissed Moore ever so passionately and briefly.

Becoming lost in the moment, he embraced her tightly and allowed a hint of raw passion to dig in deeply as he whispered her name, "Peaches," and then buried his lips into hers.

Their eyes had closed and the ardent embrace was not to be broken in that fractious moment, frozen in time. They each were without thought, having allowed their prior passion to overcome them.

Each was nearly breathless as their lips slowly parted. She

gently allowed her face and body to ease away from Moore, ever so slowly. As she did, she made a grab for the Sig Sauer. It was in vain as Moore had a firm grip on it and pulled it away from her. He had guessed that she would make a play to get the weapon. And he was right.

"That's not going to work," Moore said as he firmly pushed her away although he did enjoy the moment.

Steiner stepped back into reality. She spoke sternly, "You ruined my business in Cuba."

"I guess," Moore said as he paused. "If I'm going to ruin someone's business, I ruined the right kind of business," he stated matter-of-factly.

"You have no idea what you did. The impact your actions have had on our business. It's going to take a while for everything to come back together. Between Cuba and your nosing around here, especially in Ocean City," she fumed, "you've cost me dearly, Emerson Moore."

"You played me in Cuba," Moore told her.

She laughed for a moment as she recalled their initial encounter. "I did. You were so easy," she insisted.

"Why did you do that?"

"Baudin was the one behind that ploy. He wanted to see how long he could play with you before he killed you."

"I'm curious. When did he know about me?" Moore asked.

"The minute you entered Santa Lucha. His eyes and ears on the ground let him know that there was a stranger in town. I happened to be there working on a deal with him. He suggested that I should check you out. It was so easy to lure you in. I completely had you at 'Hello.' The thing with the purse snatching was all set up to connect you to me."

"Baudin told me about that before he died."

"You surprised him. You surprised me. He was the one who ended up dead," Steiner noted.

She was growing weary of the conversation. She wanted Moore dead.

The library door quietly opened and Clawson walked in. As Moore's attention was drawn to his entrance, Steiner shouted, "It's Moore. Kill him!"

"What?" Clawson asked in surprise. He pulled out his .45 and fired off two quick shots, narrowly missing Moore.

Moore crashed through the French doors, falling outside to the patio floor. As Clawson raced across the room with his gun, Moore scrambled to his feet and ran to the other side of the fence and shrubbery.

"Find him," Steiner yelled furiously as Clawson ran through the open door and began searching for Moore. While he did, Steiner called to Graber. "Moore's alive. Have the men find him," she ordered curtly.

Meanwhile, a cement mixer truck turned right off Hermitage Road onto Antebellum Lane. Its headlights found its path blocked by the security guard's vehicle which was parked horizontally across the lane. Two red-uniformed guards leaned against the sides of the vehicle while a third guard pointed the strong white beam of his flashlight into the truck driver's eyes.

The truck stopped, and the driver's window rolled down.

"Can I help you this fine evening?" the lead guard asked as he approached the driver's side. "A little late at night to be making cement deliveries, isn't it?"

"Special delivery, friend," Meier answered as he stuck his head out of the window. He looked from the guard below his window to the other two and back. "You guys have really dangerous jobs, don't you?"

The guard's eyes crunched up as he tried to determine where the conversation was headed.

"You guys are fully trained, professional school crossing guards, aren't you?" Meier cracked, sarcastically.

Roe, who was sitting next to Meier in the truck, laughed, but the guard just glared at Meier.

"Funny. You can back your vehicle down the road. No one is expecting a delivery tonight," the guard said firmly.

"Oh, I know that. It's a surprise delivery," Meier said as he looked at the guard's red uniform. Meier wasn't letting up. "I like your red uniform. Kind of reminds me of Little Red Riding Hood," he chuckled as his eye roved over the rent-a-cop's outfit. "Do you know who that makes me?"

"Who?"

"The big bad wolf," Meier roared. "And I think your two little piggies over there are in trouble." Meier nodded to the two guards next to the vehicle.

When the lead guard turned his head, he saw that Duncan and Richstein had snuck up from behind them and were tying up his men. As the guard reached for his radio to call for help, he felt a nudge against the back of his head. He turned and found himself staring into Roe's Kimber .45.

"We aren't going to hurt you. We're just going to tie you boys up while we get our business done," Roe said in a dangerous tone.

Within five minutes, the three guards had been secured, and their vehicle moved from the center of the road. The cement truck went to the main gate entrance to the Steiner Estate.

"I'm going to change my moniker from Big Daddy to Mr. Fourth of July," Meier said as he drove the short distance.

"Why?" Roe asked.

"Because I'm going to set off some explosions that will light up the sky like the Fourth of July!"

"Good," Roe smiled.

"Or you can check with my wife, and she can tell you why she calls me Mr. Fourth of July," Meier said with a sly wink. He drove down the lane with his lights off.

Roe chuckled quietly.

Meier pulled past the locked entrance gate and stopped the truck. The trailing SUV with its lights off contained Duncan, Richstein, Hardman and Brode. It parked on the other side of the gate. The team exited their vehicles and met in front of the gate as they eyed the compound.

"That makes it a bit easier," Meier said as floodlights started flickering on, and they could see armed men running around.

"Must be looking for Emerson," Roe guessed.

"I'd say so," Meier agreed when he heard a burst of gunfire from behind the house. "And I think someone just saw him."

"Ready to roll?" Roe asked.

"Let's get this Tikrit Express moving," Meier said as the men returned to the vehicles. He shifted the cement truck in reverse and began backing up, crushing through the gate. He drove backwards up the driveway with Roe hanging out the passenger door and firing at the armed men at the house who opened fire in return on the approaching vehicles.

The SUV followed with Duncan at the wheel. Richstein, Hardman and Brode fired their weapons from their open windows.

The cement truck flew backwards up the low steps to the front entrance of the house and crashed through the front doorway where it stopped.

Men firing their weapons ran around from the corner of the

house to the front where they were met with a hail of return gunfire, especially from Meier's SAW. Bullets whizzed through the air in both directions. Several of Steiner's men were killed during the exchange.

Within minutes, the firefight was over. Duncan and Richstein stood guard while Hardman and Brode checked the fallen for any survivors. There were none.

"Everyone okay?" Meier called.

All acknowledged in the affirmative except Richstein. He had blood oozing from a round he took in his side. "Just a flesh wound," the tough warrior stated nonchalantly.

"Sam and Jon, you sweep around the east side of the house. Russ and Charlie, you sweep the west side. Check the outbuildings and be careful. Roe and I will sweep the inside," Meier said as the men began the next phase of their rescue mission.

While the action was taking place in the front of the house, Moore had been dodging gunfire as he made his way to the caretaker's cottage to the right of the house. He was focused on reaching the garage next to it to steal one of the vehicles that he assumed would be parked there.

When the floodlights flashed on, he saw the armed men searching for him and tried to run in the shadows. It was almost like a child's game of hide and seek with him slipping into the shrubbery to hide when the men ran by. With only limited bullets in his weapon, he knew that he'd have to carefully manage his ammunition.

Besides, he was acutely aware that discharging his weapon would act as a clear signal for his whereabouts. He had to keep them guessing, but he didn't know for how long.

Moore's heart was pounding as he ran around a shrub and into one of the armed men. He delivered two quick, ferocious blows to the man's ribs and a right hook to his left eye before the two fell to the ground where they grappled. Moore was able to bring his weapon down hard on the man's skull, knocking him unconscious.

Standing, he heard gunfire break out in front of the house and correctly guessed that Meier and company had arrived. They were executing a frontal attack on the house, he thought. He ran at a crouch past the caretaker's cottage and rounded the corner. Suddenly he stopped dead in his tracks and smiled when he saw the parked Virginia State Police SUV.

"Over here, Mr. Moore," one of the two uniformed troopers called.

"Boy, am I glad to see you guys," Moore said as he relaxed.

"I bet you are," the trooper smiled. "You better get in the back here where you'll be safe until this all settles down," he said warmly.

"Sure. It's been a long day," Moore said with relief as he walked past the trooper and stepped into the rear of the SUV.

"And it's going to be a longer night," the trooper said as he quickly stuck a syringe needle into Moore's neck, knocking out a suddenly panicked Moore.

The imposter trooper reached for his radio. "Max, we've got Moore."

"Take him to Zimo. Now! Get out of here!" Steiner ordered. A vengeful smile filled her villainous face.

As Meier's team broke through the estate gate, Steiner met Graber and Clawson at the dock where her pilot had started the seaplane's engine. They boarded the plane and began moving away from the dock for takeoff.

"Take me to Norfolk. We are going to have our way with Moore," she exclaimed in evil glee.

Exiting at the rear of the house, Meier and Roe heard sporadic shots as their team eliminated Steiner's men. They also saw the seaplane taking off.

"Well ain't that the berries!" Meier grumbled as he watched its lights fade into the night sky.

"You think Emerson is aboard?" Roe asked.

"I don't really know."

Duncan and Richstein walked over from the caretaker's cottage and garage area.

"All clear. No Emerson," Duncan reported.

Hardman and Brode joined them from the west side.

"We're clear over here," Brode said.

"Chuck, did you have the state police involved on this?" Hardman asked.

"If I did, don't you think I'd have told you?" Meier shot back.

"We saw a state police car driving off the property," Hardman commented.

"I don't know anything about that." Meier was very frustrated in not having found Moore or catching Steiner. "I don't know where the zip-a-dee went for my doo-dah day."

"You mean do-do day," Roe cracked.

"Looky there!" Duncan exclaimed. "We've got a parade of flashing lights coming up the drive."

They all turned to see a stream of law enforcement vehicles approaching them.

"This is going to take some explaining," Meier said. "And we don't know where Emerson disappeared to," he added with frustration.

# CHAPTER 28

## The Warehouse
## Norfolk, Virginia

His body was beaten and bruised from the flurry of blows that Zimo had delivered to it. His left eye was half-closed, and his lips had been split open from being struck.

"You set us up, didn't you?" Zimo drilled in.

"No. I knew nothing about it," Kronsky replied. He spoke in a near whisper as he denied any knowledge about the ambush at the cabin in Chincoteague Bay.

The sounds of approaching footsteps caused Zimo to turn to face them. He saw Steiner storm into the room with Clawson at her side.

"I'm glad you made it out of there," Zimo said as he thought about Clawson's call to let him know what happened at the Kings Creek estate.

"They think they have us, but we'll let our lawyers work this out," Steiner fumed. "I'm sure there's some illegal entry and more that can be thrown at them. Did you learn anything from him?" she demanded as she walked over to Kronsky and looked down on him.

"Nothing. He said he didn't know. He thought they set him up," Zimo replied. "I can do more to him, like pulling out his fingernails," Zimo said as he reached for a pair of pliers.

"No. That's not necessary. We've got Moore," she proclaimed triumphantly.

"You do?"

"Stupid schmuck. He ran over to our police vehicle for help. He's out cold, and they're bringing him to us." She glanced at her watch. "It shouldn't be too much longer."

"I'll get back to Kronsky then."

"No, but I have an idea," Steiner mused.

"Is this the guy you said was so talented with carpentry?" Her eyes returned to stare at Kronsky. Steiner was thinking how she could finish off Emerson Moore in a manner that would ensure his certain death. There would be no escape for him now and he would suffer.

"Yes. The guy's talented," Zimo affirmed.

"I want you to get him on his feet," Steiner directed. "Take him to the carpentry shop next door. There's something I want Kronsky to build for me. He has one hour to do it." She then explained to Zimo what she had in mind.

"I'll get him right on it," Zimo said as he helped Kronsky to his feet and half walked him across the warehouse to the carpentry room.

"I'll be in your office," she said, then walked away. When she entered, she cast an eye to the aquarium where Zimo kept his dangerous critters. She was surprised by how many he had.

She ambled across the room and pulled open the top drawer of a filing cabinet. It was where Zimo kept his liquor supply. She reached in and withdrew a bottle of whiskey, then poured herself a shot. She sat in the chair behind the desk and swirled the whisky in her shot glass as she thought.

Her lawyers had been so careful in setting up her front business for the warehouse. It would be difficult for anyone to trace that she was the true owner. She liked the layers that separated her from the drug sales. She also was concerned that Moore and whatever law enforcement units were working with him would be able to pierce the veil of ownership and identify her as being behind any drug trafficking.

She raised the glass to her lips and threw it down. She then poured another. It was becoming a long night.

Forty-five minutes later, the door to the warehouse opened so that the vehicle containing Moore could enter.

Clawson walked into the office where Steiner was sitting. "They just brought in Moore."

"Good. Is he conscious?"

"He's coming out of it. Not 100 percent yet."

"Have them wake him up. I'll be out shortly," she said in a straightforward tone. Clawson turned and left the office. She allowed a narrow smile to cross her lips as she thought about the revenge she would finally bestow upon Moore.

A few minutes later, Steiner left the office and walked across the warehouse to where the police car was parked. Moore's body was on the cold concrete floor. He was trying to move to a sitting position, but was still woozy from the side effects of the injection he had been given.

"Hello, pretty boy." Steiner allowed the words to sneer out of her mouth. She leaned forward as she stopped in front of him. A disparaging smile filled her smooth face and her eyes bored holes into Moore's body.

"It's payback time, Moore!" she snapped as she struck out with her right foot, connecting to Moore's rib cage.

The sharp kick caught the unsuspecting Moore by surprise, but he quickly recovered. "Is that all you have?" he asked boldly.

The blood raced through her veins as her anger boiled over. She kicked him twice more. When Moore reached out to stop her, Zimo and Clawson moved in. They grabbed both of his arms and jerked him to his feet.

"Not so fast," the hulking Zimo warned Moore with a hateful smirk.

Steiner's forehead was twitching with fury. She planted one swift kick to Moore's groin, causing a loud groan to escape from Moore's mouth as stars burst in his head from the ensuing pain. He felt as if he were on the other side of hell.

"I'll show you what I've got," she roared. "We're just getting started," she exploded.

Moore tried to squirm free and throw himself at her but to no avail. The two men had him firmly in their grasp.

"Tie him to that post," she directed the two men, who quickly followed her instructions.

Moore's pain had subsided, and he was acutely aware of his precarious situation. His knuckles were white from clenching his fist. He gritted his teeth as Zimo moved in to hammer his body with a series of blows to the midsection. His time was now running out, so too, his luck.

"You're holding back Zimo. Hit him harder," Steiner commanded as her face raged red. She was enjoying Zimo's punishing pummels to Moore.

Despite his efforts to remain silent and take the beating, Moore's mouth opened, and a moan escaped. His frame began to hunch forward as he succumbed to the mauling and the dank smell of perspiration became noticeable. Moore was completely soaked through his shirt, and sweat poured from his forehead and face. The gravity of his situation became a stark reality to him.

Zimo moved up and began bashing Moore's face, causing blood to run from his thrashed nose and mouth. Moore passed out.

"Get a bucket of water and bring him back," Steiner said sharply.

Within a minute, Moore had been drenched by a bucket of cold water. He coughed twice and slowly raised his head to stare directly at Steiner. His eyes were filled with iron-willed determination.

"Like I said earlier. Is that all you have?" Moore sputtered, fearlessly.

"Where's Kronsky?" she snapped at Zimo.

"I left him out back. He's working on the project you gave him," Zimo explained.

"It should be done by now. Go get him and bring it out," she said. "I'll be right back." She returned to Zimo's office while Zimo rushed off to get Kronsky.

In a matter of minutes, Zimo ushered in a battered Kronsky who was pushing a wooden cart on wheels. On top of the cart was the eight-foot long wooden box that Steiner had ordered him to build.

When Kronsky spotted Moore, he hung his head in shame.

Steiner returned from the office. She was carrying Zimo's aquarium and set it on a nearby table.

"Let's see what you've built for me," she said as she walked over to the box. She stood on her tip toes as she swung open the hinged lid. "I can't see inside. This is all too tall for me."

"I'm sorry," Kronsky said, "this wooden cart was all I had to put it on."

"I really don't care." Turning to Zimo, she continued, "Gag Moore and bind his feet. Then you guys toss him into the box."

The men rushed to do her bidding. As they worked, Steiner said, "I want you to see what I have here in Zimo's aquarium." She brought it over to show Moore, whose eyes widened in fear.

"Yes. They are what you think they are. I think this is an appropriate way for you to meet your death and find the promised land. It's sort of a payback for what you did to Baudin. He died from bee stings, and you will die from the stings of Zimo's little playthings," she said as she shook the aquarium, irritating the little creatures that were scurrying around.

"That's right. Scorpions," she smiled with evil glee. "Zimo, tell Moore about them. You're the expert."

Zimo smiled as he began his explanation. "I have two kinds there. One is the deathstalker. The other is the bark scorpion. The bark scorpion is the most venomous in North America. And that's because its venom is filled with neurotoxins."

"Tell him what happens when you're stung by one of these," Steiner ordered Zimo.

"You're going to have trouble breathing. Your muscles will start twitching. You'll lose control of them. You'll get strange movements with your head, neck and eyes. You'll start sweating and drooling. Then you'll vomit. You just might choke on your vomit because your mouth is taped shut. Your blood pressure will soar. So will your heart rate and cardiac arrest will set in."

"Very well done, Zimo," Steiner smiled. "You can think of the anguish and pain that tormented Baudin when he died from the bee stings. And do you know what's different for you?" she asked.

Moore couldn't respond. His eyes were filled with fear.

"You'll have a slow, painful death. It won't be as fast as Baudin's death. You will suffer. You will suffer much more," she glowed with sweet revenge. "Toss him in the box."

The men lifted a struggling Moore high and dumped him over the edge into the wooden box as Kronsky stood behind it. They heard the thud as Moore's body hit the bottom of the box and a groan as the entire wooden cart shook.

Steiner glared at Kronsky. "I want to see inside. Someone needs to bring in a chair or stool so that I can watch him take his last breath," she stormed as she handed the aquarium to Zimo.

"Can you reach up and dump your critters inside?" she asked Zimo.

"I'll get a chair," Zimo said.

"Don't waste time now. Just dump them," she ordered abruptly.

Zimo shook the aquarium hard to agitate the two dozen scorpions and reached up. He tilted the aquarium and let them slide into the wooden box. Then he walked around to the other side and flipped the lid shut.

"We'll check him in a while," Steiner said. "And someone find me a chair to stand on so I can see inside the box."

"What about Kronsky?" Zimo asked.

"What about him?"

"He's a witness to all of this," Zimo said.

"Kill him," Steiner said as if it was an everyday occurrence.

Kronsky's face filled with fear, and he turned to run.

Before Kronsky could escape, Zimo produced a .45 from the back of his waist and calmly fired two bullets into Kronsky, killing him.

Clawson came running into the warehouse.

"We've got visitors," he yelled as he approached.

"Who now?" Steiner demanded.

"I'd guess the same people that we saw at the estate," he

said quickly in response.

"How would they have found us?" she fumed as she realized her joy at watching Moore's excruciatingly painful death was being interrupted.

They heard several shots from the outside of the warehouse.

"Give me your .45," Steiner commanded Clawson, who obediently handed over his weapon. She was standing ten feet away from Moore's wooden box when she turned, aimed and fired five rounds into it. "That should take care of my problems," she laughed uncontrollably, and she handed the gun back to Clawson.

"Take care of whoever is outside," she added with a determined look on her face.

Before Clawson could respond, a black SUV crashed through the warehouse door and its occupants fired through its open windows. Meier was wild-eyed as he quickly assessed the area. When he saw the wooden box, he drove right over to it and brought the vehicle to a screeching stop as he parked it between the wooden box and the gunmen.

It was followed quickly by the second SUV that flew in and parked behind Meier's vehicle. Gunfire exploded throughout the warehouse as the vehicles emptied and the two sides fought for control.

Seeing Kronsky's body and the red pool of blood around it, Meier yelled at Roe. "Check him. I'll go for Emerson."

Immediately Roe ran over to Kronsky and turned his body over. "Louie, are you okay?" he asked, before he saw the open lifeless eyes staring at him. "He's gone," Roe shouted between rounds striking their vehicles.

"I wouldn't say it looks too promising for Emerson," Meier said as he approached the bullet-ridden wooden box. He reached up and threw open the lid. He stood on his tiptoes and looked inside. "Nothing here but a bunch of scorpions," he said as he stared into the box.

He then heard a muffled voice and what sounded like someone kicking at the sides of the wooden cart. He looked below the box to the wheeled workbench that it sat on. He eased his fingers along the edge and found a latch which he released. The side dropped, and he saw Moore.

"That's not the safest place to hide, Emerson," he said as he knelt on the floor and pulled the tape off Moore's mouth.

"Get me out of here!" Moore said desperately as he rolled out of the cart's interior.

"Now just settle down there. I was just about to free you," Meier explained as he produced a knife and sliced through the tape binding Moore's legs and cut the plastic ties from around his wrists.

"You okay?" Meier asked as he helped Moore to a sitting position.

"Yes," Moore said in a hoarse whisper. "How did you find me?"

Meier pointed to Kronsky's body. "They made the mistake of leaving him alone in the carpentry shop. He called Roe's cell and told Roe where he was. He then said that they had him building a coffin for you."

"They killed him. They killed Kronsky," Moore repeated. He was shocked by Kronsky's death and an uncontrollable vengeance filled him.

"He died saving you," Meier said. "How did you end up in the bottom of that cart?"

"Trap door. Kronsky put in a trap door. I dropped through before they tossed in a bunch of scorpions to kill me. If you only could have gotten here sooner, he'd still be alive. He was a good kid," Moore said as he stared sadly at Kronsky's lifeless body.

"Yeah, that's what you and Roe had been saying," Meier affirmed.

Meier suddenly saw a suspicious movement out of the corner of his eye. He abruptly turned and fired two quick shots at Zimo, who had been silently working his way around the perimeter in a flanking move.

"Your buddy Zimo is trying to flank us," Meier warned.

When Moore heard Zimo's name, his adrenaline kicked in. "Give me a gun," he said as he snatched Meier's knife from his hand and a burning rage fueled his primeval instinct.

"Take mine," Meier said as he loaded a new magazine. "I have another."

Before Meier could say anything else, Moore launched himself around the wooden box. He ran directly toward Zimo, firing as he recklessly closed the distance between them. His mind was a blur as raw emotion drove his reaction to Kronsky's death. He had high hopes for the boy, and they would never be realized. The kid died saving him. Moore would make Zimo pay.

Zimo was crouched behind a stack of boxes that Moore leapt upon, knocking them and Zimo down. He rolled on top of Zimo and began striking him in the chest with the sharp knife. He continued stabbing him, over and over as relentless fury filled him.

"You can stop, Emerson. He's dead," Meier said after he caught up to Moore and saw his mental state.

Moore wildly continued stabbing. He was like a mindless robot, repeating a task over and over.

"Emerson. Stop!" Meier shouted as he reached down and

grabbed Moore's arm. With his other hand, Meier pried the knife out of Moore's hand. "He's dead. Let it go. Nothing will bring back Kronsky."

Moore's impulsive wrath gradually subsided, and he began to breathe normally. "I did that for Kronsky."

"I know that, Emerson. Now get your wits about you. We're not out of this mess yet. They've got more people here than we expected. And you need to think clearly to help us win this." Meier stared intently into Moore's eyes. "Are you back with us?"

"Yeah. I'm good." Moore still seethed emotionally at Zimo's brutal killing of Kronsky.

"Come with me and watch my back. We'll work our way around the way Zimo came at us to get at them," he explained as he crouched. "Follow me," he said as he began to move away.

As they made their way, Moore saw several bodies strewn on the warehouse floor. He also saw that some of their team had been hit. Hardman had been wounded in the thigh and Richstein had a shoulder wound.

Brode had taken two rounds to his shoulder and arm during the initial exchange of gunfire and was sitting on the floor behind his SUV. He held a bandage from his field medical kit to his shoulder to stem the blood flow.

Meier rounded a corner and opened up his SAW on a number of the gunmen. They were taken by surprise and were riddled with rounds. Their bodies crumpled to the ground.

Meier surveyed the area. "I think we got them all," he said as he straightened. He walked forward with the SAW held at waist height, its lethal barrel led the way.

"Do you see Steiner or Clawson?" Moore asked as his eyes scanned the warehouse.

"I saw a woman run for cover when we crashed in here, but not since," Meier replied as he looked around with a wary eye.

Moore heard a noise from behind them. He whirled and saw a gunman raise an Uzi and point it at Meier. Moore fired twice with the .45. One round hit the man in the chest and the other struck the side of his skull. The man instantly fell to the floor.

"Nice shooting, Emerson," Meier said as he turned his head back to the area in front of them.

"Are we clear?" Roe shouted from across the room.

"Give us a few. We're mopping up," Meier said.

"There!" Moore yelled as he saw a flight of steps through one of the office windows. He caught a glimpse of Steiner as she fled up the stairs. "I'll get her," he yelled as he opened the office door and set off in pursuit.

He ran up the stairs to the first landing where he turned the corner and was yanked off of his feet by Graber, who slammed Moore to the floor.

"You've been a real pain in the ass," Graber roared as he jumped on top of Moore and the two grappled.

As they fought, Moore twisted forcefully to Graber's back. He popped Graber's right arm behind his back and suddenly yanked up, snapping the bone. The man screamed in agony.

Out of the corner of his eye, Moore sensed movement. He turned his head slightly while still trying to subdue Graber and saw a gun barrel poking around the stairwell.

Reacting quickly, Moore rolled over, pulling Graber's body on top of his as the weapon fired. The first bullet missed, but the second bullet ripped off the left side of Graber's skull, splattering blood and brain matter on Moore.

As the gunman descended the stairs, Moore aimed his .45

at him and fired, striking him in the chest and killing him. The man's body fell onto the crowded landing. Moore eased himself out from under Graber's body and stood. He then continued his race up the stairs as another warm wash of adrenaline filled him with energy.

When Moore raced around the corner at the top of the stairs, a stream of rounds sent him diving for cover as a stream of lead pocked the wall, tearing through the plaster just inches above his head.

Clawson advanced on Moore, firing his MP7 at thigh level across the room and pinning Moore to the floor. Moore crawled forward, but was running out of cover.

A sudden gunshot from the stairwell struck Clawson. He fell to the floor, wounded in the left shoulder, but still alive.

"It's safe now, Emerson," Meier's deep voice boomed as he approached Clawson and kicked the MP7 away.

Moore rose to his feet and joined Meier to stand over Clawson.

"Thanks, Chuck."

"That's what I'm here for," he said. "Help me get this piece of shit into that chair."

Moore reached down. They lifted Clawson and carried him over to a straight back chair where they dropped him.

"Where's Steiner?" Meier demanded.

Clawson didn't respond.

"Tell us where she is or, my friend, it's going to get real ugly around here for you," Meier warned.

Clawson's lips were sealed.

"Okay, then," Meier said as he pulled a taser from his belt. He held it against Clawson's neck for a three count while Clawson screamed.

"Ready to talk?" Meier asked.

Drained but still resistant, Clawson grimaced. His lips closed tight as he clenched his hands.

Meier sent another round of voltage through for three seconds. Clawson's tightly closed lips opened as he screamed in terror. He knew that he had to buy time for Steiner to escape.

"Got anything for me now?" Meier asked.

Hearing the seaplane's engine start, Clawson relaxed. "You're too late. She's gone," he laughed as he kicked sharply at Meier's groin and rolled off the table. Meier was caught by surprise and took two steps backward as he recovered from the kick.

Clawson dove to the floor and grabbed his weapon. As he rolled over, he aimed its barrel at Meier. Before he could pull the trigger, Moore fired his .45 once, striking Clawson in the chest. Clawson dropped his weapon and groaned as blood appeared on his lips. He was dead within seconds.

"Nice shooting," Meier said appreciatively.

"That all goes back to my training in Cedar Key," Moore said.

"And I'm glad you had that training," Meier said as he hefted his taser. "Lucky for my kids that they were born when they were."

"Why?" Moore asked.

"I had to use a wooden spoon on them back then. Today, I would have used a taser," he grinned. Turning serious again, he said, "We better get downstairs if we're going to have a chance to catch Steiner."

Moore opened a door and saw an outside staircase. "I bet she ran down here."

"You go that way, and I'll head down the inside stairwell.

I'll see you on the other side," Meier said quickly as the two men swept into action.

Moore stepped out onto the outside stairwell, which was bathed in light. He took three steps when a bullet smashed into the wall next to his head. He looked toward the seaplane and saw Steiner. She was standing on the seaplane's pontoon and taking her last shots at Moore.

Steiner was raging like a wildfire. Waves of fury filled her as the blood rose in her cheeks. The whites of her eyes had turned a pure black as she stared lethally at Moore on the staircase. Her eyes squinted like a pit viper's slit-like pupils, and her heart turned ice cold, robbing it of any feelings other than a cool hatred for Moore. She fired twice again and missed striking Moore.

"We've got to go," Henley called from inside the plane.

She again fired wildly at Moore as she emptied her gun. Throwing it into the channel, she turned and climbed into the plane much to the pilot's relief. He pushed the throttle forward to taxi the plane down the channel and into the harbor where they could take off.

As the seaplane moved away, Moore reached the bottom of the stairs where he met Meier.

"She's getting away," Moore lamented.

"Not quite yet," Roe called as he ran out of the warehouse.

"What do you have there, partner?" Meier asked although he already knew the answer.

"They should never have blown up my cabin. Payback is a bitch, isn't it?" Roe asked firmly as he lined up the RPG that he had found in the back of Meier's SUV. When he heard the seaplane engine start, he remembered seeing it in the trunk and ran to get it.

Calmly, Roe sighted the RPG. "It's been awhile since I fired one of these, but there are some things that come back to you real quick," he said as he pulled the trigger.

The grenade shot out of the tube at 384 feet per second. Its warhead connected with the seaplane an instant later with a blinding flash as a fiery ball of yellow flame billowed outward. The plane blew apart, killing Steiner and the pilot.

"They're gone," Roe said, satisfied with his action.

"Yeah. All over the place," Meier added before turning to Moore. "Confetti. She just got a case of IED."

"What?" Moore asked with a confused look.

"Intermittent Explosive Disorder," Meier teased as only he could at times like these. "They won't be doing a chalk outline of either of them two," Meier added as the men turned and walked back inside the warehouse.

"Being in Tikrit sure did give you a morbid sense of humor," Moore said as they walked.

"You can't let your undies get in knots about things. Remember, I put the fun in dysfunctional," Meier joked as they saw several uniformed police officers enter the other side of the warehouse. They had been contacted by neighboring business owners after hearing the initial gunfire. The officers were quickly greeted by Hardman and Brode, who explained what had transpired.

As Moore looked at the number of bodies scattered on the warehouse floor, he thought about Steiner and her death. In some ways, he felt sorry for Steiner's demise. But then again, she got her just rewards for what she'd been involved in. Still, he didn't like seeing someone die even though he'd been responsible for several deaths that evening.

"Roe," Meier called.

"What?" Roe asked as he looked at Meier and saw that Meier was watching Moore.

"I think I saw a bottle of whiskey in that office when I ran by. Could you grab it?

"Are you going to give Emerson a drink?" Roe asked as he started walking to the office. Meier and Moore followed him.

"Hell no. It's for me," he grinned. "I earned it today."

"You've more than earned it," Moore said as he snapped out of his melancholy mood.

"Roe, you should have seen Emerson go dog crazy stabbing that guy a few minutes ago," Meier said as they entered the office.

"What? Emerson, is that true?" a stunned Roe asked.

"Yeah," Moore admitted reluctantly. "I really lost it. I couldn't stop stabbing the guy. He killed Kronsky," he explained as he found the whiskey and three glasses. He began filling the glasses.

"I'm surprised," Roe said, taking one of the filled glasses.

"I'm not usually like that. I just lost it," Moore explained.

"What do you think we should do with those scorpions?" Meier asked with raised eyebrows.

# CHAPTER 29

## Two Days Later
## Roe Terry's House

Things had finally settled down. Moore and the guys went through a debriefing with the Norfolk police, and everyone had departed for their homes. Moore planned to catch a flight out of Baltimore for Cleveland in a couple of days to return to Put-in-Bay. It seemed like he'd been gone for months. He had also called Sedler and filed a story for *The Post*. Meier had left for the long drive to the Keys.

Moore was relaxing on the deck while Roe grilled some freshly caught flounder for dinner. His phone rang, and he looked down. He saw that it was "Mad Dog" Mike Adams calling and answered on the second ring.

"Hi Mike," Moore said. "What's happening?"

"You staying out of trouble?" Adams asked in a serious tone.

"Of course I am," Moore responded, not wanting to disclose what he had been through. "Are you on the island?"

"Yes. I just walked off the Miller Ferry at the Lime Kiln dock. I'm standing here with Billy and Liam," Adams answered.

Before Adams could continue, Moore interrupted him. "And how is little Liam doing?"

"I'll let him tell you himself," Adams said as he bent down

and held the phone up to four-year-old Liam. "Tell my friend about the ferry, Liam," Adams said in an encouraging tone.

"That's my boat. One day I'm going to drive it," Liam said without any hesitation.

Adams chuckled and started to stand up, but Liam reached for the phone. "You want to tell him something else?" Adams asked as he leaned down again.

"My mommy plays the guitar and sings. I get to do the train whistle," he spoke proudly to Moore.

"I know you do. I've seen you on stage with her. And you play the tambourine so well," Moore responded to Liam's comments as he thought back to the two of them singing Johnny Cash's *Folsom Prison Blues*.

"Okay Liam, I need to talk to my friend," Adams said as he straightened and walked a short distance away.

"Okay. I can talk now," Adams said.

"What's up, Mike?" Moore noted the serious tone in Adams' voice.

"It's about your aunt," Adams started.

"What's wrong? Is she okay?" The words gushed out of Moore's mouth.

"I'm on my way over to her house now. Or what's left of it."

"What do you mean?" Moore asked urgently.

"I saw black smoke rising from the island as I rode over on the ferry. Then I spotted Billy when I walked off and asked him if he knew where the smoke was coming from. Billy told me there was an explosion at her house about twenty minutes ago. The fire department is there and trying to put out the fire. I'm catching a ride to check it out. I'll let you know what I find shortly."

"Is my aunt okay?" Moore asked as fear began to fill him.

He gripped the side of his chair as he tried to remain calm.

Adams answered in a solemn tone. "No one has seen her."

Coming Soon

The Next Emerson Moore Adventure

***Sunset Blues***

Out of the Emerson Moore series

***Memory Layne***